CW00867183

Ivy
and
Roses

Suzy K. Quinn

Suzy K.Quinn
UK

Copyright © by Suzy K.Quinn

First Edition 2016

Published by: Devoted Books
Manufactured in the UK.

For my two angels, Lexi and Laya

DEVOTED BOOKS

Devoted to our readers?
Seriously. We *love* you…

Welcome to the world of bestselling romance.
If you love hot heroes and page-turning
plots, we're glad you found us.
We love our readers, so we offer
MORE than just great stories.
When you finish a Devoted book, you'll
be given lots of **free extras**, including **secret
scenes** and **pictures of characters**.

So **turn the page**, and get ready for
a book that will love you back …

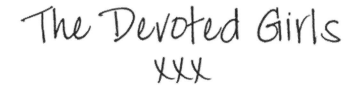

The Devoted Girls
xxx

Preface

Yay!

You picked up my book. Which at least means the cover is good …

I still can't believe so many people read my stories.

Each and every day, I am humbled by this fact.

There are hundreds of thousands of DEVOTED readers now, and I love each and every one you. I never in my wildest dreams expected to ever reach this many readers, but I am SO honoured that you bought this book.

See you at the end.

Huge kisses,

Love, Suzy xxx

\

1

The silver box glimmers from the mantelpiece.

It's large and thick – the size of a heavy coffee-table book and just as heavy.

I've been ignoring it for days now.

You have to open it some time, says a little voice.

I know.

Through the farmhouse windows, I see rose buds on thorny stems. The grass is taller than it's been in a while, and pink and white blossom decorates the fruit trees.

Spring.

A time of new beginnings.

I glance at Ivy, sleeping in her woven basket.

She's getting too big for that basket now, but I like to have her with me. As close as possible, wherever I am.

Sometimes, life feels so perfect that I can't believe I got so lucky.

I'm married to one of Hollywood's greatest actors – my former teacher, and a man I am deeply, obsessively in love with.

Marc Blackwell dotes on me, and is the perfect, protective father to our beautiful baby, Ivy.

Our luxurious farmhouse is set on five acres of land, and surrounded by flowering, grassy gardens.

Some of the bigger fruit trees will be perfect for a rope swing when Ivy grows up. And then of course, there are the horses for her to ride on.

Security around the farmhouse is the best there is – no photographer or journalist can get near us.

All in all, things should be amazing. And they are. Most of the time. But sometimes I feel like … oh, it's silly.

Everything *is* perfect.

And yet still the silver parcel glimmers.

I watch the pink sun setting over farmland.

Marc will be home soon.

I long for him when he's in the city, and often wait by the window, watching the darkening sky and listening for the crunch of his car on gravel.

Wandering into the kitchen, I take a bowl of pasta dough from the fridge. It's covered with lightly olive-oiled cling film and perfect for rolling.

Dough should relax a little before it's rolled – that was one of my mother's many secrets for perfect pasta.

I've prepared so much food today, it's just crazy.

Strings of spaghetti hang from the pan rails, the tea towel hooks and rolling pins bridging cans of tomatoes.

I've made sheets of pasta too, for lasagne or ravioli – I haven't decided which yet.

There's already enough pasta for twenty people, but that's not the half of it.

In my new wood-burning oven, three pizzas bubble and cook.

A giant tiramisu, covered in hand-tempered chocolate shards, waits in the fridge.

I keep telling myself I'm loving my new role as a house-wife. That my overcooking means we'll never go short of pasta.

But the truth is, I'm a little bored at home.

Rodney manages the cleaning, so the whole house is always polished, hoovered and smelling faintly of lemon.

A fancy laundry service washes all our clothes and delivers it back, wrapped in lavender-scented wax paper.

Being a mother is wonderful, but …

No.

I love Ivy to death and want to be with her always. Every minute of the day. That other life I had … it's a million miles away now.

I'm just checking the pizza, when I hear the low growl of Marc's car.

Marc.

I catch my reflection in our shiny, wood-burning oven, and see a smile light my face and brighten my eyes.

'Perfect timing,' I call out, when I hear the front door.

Hearing the clip of Marc's shoes, I open the oven door and slide a long, wooden pizza spatula into the fiery insides.

I've made Marc's favourite – spiced olive, spinach and feta.

Anticipation warms my chest as Marc strides into the kitchen.

My husband.

2

Marc wears a sharp, black suit and white shirt, open a little at the neck. His hands are in his pockets and he's frowning, his jaw hard and tight.

For a moment, Marc takes in the metres of pasta hanging in sheets and strands around the kitchen.

His thick, brown hair is a little dishevelled. And his dark eyebrows are pulled together over extremely serious blue eyes.

'Is something wrong?' I drop pizza onto a long olive-wood board, then dust floury hands on my striped chef's apron.

Marc's lips twitch into a smile. 'Sophia, this restaurant of yours gets more productive by the day. How many customers were you expecting tonight?'

'Just you. Rodney's sorting the car.'

His smile grows. 'Twenty portions of pasta for two people? And pizza too? I'm happy to see that your commitment to freezer stocking continues.'

'I like cooking. Ivy's sleeping in the living room. Do you want to see her?'

'Do you need to ask?'

I put my finger to my lips and lead him into the lounge, pointing to our beautiful baby girl asleep in her woven basket.

Ivy's tiny little face is still and peaceful.

We both watch her for a moment. Then Marc crouches down and puts his ear to her chest.

He sits back on his knees, taking her in.

I smile, knowing the craziness of checking Ivy's breathing. She's fine. We both know she's fine. But still we check.

'She'll sleep for hours now,' I whisper. 'Dinner's ready.'

'Ah yes,' says Marc, getting to his feet. 'I forgot. Restaurant Sophia hates serving cold food.'

'It tastes fresher when it's hot.'

Marc frowns as he passes the mantelpiece. 'You still haven't opened your parcel?'

'Not yet.'

'Any particular reason?'

'Just … what's the hurry? It's only going to be something I can't do. Or won't do. So why torture myself? My life is here with Ivy. The real world … it's not for me right now.'

'The *real* world?' Marc raises an eyebrow. 'Here was I thinking you already lived in the real world. With Ivy and me.'

'You know what I mean. You go out to work. I stay here. That's just how it is.'

In the kitchen, Marc watches me, forearm rested on the breakfast bar. His fingers drum the polished oak. 'You know, I love having you here. At home.'

'I love being here too,' I say absentmindedly, slicing up pizza with a rolling cutter, then carrying the board to our kitchen table.

We have a formal dining room, but we almost always end up eating in the kitchen. The table is big enough to seat six anyway – it's not like anything in this house is small.

'You don't sound overly convinced,' says Marc, eyebrows pulled together as he joins me at the table.

I shrug. 'Maybe I'm a little lonely in the day sometimes.'

Marc pulls out a solid, wooden chair, still watching me with those intense eyes of his. 'Perhaps you should have some friends over.'

'Everyone's too busy with their own lives. Tom and Tanya are studying. Jen is busy in London. I don't like to ask people.'

I couldn't be happier for Jen, my best friend for so many years. Her business is really working out. And Tom and Tanya – I only met them last year at Ivy College, but they're now two of my best friends and wouldn't want them missing study because of me.

I take a seat, and Marc leans over to kiss the top of my head. 'So how about I arrange a trip?' he murmurs into my hair. 'Just the two of us. Cure this loneliness of yours.'

'You mean the *three* of us.'

'Actually, I meant just you and me. You've been distracted ever since that parcel arrived. Perhaps a break from child-care would do you good. Give you some perspective.'

'I couldn't leave Ivy.'

'Plenty of people employ a nanny, Sophia. Everyone I know with children, as a matter of fact.'

'I just couldn't. Not yet.'

Marc frowns, turning his attention to the table. 'You've been folding napkins again.'

I eye the swan napkins at each place setting. Only Marc and I are eating, but I've made swans for all six places. Just to make the table look neat.

I've also filled three vases with fresh daffodils from our garden. They'll be the last we see this year, so I wanted to make the most of them.

'Sophia—'

I sit down forcefully, grabbing a swan napkin and flapping it out on my lap. 'Yes, I folded some napkins. So what?'

Marc sits opposite, his dark eyes playful. 'I think you're right about this loneliness. You obviously need something to fill your time. I have a few ideas.'

'I'm just … playing at being a good housewife. It's all I've ever wanted to do. Make a nice home for you and our baby.'

'And you do a wonderful job of it.' Marc serves me pizza.

'Oh wait! There's salad too.' I spring up.

'Sit down. You've done enough running around today. I'll get it.' Marc goes to the fridge.

'I've hardly run around at all,' I tell him, dropping down in my chair. 'Rodney does such a good job of managing this house. All I have to do is take care of Ivy.'

'Still a challenging job. And you're up all night.' Marc opens the fridge and laughs. 'Sophia – what time does the party start?'

'Party?'

'There's a giant dessert in here.' He shakes his head at the fridge.

'I was just …'

'Looking for something to fill the time?' Marc finishes.

'Like I said, I'm probably just a little lonely in the day.' I busy myself cutting up pizza. 'I miss you. That's all.'

'That's all?' Marc asks, fixing me with intense eyes.

'That's all.' But I can't meet his eye.

3

I can feel Marc's eyes on me, but I can't look up.

It's true. I do miss you. But that's not all I miss. I want to act again. And I can't open that envelope on the mantelpiece because I think it will break my heart – being offered a part I can't take.

'There's nothing else you want to tell me?' Marc asks, closing the fridge door.

'No.'

Probably I am just lonely. It's so hard to make sense of what I'm feeling right now, with Ivy so young and needing me so much.

Marc sets a bowl of green salad on the table. 'Do we need another little talk about lying, Sophia? Or would you rather I put you over my knee?'

I would laugh, but I know he's being serious.

'Really, Marc. I'm just alone a lot. That's probably all it is. Jen's so wrapped up in her new business. And Tom and Tanya … you're being very strict on your class this year, Mr Blackwell. I hardly ever see them.'

'You want to be the best, you have to put in the hours. Come the summer, they'll be some of the most sought-after young actors in London. So Mrs Blackwell.' Marc takes a bottle of red wine from the rack. He runs a corkscrew spiral blade around the metal wrapping. 'What are we going to do with this loneliness of yours?'

I love watching his fingers work.

'It won't be forever,' I say, as Marc twists the screw into the cork. 'Ivy will be all grown up one day.'

Pop!

The cork comes free, and Marc pours red wine into my glass, then his.

'And what about when her brother or sister is born?' Marc asks.

My eyes widen. 'You're thinking of more babies already?'

Marc sits, taking a sip of wine. 'Of course. Aren't you?'

'Not quite yet.'

'If you're missing your friends,' says Marc, 'how about we move to the city for a while? You'll see more of them if they're on your doorstep.'

'Maybe.'

He watches me over his wineglass. 'Not the enthusiastic response I was hoping for. What are we going to do with you, Mrs Blackwell?'

My eyes wander to the living room. 'I … think I miss acting.'

Marc places his glass firmly on the table. 'No more rushing into things, Sophia. You still have a lot to learn. The classroom is open, when Ivy is old enough for you to be away for long stretches. Until then, your place is here.'

I look down at my pizza slice.

That's exactly what I thought you'd say.

I know Marc doesn't want me to act. He doesn't want me doing anything that puts me out of his sight or control.

He'd be happy if I stayed home all day, every day, a little bird in a cage.

'Sophia, look at me,' Marc snaps. '*Look* at me. I hate seeing you sad.'

I know my eyes are heavy.

My perfect baby, house and husband … what more could I wish for?

Pushing on a smile, I say, 'I shouldn't have said that about acting. And you know, I'm really not that lonely. Everything is fine.'

'That does it.' Marc stands and closes the kitchen door. 'Mrs Blackwell, lying to your husband is a very serious matter.'

'Who says I'm lying?'

'I do. You know it. I know it. The pasta knows it. Something is wrong. And something needs to be done.'

'Marc—'

'Here. Now.' He beckons me.

I shake my head, smiling now, but I get to my feet and go to him.

We grin at each other as he pulls me onto his lap.

'Now Sophia.' He sweeps my long, wavy brown hair around my neck. 'As I'm sure you're aware, a husband must discipline his wife from time to time.'

'Must he indced?'

'He must. And I take my husbandly duties very seriously.'

'Thank goodness,' I smile. 'What would I do without you?'

'I imagine,' says Marc, 'that you'd be totally, utterly out of control.'

I close my eyes.

'Lie over my lap.' The words are firm and low.

Oh god.

After all this time, I'm still putty in Marc's hands. Sometimes, I think I would do *anything* he asked.

Perhaps that thought should be frightening. But I know he would die to protect me. And I love him, just as fiercely.

There's something about this kind of love – this obsession we have with each other, and the darkness we explore. I'm incomplete without him, and he without me.

And I want Marc's instruction more than ever.

Marc lays me over his legs, and my fingers graze the kitchen floor tiles.

'Very good, Mrs Blackwell.' I can feel the smile in Marc's words.

God.

He can still send shivers through me with a few well-chosen words.

I don't see him raise his hand. Only feel and hear the sharp smack as his palm comes down on my buttocks.

Smack.

Smack.

Smack.

His hand is firm and heavy, sending flashes of pain around my backside and down my legs.

My whole body burns hot.

Smack.

Smack.

Smack.

I am so tuned into him now. Every sense is alert. The sound of his hand is electric, and my skin sparkles under his touch.

Marc spanks me rhythmically and precisely, with enough impact to make me flinch.

I enjoy the spanking as it gets harder and more intense, and I love the thought of Marc – his handsome face frowning in concentration – enjoying the control he has over me.

Then he stops.

'Now stand up.'

I wriggle onto my feet, face flushed, my backside burning.

Marc reaches up to stroke the ends of my hair. 'You get more beautiful by the day. Do you know that? Sit down and eat your dinner.'

'That's it?' I laugh.

'For now,' says Marc. 'Need I lecture you again about anticipation?'

With difficulty, I drop back into my chair, my backside sore.

I'm breathless, watching Marc and wanting more.

'Patience Sophia. All good things come to those who wait. Eat your dinner.'

'Suddenly I'm not all that hungry.'

'Really Mrs Blackwell? Why is that? Something on your mind?'

4

'You know full well what's on my mind.'

Marc reaches over and cuts my pizza, holding out a forkful. 'You should eat something.'

I take a bite.

'I have an idea,' he says, cutting more pizza for me. 'Of how to cure your loneliness.'

'You do?'

'Yes. I'm going to take you on a trip.'

'What sort of trip?'

'A trip where I can lavish you with attention. I have some important business to attend to overseas. So I'm going to take you along, and remind you what it feels like to have my personal, undivided tuition all day, every day.'

'What important business?' I ask, accepting another piece of pizza.

'We can leave tomorrow. You'll find out then.'

'Tomorrow? Marc, we can't go on an overseas trip tomorrow. What about Ivy? She's never even been on a plane before – she might hate it. And she'll need a passport. Travel medicine just in case. The right things to sleep in—'

'Rodney will take care of everything.'

'But Marc, *tomorrow*? We've never even taken Ivy to London before.'

'You're not content, Sophia. A trip is exactly what you need. And while you're away, you can start thinking about the *real* world. And your place in it. At home with Ivy. Once you've had chance to rest and see things in perspective, everything will be clearer.'

That's what I'm afraid of.

'Marc—'

'And another thing. I think you should return to Ivy College next year.'

'Ivy College? I've been in a movie, Marc. What else do I need to learn?'

'Plenty. I've told you before – you rushed into that movie. You need to go back and lay some foundations.'

'Even if you're right, everyone knows about the two of us. It would be weird.'

'You care so much what people think?'

'No. But how will the other students feel, knowing one of their classmates is married to the teacher? We'd have to work so hard to show everyone I'm not your favourite.'

'You'll always be my favourite.'

'You know what I mean.'

Marc stands up, dusting his hands on a napkin. 'I'm telling you Sophia, it will do you the world of good to be a student again. When Ivy is old enough, of course. Now listen – that parcel has sat on the mantelpiece long enough. It's time to open it.'

Marc goes to the living room and returns with the silver box.

24

He pushes my plate to one side, and puts the parcel on my reed placemat, where it glimmers under the bright kitchen lights.

'Perhaps you can explain why you've walked past this for weeks and been too afraid to open it up?'

'It's not that I've been afraid, exactly.'

'Do you have any idea what's inside?'

'It has a lotus flower on the box.' I stroke the silver stem and petal prongs embossed on cardboard. 'So ... something to do with the Riviera Film Festival?'

'That would be my guess too.' Marc frowns. 'Although it feels a lot heavier than mine.'

'Did you get an invitation?' I ask.

'Of course. I'm invited every year.'

I push the box on the table and stand, wiping my hands with a napkin. 'What's the point in torturing myself? Film festivals. Awards. I can't do any of that stuff right now.'

'It's good manners, for a start,' says Marc. 'Whoever sent you that invitation will want a reply. The sooner you let them know, the better.'

'Okay, fine.' I pull off the lid, frowning at the folded card and sheaf of papers inside.

Then, just like that, I realise what the papers are.

Quickly, I push the lid back on, my heart yammering.

Marc frowns. 'Sophia?'

I shake my head. 'It's nothing. Just ... like you said, an invitation.'

'What else?' Marc asks.

I blink at him. 'Does it matter?'

'Yes it matters,' he insists.

'There's a script in there.'

'A script? From whom?'

'Who cares?' I say. 'I'm not doing it anyway.'

'I'm glad you see sense about that.'

'See sense?'

'Christ Sophia – you were barely ready for *Rapunzel*. And now you have a baby. Movies are the last thing you should be considering.'

'Barely ready? *Rapunzel* turned out great. Everyone said so.'

'You still had a lot to learn, making that movie. Everything was moving too fast before Ivy came along. It makes sense to slow down now. And when the time is right, go back to your studies.'

'What if I want to act in a movie?'

'A moment ago you were saying you couldn't possibly be away from Ivy. That a nanny was out of the question.'

'I know, I know. I just …'

'You love acting,' Marc finishes for me.

I nod.

'And when Ivy is a little older, you can act at Ivy College. In a safe, nurturing environment. And when you're ready, you can start taking movie roles. Perhaps when Ivy is at school. There's plenty of time.'

'Is that what this is all about? Keeping me safe?'

'In part. And stopping you from exhausting yourself. Taking on things you're not ready for.'

I sigh. 'This argument is pointless. Ivy's too young to have a nanny. So I can't act anyway. You got your wish.'

'It's not my wish for you not to act. And I disagree with you – Ivy isn't too young for a nanny. As a matter of fact, a nanny might help solve this loneliness of yours. Give you time to see friends in the city.'

'I don't want a nanny.'

I hear the tiniest little noise and know that Ivy has woken up.

'A mother's hearing,' I tell Marc, standing up. 'No nanny on earth would be able to hear like that.'

5

'Sophia,' says Marc, striding after me. 'We still need to talk about this.'

I kneel down by the Moses basket, and smile like an idiot as Ivy sleepily opens her big, blue eyes.

'Hello gorgeous girl. Mummy's here.'

Marc kneels down beside me, and puts a large, gentle hand on Ivy's head. 'Perhaps this discussion is best saved for later.'

'There's nothing left to say,' I insist. 'Okay – I admit it. I miss acting. But it's something I'm going to have to live with.' I lift Ivy up into my arms, laying her against my chest.

'You're tired and you're not thinking straight. We'll talk on our trip tomorrow.'

'I already told you.' I stroke Ivy's downy head. 'There's nothing to talk about.'

'Sophia, you're being childish.'

I stand and walk with Ivy, swaying her back and forth. But she doesn't stop crying.

'Here.' Marc comes beside me. 'Let me take her. You're exhausted.'

'I'm really *not* that tired.'

'You haven't had a full night's sleep in months.'

'I'm her mother, Marc. I'm with her all day. I know what she needs better than anyone.'

Marc puts a firm hand on my shoulder. 'Just … for a moment, let me try. I had a little sister, once upon a time. I'm not too terrible with babies.'

Ivy won't stop crying, and I begin pacing faster, rocking her back and forth. 'Something's wrong with her,' I decide. 'She never usually cries when she wakes up. Maybe we should call a doctor.'

'Before we enlist the medical profession, would you just let her father try?'

Reluctantly, I put Ivy into Marc's arms.

Her cries get louder and more frantic.

'See?' I say, reaching out to take her back.

'Wait a minute.' Marc takes Ivy to the window, and shows her the sunset.

Instantly, she stops crying.

'Will you look at that?' says Marc. 'She was just a little bored. Like her mother. Rodney will pack everything for our trip tomorrow. We'll leave at nine o'clock.'

'But Ivy usually naps just after nine—'

'I know. She'll fall asleep in the car seat and wake at the airport.'

Ivy wakes a few times in the night. The third time, she just won't settle, and I am in tears, walking her around the nursery.

It was never like this with Sammy.

I'm startled by the shadow of Marc, his toned body lit by the hallway light. He wears loose black pyjama bottoms and nothing else.

'Sophia—'

'I don't know what's wrong with her,' I sob. 'She's had milk. I just …' I burst into tears.

Marc puts his arms around us, then takes Ivy. He lifts her high in the air, and she goes limp and stops crying. Then he folds her against his shoulder and walks around.

Within a minute, she's asleep.

'How did you do that?'

'Because I'm not overtired and irate. This is getting ridiculous. You doing this all on your own, and it's wearing you out. All this talk of acting – a rest if what you need. It's time to hire professional help. You should go to bed. You're exhausted.'

'But—'

'No arguments.' He lays Ivy gently in the cot, and she turns her head. 'Things have to change.'

Ivy is so absolutely beautiful when she sleeps. I could watch her forever.

'Bed,' Marc tells me. 'And tomorrow, we're going to revisit this subject of hiring a nanny seriously.'

I rub my eyes, feeling tears on my knuckles.

'Now.' Marc's voice is softer as he guides me out of the nursery. 'Ivy is fine with her father. You have a big day tomorrow and for once you need to sleep.'

'Are you going to tell me where we're going?'

'No. You're going to have to wait.'

6

In the early hours of the morning, Ivy wakes again.

I push off the duvet, ready to run to her, but Marc grabs my wrist.

'Where do you think you're going?'

'To get Ivy milk.'

'No,' says Marc. 'I'll do it. You need to sleep.'

'*You* need to sleep too.'

'I'll be fine.'

The next morning, I wake in a panic.

Ivy.

Blinking at the bedside clock, my heart turns to ice.

Eight o'clock. Oh god.

Ivy will have woken by now. I should have heard her cry. Something must be wrong. And Marc isn't beside me …

I spring up and run to the nursery.

The cot is empty, so I tumble downstairs and find Marc and Ivy in the sitting room, on our big, squashy sofa.

Ivy is lying on Marc's bare chest, sleeping contentedly, while he reads a newspaper and drinks black coffee.

My face softens.

'You didn't wake me,' I say, bare feet feeling polished floorboards.

Marc's blue eyes look up from his newspaper. 'You needed to sleep. Rodney made breakfast. It's laid out in the kitchen.'

'Is Ivy okay?'

Marc tilts his chin to look at the sleeping baby on his chest. 'She's perfect.'

I sit on the edge of the sofa. 'I'm sorry. About last night. I was just tired.'

'I know you're tired. That's why I'm arranging some extra help for you.'

'Marc. Listen. I think maybe I just miss you during the day. Perhaps if you just came home earlier—'

'It would only solve half the problem,' says Marc. 'You're tired, Sophia. You need someone to share the burden.'

'Ivy's not a burden.' I drop onto the sofa beside him.

'No. Of course she isn't. But she is tiring. And when you're exhausted like this, you're not thinking straight. You think you want to act, when all you really want is a good night's sleep.'

Maybe Marc's right. But …

'I see the cogs ticking, Mrs Blackwell,' says Marc, stroking a finger down my forehead. 'What is going on in there?'

'I'm thinking about acting,' I admit.

'Don't.'

'Oh so patronising.'

'But right.' Marc puts down his coffee cup. 'Now listen. I've arranged to have a nanny accompany us on this trip. Just temporarily. So you can get used to the idea of accepting help.'

'Marc—'

'Sophia. You are exhausted. It isn't healthy – taking all this on yourself.'

'Millions of women—'

'Millions of women have mothers, sisters to help out,' says Marc. 'You have no one. That's going to change. As of today. Our new nanny will accompany us on the plane. And when we reach our destination, she can look after Ivy while we make our appointment.'

'You expect me to let someone I've never met look after Ivy?'

'Do you think I'd let anyone near our daughter who hadn't been properly vetted?'

'I'm her mother, Marc. The most important vetting comes from me.'

He folds up his newspaper. 'You should know to trust me by now.'

'Ivy's so young. It's way too soon to have someone else helping out.'

'It's not too soon.'

I feel tears coming again, and swipe them away. Why do I keep crying *all* the time?

Marc rearranges Ivy and pulls me against his chest. 'You are a good mother, Sophia. A wonderful mother. But it's time to loosen the reins.'

'And get help from someone I've never met?'

'The new nanny comes highly recommended. I promise you – she's the best there is. Look, this is just for the trip. Okay? If you don't like the nanny, we'll send her home. Now eat some breakfast. The car will be here soon.'

7

'So tell me about this nanny,' I say, as we drive towards City Airport. 'Have you met her?'

'No,' says Marc. 'I've never met her. But I know her husband. And Denise gave me the recommendation. There's no one I would trust more. This nanny has worked for some prominent London families.'

Which means she's probably very snooty, I decide. *Well, if she's not my sort of person, I'll say so straight away. I'm not having anyone I don't like looking after my baby.*

'This is a favour,' Marc continues. 'Technically, she doesn't work anymore. Not since she was married.' He raises a teasing eyebrow. 'But her husband let her off the leash for our trip.'

'Let her off the *leash*?'

'Just a turn of phrase,' says Marc, his lip twitching. 'Of course, if you're interested in leashes …'

I can't help smiling. 'Stop that.'

'I have a feeling you're going to enjoy this trip,' says Marc. 'We had some unfinished business in the kitchen yesterday, didn't we?'

My cheeks redden. 'You can't talk like that with Ivy around.'

'All the more reason to hire a nanny.'

The private jet is as beautiful as ever – soft, white leather seats and a tan cushioned interior.

I smell coffee and freshly baked pastries as we climb aboard.

Marc has arranged for a baby cot to be placed by our seats, but Ivy is wide-awake as the engines start, staring at everything.

I hold her in my arms, so she can look out of the window.

As the ground crew load the plane, a limo pulls up.

'That's weird.' I frown. 'How can the engines be starting if the pilot's only just arrived?'

But it's not the pilot.

A young, red-haired girl steps out of the limo. She hands a duffle bag to a man in a neon-yellow vest, then climbs the plane steps.

'This is her,' says Marc, standing. 'The new nanny.' He strides down the plane.

My heart pounds.

'Welcome onboard,' Marc calls down the steps. 'Sophia has been waiting to meet you. Come this way.'

I cuddle Ivy close to my chest.

'Well this is her,' I whisper. 'The new nanny. Listen – cry if you don't like her. And then mummy will know. Okay?'

The red-haired girl steps onto the plane, and I scrutinise her from head to toe.

She's younger than I expected – I suppose I think of nannies as old dragons. And she's pretty, with pale skin and freckles.

She can't be very experienced, I decide. *She's barely older than me.*

I like her clothes, though. She wears jeans, which are embroidered with black sequins, and a baggy off-the-shoulder sweatshirt with a hand-printed Scottish flag on the front.

I'm glad she isn't formally dressed – that would have been an instant black mark.

The girl smiles when she sees me.

'Hi.' She marches along the plane and sticks out her hand. 'You must be Sophia. I'm Seraphina. Seraphina Mansfield.'

8

'Um … hi.' I let the girl shake my hand.

Seraphina seems … nice. Natural. Not stiff or stuck up.

Her red hair falls about her shoulders, and Ivy reaches up to grab a handful of it.

'Babies always do that,' Seraphina laughs. 'Must be something to do with the colour. So this is Ivy? She's beautiful, isn't she?'

Seraphina perches on the chair arm and strokes Ivy's head. 'Gorgeous. And she looks just like you. Marc tells me you're an actress.'

'*Was* an actress.' I turn to the window.

'Listen, I know it's tough.' Seraphina slides into the chair beside me. 'Having someone else look after your baby. I'm not here to try and take over. But I'm great at giving tired mothers a few nights off. I don't mind waking up. Not at all.'

Ivy is really staring at Seraphina. And smiling.

With a clunk, the plane door swings closed, and our air steward pulls the lock into position.

Marc watches me from the front of the plane, arms folded, a tiny smile on his lips.

'I'll leave you three to get to know each other.' He takes a seat near the cock pit.

'You know what?' says Seraphina, stroking Ivy's cheek. 'If you're not comfortable with anything at any point, just tell me. Okay? I kind of get the feeling this was arranged over your head.'

I laugh. She really is nice. And Ivy seems to like her.

'Marc arranged it,' I admit. 'He's so convinced that a break will do me good.'

'And what do you think?'

I find myself chewing a fingernail. 'Marc's often right about things.'

'You sure about that? Or does he just think he's right?'

I laugh again. 'No, he honestly is right a lot. I should give this a try. It could be that after a few night's sleep, I feel like myself again.'

'You don't feel like yourself?'

'We-ell, I love being a mother,' I say. 'I love Ivy.'

'But?'

And then I hear myself tell this total stranger the truth. 'I miss acting.'

'Makes sense,' says Seraphina. 'When you have a passion, it hurts not to do it.'

'How long have you been a nanny?' I ask her.

'Since I was sixteen. Well.' She lowers her voice. '*Eighteen*, officially. But I started work young.'

'Marc says you don't work anymore.'

'Oh, I *so* do work!' she laughs. 'I mean, just on temporary placements these days. There's a little boy back home I've fallen in love with, so I can't leave him for long. Did Patrick say I don't work any more? I'll kill him.'

'Who's Patrick?' I ask.

'My husband. He's what you call traditional. If he had his way, I wouldn't lift a finger.'

'Sounds familiar,' I say, my eyes wandering to Marc.

'But I couldn't imagine not working,' says Seraphina. 'It's who I am, you know?'

'I know what you mean.'

Ivy is being so good and still. I feel a wave of guilt. How could I even think about acting when I have this beautiful baby?

'Would you like to hold her?' I say, offering Ivy to Seraphina.

'I'd love to.' Seraphina takes Ivy and makes faces at her.

Ivy lets out a little giggle, and my heart melts.

'She likes you,' I say. 'I suppose all children do.'

'Eventually,' says Seraphina. 'But not always at first. Ivy here is very friendly. Must have a good mother.' She winks.

'Oh, I don't know about that.'

'Of course you're a good mother,' Seraphina insists. 'Now listen. Don't feel guilty about someone else helping out with your daughter. You know what? Half the world share their babies around. Mothers aren't designed to do it alone.'

I sigh. 'I already have so much help around the house.'

'Being a mother is always tiring,' says Seraphina. 'No matter how much help you have. When was the last time you had a whole night's sleep?'

'Before Ivy was born,' I admit.

'See? Your shift never ends.'

'I love it though,' I insist.

'Of course you do. But that doesn't mean you're not allowed to love other things. And still want to act. Anyway, listen. I'm here to help on this trip. So let me help. Okay?'

9

As the plane comes in to land, I see miles of fir trees, snowy mountains and blue lakes.

Where are we?

Ivy is sleeping now, strapped into her cot.

At the back of the plane, Seraphina naps on the daybed.

I unbuckle myself and wobble down the aisle towards Marc.

'So where are we?' I ask him.

Marc pulls me onto his lap. 'Nice to see you're as curious as ever.'

'Who wouldn't be?' I say.

He strokes hair from my face. 'You know, we have some unfinished business. From the kitchen table yesterday. I'm hoping to settle that business later today. After we land.'

'But WHERE will we land?' I insist.

He smiles. 'Switzerland.'

'Oh *wow*.' I lean towards the window. 'That's amazing. Why didn't you just tell me where we were going?'

'It would spoil the anticipation,' Marc's lips twitch. 'And you know how I feel about anticipation.'

'You are infuriating. Do you know that?' I lean into his hard chest, and his arms come tight around me.

'We work well together, don't you think?' he whispers into my hair.

'Mostly, yes.'

'Mostly?' Marc pulls me back so I'm looking right up at him. 'Careful, Sophia. Don't make the punishment even worse.'

I give him a warning 'not here' look, and pull myself off his lap.

'I'd better go check on Ivy.'

A shiny black 4x4 people carrier picks us up from the airport, its huge tyres holding us high off the road.

We drive up a winding mountain trail of fir trees and blue rock.

From time to time, I catch flashes of a sparkling blue lake below us.

Leaning against the window, I smile at green trees.

'I love this place,' I whisper to Marc, who sits beside me, his hand firmly on my thigh.

Seraphina is on the other side of the car, with Ivy beside her in a baby seat. She's spent the whole journey so far talking to Ivy and making her smile.

I'm really getting to like this girl. She's so at ease. And so natural with Ivy. If I were a baby, I'd like her too.

A few jaunty wooden houses are set into the mountainside, and I see signs for shops and restaurants in several different languages – French, German and Italian.

Soon, mountainside gives way to shops, cottages and restaurants, and we drive into a stunningly beautiful chocolate-box town set around a crystal-clear lake.

'So where *exactly* are we?' I ask Marc.

'Montreux,' he replies, squeezing my thigh. 'By Lake Geneva.'

'Are we going skiing or something?'

His lips twitch. 'Not quite.'

The 4x4 drives along the lake, and I see a beautiful, yellow wedding-cake building overlooking the water. It's huge, with a hundred twinkling windows.

'This is where we're staying,' says Marc, as the car pulls to a stop.

'*Here*?' I say, looking up and up. 'It's like a castle.'

Marc's lips flicker into a smile. 'Very fitting, don't you think? For a princess.'

'And *why* are we here, exactly?' I ask.

10

Marc unbuckles his seatbelt. '*That* you will find out later.'

I roll my eyes, but can't help grinning.

'Look, Ivy,' I say, leaning over to unclip her baby seat. 'This is where we'll be staying tonight.'

The chauffeur opens our car door.

'Here.' Seraphina reaches for Ivy. 'Let me take the baby while you get out.'

'Thanks,' I say, surprised by how willing I am to put Ivy into her arms.

I really do like her, I realise. *Maybe a nanny isn't such a bad idea after all.*

The hotel lobby is astonishing – a stretch of diamond marble tiles, leading to a sweeping, gold-railed staircase.

Yellow-suited bellboys hurry across the marble with a trolley for our luggage, the wheels gliding silently on the smooth floor.

'Mr and Mrs Blackwell.' A black-suited gentleman steps from behind the lobby desk. 'A very warm welcome to our hotel. I've been sent to greet you personally, as your butler and concierge. Anything you wish for, you only have to ask me.'

The man wears a round, yellow cap, and his white-black hair is neatly cut around his ears.

I detect an Italian accent, and reply, 'Molte grazie,' without thinking.

The man's face lights up. 'You speak Italian?'

'A little,' I say. 'My mother taught me. A long time ago.'

He grabs my hand and shakes it warmly. 'Benvenuto! Benvenuto. A pleasure to have you here. Please, allow me to show you to your suite. The *best* room in the hotel.' He puts his fingers together and gives them an extravagant Italian kiss. 'Bellissimo! Please come with me, Mrs Blackwell. My name is Phillipe. As I say, ask me for anything at all.'

I notice Marc smiling at me.

'What?' I ask.

'It looks like someone else has fallen in love with you,' he says, stroking hair from my face.

Phillipe leads us up the black-carpeted staircase.

Marc and I follow.

'The nanny quarters are just down there,' Phillipe says, gesturing down the hallway.

'Great,' says Seraphina. 'I'll go unpack.'

'No need madam.' Phillipe gives her a bright smile. 'The housekeeper will be in attendance soon.'

'Well, maybe I'll just check out the view or something.' Seraphina winks at me. 'I'll leave you two to get settled. Let me take Ivy.'

'Oh, Ivy can stay with us,' I say. 'Honestly, it's fine.'

'Sophia.' Marc replies with a warning voice. 'You need to practise letting go of Ivy from time to time. Starting from now.'

'He's right, you know.' Seraphina takes Ivy and sways her back and forth. 'But if you're not comfortable with anything, just let me know, okay? I'm right down the hall.'

I nod, feeling my heart tug.

'It'll be okay,' says Seraphina, giving me a kind smile.

My heart softens a little.

'Mr and Mrs Blackwell?' Phillipe waves us towards silky double doors. 'Here is your room.'

I turn, as Phillipe opens the doors.

Wow.

Our suite is enormous. Soft, white furniture, a four-poster bed, dishes of chocolates and six gleaming sets of balcony doors.

Goodness, the *view*. Panoramic and astonishing – the lake, blue and perfect, glimmers beside snow-topped mountains.

'There's just one thing,' I say. 'We need a cot. For Ivy.'

The butler puts a hand to his chest. 'Mrs Blackwell! A thousand apologies. This should already have been arranged. Please let me—'

'Actually, there's no mistake,' says Marc. 'I didn't request a cot. Ivy will sleep in Seraphina's room.'

'*Sleep*? No Marc, I couldn't,' I insist, shaking my head. 'Not yet. She's never even been abroad before.'

'She'll be no further away than when you're at home with the baby monitor,' Marc says, sliding hands into his pockets. 'You can see her any time you like.'

'You have nothing to worry about in this hotel, Mrs Blackwell,' offers Phillipe, fussing with the thick, silk curtains. 'It's a very safe place. Excellent security. And so romantic. Take some alone time with your handsome husband. Enjoy.'

Marc strides over and gives our butler a folded note. 'Thank you, Phillipe. There won't be anything else.'

'You don't want I unpack your things?' Phillipe's hands drop from the curtains, his eyes crinkling with concern.

'Not right now.'

Phillipe looks between us, then swiftly crosses the room, closing the doors behind him.

When the double doors are closed, I turn to Marc. 'That seemed a little curt. Even for you. He was only trying to help.'

Marc locks the door. 'You didn't see how much I tipped him.'

'Money doesn't make up for good manners,' I say, sitting on the soft bed.

'I wanted to talk to you. Alone.' Marc tests the door to make sure it's locked. 'Sophia. We have an appointment tomorrow. And dinner this evening—'

There's a gentle knock at the door.

'Who is it?' Marc barks.

'Oh. Um … hi,' calls a soft voice. 'It's just me. Seraphina. Is this a bad time?'

'Come in,' I call out.

Marc unlocks the door, and Seraphina leans tentatively into the room, Ivy tight against her chest.

'Are you two settling in okay?' she asks.

I give a tired smile. 'Fine.'

'I thought I'd take Ivy for a little walk. Is that okay?'

I look at my baby, sleeping in Seraphina's arms. She's screwing up her face in her sleep, which tells me she's uncomfortable and will wake soon.

I feel a wave of tiredness wash over me, knowing that usually I'd have to rock and shush her, or push her in the pram over something bumpy for the best part of an hour.

But today I *don't* have to.

Seraphina is offering to help.

'The hotel have a special stroller all ready for us,' Seraphina continues. 'It's fur-lined, would you believe. Luxury!'

I smile.

'That sounds great,' I say, relief softening my shoulders. 'A walk is exactly what Ivy needs.'

'You needn't worry,' says Seraphina. 'I'll pack plenty of bedding. And milk. She won't be cold or hungry. You can trust me.' She gives me a big smile.

'I know,' I say. And I mean it.

11

'You look exhausted,' Marc observes, the moment the door closes. 'Why don't you catch up on some sleep? The beds here are said to be the most comfortable in the world.'

My eyes wander to the big, downy white bed. 'But we're in Switzerland,' I protest. 'I want to see things.'

'There'll be time for that later.' Marc locks the door again.

I feel myself yawn, quite without meaning to.

Marc laughs. 'Bed, Sophia. Right now.'

I climb out of my jumper and jeans, sliding under the duvet in just a t-shirt and underwear.

Lying on the huge, soft bed, I'm stroked by silky cotton.

Soon, I'm lost in sleep.

When I wake, Marc is sitting on the edge of the bed, watching me.

'How long did I sleep?' I ask, rubbing my eyes.

'Most of the day.' Marc is looking at me intensely, like I'm some precious thing that might break if he doesn't pay attention.

'Really?' I sit up. 'Is Ivy okay?'

'She's fine.' Marc runs a hand up and down the duvet, stroking my legs. 'She's still with Seraphina.'

'You let me sleep *all* day?'

'Almost all day,' says Marc, turning to the window. 'You needed it.'

'You can't have been sitting there the whole time?'

'I was. More or less.' Marc turns back to me. 'Did you sleep well?'

'Really well.' I notice a pinky sunset through the tall windows. 'Wow. It really is late.' I swing my legs out of the bed. 'Is Ivy in Seraphina's room?'

'Yes. But you're staying here. Rest and recuperation is your job today. Husband's orders.'

I laugh. 'I've just *had* a rest.'

Marc frowns, shaking his head. 'Not nearly enough.'

I push the duvet back. 'How many hours have you been watching me, exactly?'

His lips twitch. 'Five.'

'And you've just been sitting here with me?' I say, eyebrows lifting in disbelief. 'Didn't you want to explore this amazing hotel?'

'I've seen hundreds of amazing hotels.' Marc reaches forward to stroke hair from my face. 'You're more beautiful than all of them.'

'This room is incredible,' I shield my eyes against the setting sun.

Feeling soft carpet under my feet, I stretch again.

Marc's lips flick into a smile. 'There's more.' He stands, opening a door by the bed. 'Take a look.'

'Oh my god.' I hop onto thick carpet and wander towards the door. '*Wow*. It's like being in a spa.'

The whole room is white marble, flecked with silver and blue. Essential oils sit on a glass shelf, next to plate of fish-shaped chocolates.

Sinks are cut into the wall, and a giant round bathtub rests on golden feet.

'This can't be all for us,' I breathe. 'It's huge.'

'For us and nobody else,' says Marc. 'I want you to take a long, relaxing bath before dinner tonight.'

'But Ivy—'

'Is absolutely fine.'

Marc turns a tap, and hot water gushes into the bath.

I catch a glimpse of us in one of the mirrors – me in my t-shirt and underwear, looking startled and sleep-crumpled.

Marc is handsome and stern beside me, sliding hands under my t-shirt and lifting it over my head. He drops my clothing over a towel rail, then undoes my bra, watching me in the mirror as he pulls it free of my arms.

Behind us, the bath steams and bubbles.

'Are you intending to join me in this bath?' I whisper.

Marc's hands drop to my waist, pushing my panties from my hips.

I feel the skin-warmed fabric drop to my feet.

'Perhaps.' Marc is still watching me in the mirror, and I see my naked breasts rise and fall. 'Into the tub with you, Mrs Blackwell.'

He helps me climb into the high marble bath, holding my arm firmly as my feet find hot water. 'Sit down.'

I laugh. 'What's my next instruction? Beg? Roll over?'

His lips twitch into a smile. 'I might make you beg. I'm not sure yet.'

My body gives a little shiver. 'Well, if you could warn me now. So I can get used to the idea.'

'I don't give warnings.' He guides me down into the bath, and I go where he wants me, sinking into hot, bubbling water.

Heat stings my skin as I stretch out my legs.

'It feels amazing in here,' I say, feeling bubble jets massage my legs.

The water level is rising by the second and my body gets lighter.

Marc watches me, a half smile on his lips. 'Lie back in the water.'

'You don't want me to beg yet then?' I ask.

'Not yet.'

I lie back, feeling my hair spread out underwater, loose and swaying like a mermaid's.

Marc unbuttons his shirt, watery light dancing over his firm chest.

I watch as he pulls his shirt free, mesmerised by his perfect, long, toned body.

'So *are* you joining me in here?' I ask.

'I think I should. Just to make sure you don't drown.' He continues to undress, and I see the size and length of him rigid in his black underwear.

When he pulls his jockey shorts free, I can't take my eyes off him. Or more specifically, the rock hard part of him that's pointing right at me.

'You know I can swim, don't you?' I say.

Marc's long, tall body steps into the bath. 'All the same, I think for your safety I should join you.'

His eyes are intense, and he is long and hard, casting a shadow over my stomach as he straddles my body.

God, he is perfect. Toned, rippling abdomen and hard pectoral muscles move under the low light as Marc kneels between my legs and dips his head.

'Oh god,' I moan, as his tongue finds me. 'Oh god Marc.'

Marc quickens his movements, sending electric shocks over my whole body.

I moan and cry out.

He moves back on his haunches. 'Now then. We had a lesson about anticipation yesterday, isn't that right?'

I can't speak. My whole body is tense and throbbing and begging for him to put his mouth back.

Marc smiles, one eyebrow raised. 'Good things come to those who wait.' He turns me over in the water and rests me along his thigh. 'Comfortable?' he asks, his hands firmly on my hips.

I feel his knee between my breasts. 'Depends how you look at it,' I gasp, desperate to feel him inside me.

'From this position,' says Marc, 'You look very good indeed.' Gently, he slides me back and forth over his leg.

'Oh Marc,' I moan. 'Oh god.'

'I hope you understand,' Marc murmurs, running a warn, wet hand up and down my back, 'that lying to your husband has consequences.'

12

'I do. I do understand.' I gasp, my eyes squeezing tight shut. All I can feel is Marc's hard thigh rubbing between my legs.

'You won't lie to me again, will you?' says Marc, his voice stern and authoritative.

'No,' I moan. 'Oh *god*.'

'Good.' Marc moves me back and forth. 'As you know, I punish bad behaviour.'

He slides me around on his hard thigh, his hands tight on my hips.

'If you promise me you'll behave yourself,' Marc whispers, 'you'll get a reward.'

My body is so hot. I can barely breathe.

'Will you behave yourself in future?' says Marc, clenching my hips tight in his fingers.

'I will,' I gasp. 'I will behave.'

'Good.' He turns me around in the rapidly rising water, pulling me against his hips and sliding himself inside me.

'Oh god Marc.' The length and heat of him burns between my legs, and I stare into his eyes, unable to look away.

'I love you,' I moan.

'I love you too.' He moves hair around my shoulders. Then his hips pivot back forth, back forth.

I'm weightless in the water, and all I can feel is Marc, hard inside me, sliding in and out.

'Oh god Marc,' I cry out. 'Oh god. Please. Oh god.'

'More?' he murmurs, quickening his pace.

I nod, eyes squeezing closed again. 'More. Oh god, yes. More. *More.*'

He thrusts his hips firmly against me, waves of water flowing around us as he moves over and over again.

Hot water splashes, and I lean back, feeling Marc's hands holding me tight at the small of my back as he pulls me onto him, going deeper every time.

A dull, bruisey pleasure builds up inside me, ebbing and flowing like the water, and I begin to open into warmth and ecstasy.

Marc watches me, his eyes hard and merciless, his strokes firm until I yield to him totally, my whole body softening as an orgasm floods my body.

'Oh *god.*'

I go momentarily limp.

Marc catches me, pulling me against his chest. I feel his damp torso, hard and firm and oh so safe – my haven. The place I can rest.

Arms wrapped tightly around me, Marc asks, 'Was the anticipation worth it, Mrs Blackwell?'

I nod against his damp skin. 'Totally.'

Marc reaches for a fluffy towel and wraps it around my shoulders, then lifts me out of the water.

In the bedroom, he lays me on the bed, watching me with intense blue eyes.

'I hope you're feeling rested, Mrs Blackwell.'

'Very.' I smile sleepily up at him.

Marc carefully dries my hands, and between my fingers. 'You are a wonderful mother to our daughter. But it's time you had a night off. There will be no decisions for you today. No responsibilities or worries. I will take care of everything, and you will do as you are told.'

I laugh. 'Is that so?'

Marc strokes my arm dry with the towel. 'There's always a first time.'

'You said we were going to dinner,' I point out, enjoying the feeling of soft cotton as Marc pats my shoulders dry.

'Yes,' says Marc, stroking long pieces of my hair with the towel. 'In the hotel ballroom restaurant. One of the finest in Switzerland. You'll need something special to wear.'

'I didn't pack much special,' I admit. 'Rodney suggested evening clothes, but I told him I'm be in motherhood mode. Nothing to dress up for.'

'Lucky I planned ahead.'

When Marc has finished drying me, he carries me into the huge walk-in wardrobe, which is spot-lit and decorated with vases of fresh, white roses.

Hanging in a mirrored show panel is a beautiful silk and lace gown. It's a mysterious midnight blue colour and flecked with star-like sparkles.

Marc lifts the dress by its hanger. 'I had a local clothing boutique send up an outfit for dinner.'

I feel myself smile. 'That's for me? It's gorgeous.'

'I'm glad you like it. Try it on.'

I'm grinning now. 'I'd love to.'

'No underwear tonight.' Marc helps me step into the gown and buttons up the back. 'Understood, Mrs Blackwell?'

I close my eyes at the feel of his fingers. 'I don't know about that,' I breathe. 'I might feel a little safer with panties on.'

'You'll always be safe with me,' says Marc doing up the last button. 'You should know that by now.'

The dress is so pretty and light, and it fits me like a glove. Sheer sleeves end in embroidered points, like a medieval princess.

Marc slips shoes onto my feet and ties silk around my ankles.

'Stand up,' he commands.

I do, turning back and forth, letting the loose skirt spin a little. I catch sight of myself in one of the full-length mirrors and see a silly grin on my face.

'It's beautiful,' I tell him.

Marc takes my arm. 'Shall we go to dinner?'

13

'Marc?'

Marc's arm, looped through my own, squeezes tight as we descend the sweeping staircase. 'You're thinking about Ivy.'

I nod. 'Are you sure she's okay with Seraphina?'

'Yes,' says Marc. 'Positive.'

'How do you know?'

A smile twists Marc's lips. 'I called. Every half hour while you were sleeping.'

I laugh, checking to see my feet are meeting the steps. 'You're as obsessive as I am.'

'Possibly more so.'

We reach the marble-floored lobby area, walking under a magnificent chandelier.

'You know, I think it might be okay,' I decide, learning into Marc's firm body. 'Ivy staying away over night. I trust Seraphina. And today has been … needed.'

'Ivy won't be away,' says Marc, sliding his arm free and taking my hand. 'She'll be just down the hall.'

'You know what I mean.'

'I do.' Marc squeezes my fingers. 'But I agree with you. I think she'll be fine. I wouldn't have set this up if I felt any other way.'

Phillipe meets us in the lobby with a jerky bow. 'Mr and Mrs Blackwell! I am hoping you are enjoying our hotel *so* much. I have your table, as promised. No request is too difficult for such important guests. Please come with me.'

'Request?' I ask Marc.

'I have something special planned,' say Marc. 'To ensure your continued relaxation.'

Phillipe leads us into the hotel ballroom restaurant – a huge, domed space of crystal chandeliers, cream-marble statues and pillars. Gold-framed mirrors decorate the walls.

It must be the hotel's main restaurant. I mean, it's just magnificent. Yet only one small table sits in the grand space.

The table is set for two.

'Is this … just for us?' I ask Marc, looking around the empty ballroom.

'Just for us.' Marc squeezes my hand again. 'I didn't want you disturbed by other guests this evening. So I booked out the whole restaurant.'

I laugh – more out of surprise than anything else. 'You didn't have to do that.'

'You're right. I didn't have to.' Marc leads me to our table. 'But I wanted you all to myself.'

'This room is amazing.' My voice echoes around the domed ceiling.

'It's hosted kings and queens,' says Marc. 'So you'll fit in just fine.'

'I'm not so sure,' I say, as Marc pulls out my chair.

The table is set with flickering candles, napkins folded to look like roses, an orchid centrepiece, bone china plates and crystal wine glasses. There are eight pieces of cutlery around each plate.

'Marc, you'll have to help me,' I whisper, taking a seat. 'I don't understand Swiss cutlery.'

'The cutlery here is the same as at home.' Marc pushes my chair in. 'There just happens to be a lot of it.'

'How will I know what to do with *all* that cutlery?' I ask. 'And the glasses …'

'Sophia, relax.' Marc takes a seat opposite, fixing me with intense eyes. 'There's no one else here. It's just you and I.'

'*Phillipe is here*,' I whisper, glancing back at our butler.

Phillipe, standing by the golden double doors, smiles and gives a little wave.

Marc frowns. 'Not for long.'

'I hope you're not jealous of our butler,' I say, turning back to Marc.

'Not yet.' His blue eyes darken. 'Do I have any reason to be?'

I laugh. 'Don't be ridiculous.'

While I'm mentally counting the cutlery, I have a thought. 'Wait Marc. Maybe I should check on Ivy before we eat.'

'She's fine.'

'But what if she's—'

'Seraphina would call,' says Marc, opening a bottle of mineral water. 'Everything is under control.'

'Aren't *you* worried about Ivy?' I insist.

Marc pours fizzing Berg mineral water into my glass. 'Every minute of every day. But I learned to delegate years ago.'

'Delegate? Is that code for bossing people around?'

'Careful Mrs Blackwell.' Marc places the Perrier bottle on the table, then fixes me with his intense eyes. 'I haven't nearly finished with you yet. That bath earlier was just the beginning.' He opens up his hand. 'Take a good look. You'll be feeling more of this later if you continue to talk back.'

Suddenly, Phillipe appears by my elbow.

'Oh!' I turn to him, blushing.

'Wine, madam?' Phillipe holds out a chilled bottle of white wine, wrapped in a white napkin.

I wonder how much he heard.

Marc remains totally unembarrassed, his palm still resting on the table.

'Fill both our glasses,' says Marc, his eyes not leaving mine.

'Yes sir.' Phillipe pours wine with a flourish.

'And you can serve the food now,' Marc tells Phillipe.

'You're sure, sir?' Phillipe looks between us, wine bottle in mid-air.

'Certain,' says Marc, dropping his hand, blue eyes holding me still.

Phillipe looks between us, then gives a jerky bow and trots out of the ballroom.

'What if I hadn't have wanted wine?' I ask Marc.

'I've already told you.' Marc holds his wine up to the light, swilling it around. 'This evening, you won't be making any decisions. I'll be deciding everything for you.'

I cock my head at my own wine glass. 'Says who?'

'Me.' Marc puts his glass firmly on the table. 'And any failure to follow my instructions will be met with swift and direct punishment.' He gives me that handsome half smile of his. 'Which I have a feeling you'll enjoy.'

I push my wine glass away. 'I shouldn't drink alcohol. What if Ivy needs me?'

'Seraphina is on hand.' Marc pushes the glass back towards me. 'One glass of wine is perfectly acceptable. As a matter of fact, I am going to insist you drink two glasses of wine. For being so disobedient.' He's smiling now.

'And how exactly are you going to make me do that?' I can't help smiling too.

'I can't *make* you do anything. I can only teach you how to behave. By punishing you if you step out of line.'

I feel a little shiver.

The truth is, I love seeing this side of Marc. I have no idea what that says about me. All I know is that when he takes charge, I enjoy it.

I pick up the wine glass and take a sip. 'Happy now?'

'Very.'

'It's nice,' I say, feeling the chilled liquid on my tongue.

'*Nice?*' Marc raises an eyebrow. 'Your vocabulary disappoints me.'

'Okay, it's … delicious. It tastes like … apples. And … maybe blackberries?'

'Better.'

'What kind of food do they have here?' I ask.

Marc's lips twitch into a smile. 'The Swiss-French kind.'

'Will the menu be written in French?' I ask.

'Yes.'

I feel a sudden need to chew my fingernails. 'So how will I—'

'I've already ordered for us.' Marc takes another sip of wine. 'I phoned ahead while you were sleeping.'

'Okay. As long as it isn't foie gras.'

We smile at each other.

'Funny you should mention that,' says Marc, leaning closer. 'It *was* on the menu.'

'Marc, you didn't!'

'Of course I didn't.' He watches me with amusement. 'Drink your wine.'

I take another sip. 'This really is nice.'

'There's that word again.'

I hear a loud cough, and see Phillipe trotting across the ballroom, two white plates balanced carefully on his hand and wrist.

'Excuse me Mr and Mrs Blackwell. Your first course.' Phillipe places what looks like dessert in front of us – a piped swirl of pastry – then quickly backs away and trots out of the room.

I look down at my plate, not sure what to make of the C-shaped puff of pastry, filled with white, foamy cream.

'Do they start with dessert here?' I ask, hovering my fork over the pastry.

'No.' Marc's lips twitch. 'This is savoury.'

My cheeks flush red. 'It's not funny. Not all of us have eaten in fancy restaurants all over the world, you know.'

Marc's smile grows. 'I'm not laughing. I'm just enjoying you. Now eat.'

Tentatively, I touch the pastry with my fork. 'What is it?'

'Cod and a savoury cream in a choux bun.'

'Shoe bun?' I say, still not sure how to cut my food. 'Like the ones you wear on your feet?'

'No Sophia.' Marc steeples his fingers together. 'A different kind of shoe. It's a light, French pastry.'

'Oh. Um …' I try to cut the pastry with my knife and fork, but it all crumbles.

Marc reaches over. 'You're using the wrong cutlery. Let me help you.'

Gently, he takes the fork from my hand, then gives me the smallest knife and fork to hold.

'Thank you,' I say, making neat cuts. When I taste the food, I feel myself smiling. 'It's … nice.'

'You're skating on thin ice, Mrs Blackwell.' Marc leans further forward, elbows on the table. 'Very thin ice.'

'Marc?'

'Yes Sophia?'

'You were right.' I take another mouthful of pastry. 'I needed a rest. It's been okay having someone else help out with Ivy.'

'I hope you're seeing things more clearly now.' He drums his fingertips together. 'And that you'll consider coming back to Ivy College next year. I'm extremely interested in your continued education.'

'It would be weird going back,' I say. 'Not just because you're there. But … I mean I've already been in a movie. What is there left to learn in a classroom?'

Marc frowns. 'Don't get arrogant, Sophia. You still have a lot to learn.'

'I wasn't being arrogant.' I shake my head, cutting more pastry. 'I just feel like … I've come a long way since

I took classes with you.'

Marc cuts his own food. 'You rushed into *Rapunzel*. And the musical. Don't you remember how hard you found things? Christ – you passed out at one point.'

'Yes,' I say, 'but I learned on the job.'

'You still need a good teacher.' Marc makes firm strokes with his knife. 'You're young.'

'So are you,' I point out.

'But I started younger.' Marc takes a swift mouthful of food, chews and swallows. 'Look, perhaps now isn't the best time to discuss this. We'll talk again in a few months. When Ivy is sleeping better and you're in a more agreeable frame of mind.'

I put down my knife and fork. 'You're saying I've been disagreeable?'

'No. I'm saying you're preoccupied. Tired. Not yourself.' He takes another forkful of food.

'I'm a little tired,' I admit, cutting pastry. 'But that doesn't mean I'm not thinking straight.'

'I beg to differ. If you can't see how tuition would benefit you … listen, we'll talk another time. I want you to relax. Enjoy your break.'

'You make our daughter sound like a job,' I say.

'Well she's certainly hard work.' Marc cuts more food. 'There's no shame in taking some time for yourself. Has it been bad so far?'

'You mean aside from the last couple of minutes? No. Not at all.' I chew another mouthful.

'Don't do that.' Marc shakes his head at me.

'Do what?'

'Feel guilty.' Marc puts down his fork, and slides his hand over to take mine. 'I know that look. Ivy will be sleeping right now. And *if* she wakes, in those brief moments, Seraphina will take care of her. You are a moment away if Ivy needs you.'

'I know. You're right.' I manage a smile, squeezing his hand over the table. 'Shall we start the dinner again? Forget about acting and teaching?'

'Good idea. Have you finished your starter?'

'Yes. It was delicious. Astonishing.' I throw him a teasing smile. 'Are those better words?'

Marc holds my gaze. 'Much better.'

I push my plate away, and Marc summons Phillipe to clear the table. To my surprise, Phillipe clears not only our plates, but the orchids and some candles too.

'Is dinner finished?' I whisper to Marc.

'It's only just beginning.'

14

A moment later, Phillipe returns with a giant half-wheel of cheese, mounted on a wooden trolley.

The cheese is so big that the trolley shudders beneath its weight.

Under the trolley are various dishes of food – toasted bread slices, daintily carved carrots, puffy pretzels, crisp-bread triangles, smoked ham and folded salami.

'I hope all that cheese isn't for me,' I say, eyeing up the giant half-wheel.

'I thought,' says Marc, 'seeing as we're in Switzerland, you should try a raclette.'

'What's that?' I ask, still surprised by the sheer size of the cheese. It's enough for twenty people.

Marc strokes my fingers. 'Flame-grilled cheese, melted at the table. Phillipe – get us started, would you?'

'Of course, sir.' Phillipe lights a blowtorch, holding it against the long, flat edge of the cheese wheel. Instantly, the cheese begins to bubble and melt.

Marc nods at the Phillipe. 'Thank you Phillipe. I can take it from here.'

'You're okay to operate the fire, Mr Blackwell?' Phillipe turns off the blowtorch and hands it to Marc.

'Yes.' Marc runs fingers up and down the torch handle,

raising an eyebrow at me. 'It's not a problem.'

'More wine before I leave?' Phillipe asks.

Marc nods. 'One more glass for my wife. Thank you.'

I smile and roll my eyes, but I don't object as Phillipe refills my glass.

'You finished the first so quickly,' Marc points out.

'Well it was so *nice*,' I laugh.

When Phillipe leaves, Marc takes my plate and fills it with bread slices, vegetables, ham and salami. Then he uses a long knife to push the melted cheese over my plate.

'What did you say this was called?' I ask, watching a mountain of food grow on my plate.

'Raclette.' Marc scrapes more melted cheese over perfect crisp-bread triangles. 'Technically the name of the cheese, but everyone here understands it should be served this way.'

'It's such a perfect little meal. I can't wait to try it.' I bite into a triangle of bread, topped with nutty, melted cheese. Then I try pretzels, pickles and salami.

'This is so *nice*.' I'm grinning now.

'That does it.' Marc stands, grabbing a napkin. He dabs my fingers and lips carefully with the soft cloth, then places my hands behind my back.

'What are you doing?' I whisper.

'Disciplining you.' Marc spins the napkin into a long, thin strand then wraps it around my wrists.

'Marc?' I'm still whispering, but it's an urgent whisper. 'Here? You're disciplining me *here*?'

'Yes.' Marc binds my wrists tight with the napkin, then sits back down.

'*Marc*. We're in public.'

'You should have thought of that before you decided to overuse a very boring and ordinary word.' Marc leans back in his chair, smiling.

'Untie me.' I struggle back and forth, but of course, Marc being an expert with a rope, has done an excellent job of immobilising me.

'Phillipe won't be back for a while.' Marc's eyes sparkle.

'This isn't funny.'

'I'm not trying to be funny.' Marc slides his chair closer. 'I did warn you about misbehaving.' He picks up a triangle of crisp bread with cheese on top. 'But just because you've misbehaved, doesn't mean you shouldn't eat. You need plenty of energy for what I have in mind.'

'Marc—'

'I'll untie you if you want me to. You know I will.' Marc holds out a piece of cheese-topped bread. 'But you'll find tonight much more relaxing if you just let me take charge.'

A marriage and a baby later, and he still does this. He still tests me.

I feel the napkin cutting into my wrists.

We both know I made my decision months ago.

I take a bite, chewing the crunchy bread and delicious melted cheese. Then I take another bite. And another. Piece by piece, Marc feeds me little squares of bread, washing them down with soft, fruity wine.

Between bites and sips, Marc dabs my mouth with a napkin.

After a while, I forget we're sort-of in public. The only thing in my world is Marc, Marc, Marc.

When my plate of food is finished, Marc sits back in his chair.

As if on cue, Phillipe appears and clears the table.

Dimly, I wonder if Phillipe has noticed my hands are tied. He's not letting on if he does; his face is totally impassive.

Perhaps I should be embarrassed. But … I'm not.

As Phillipe goes to leave, Marc raises a hand. 'Bring the dessert Phillipe, and then you're dismissed for the evening. I can take it from here.'

Phillipe bows. 'Very good sir.'

15

Dessert is a trough of strawberries dipped in Swiss chocolate, balanced on a dish of ice chips.

Phillipe also brings two shots of cloudy pink schnapps. 'Good night, Mr and Mrs Blackwell.' He offers an anxious smile. 'Are you sure I can't get you anything else? Champagne, perhaps?'

'That will be all for this evening,' says Marc. 'Thank you Phillipe.'

'Very good sir.' Phillipe bows again and trots away.

Marc lifts a chocolate strawberry with silver tongs and feeds it to me.

'Nice,' I murmur, as chocolate and strawberry flavours explode in my mouth. I taste champagne, dark chocolate and honey.

'I'm warning you, Sophia.' Marc takes my bottom lip in the tongs and twists it, just a little. Not enough to hurt. But close.

Suddenly, I'm very aware of my own breathing.

My chest begins to pound.

Marc squeezes the tongs tighter until I give a little gasp.

We watch each other, my lips throbbing between the silver. Then Marc releases my lip and taps the tongs purposefully on the table, watching me with hard, blue eyes. He stands, coming behind me. 'Don't turn around.'

Marc's fingers drop firmly on my shoulder, and I feel the cool metal tongs on my collarbone.

My breathing becomes fast and ragged.

Lowering his face to my neck, Marc presses his lips along my shoulder. He slides the tongs inside my dress, finding my breast and closing down hard on vulnerable skin.

I suck in air.

It doesn't hurt at first. But then he squeezes harder.

'*Ooh.*' I flinch, my eyes squeezing shut.

It's delicious agony – the tenderness and the pain. The anticipation of more.

Just as the red-hot burning at my breast becomes unbearable, Marc squeezes and releases, squeezes and releases the tongs.

It's enough to keep me on the edge of agony. The stinging pain ebbs, becoming a pleasant wave that burns hot again.

I am totally still. I can't move, even as Marc's hand slides from my shoulder.

He begins to unbutton my dress.

'Marc.' I shake my head at him. 'Not here.'

'Your opinion isn't necessary right now.'

Once Marc has unbuttoned my dress, he unties my wrists and rubs my sore skin with strong fingers. He slides the dress from my shoulders, pulling sheer sleeves over my wrists.

My heart thuds in my ears as Marc takes my reddened breast and covers it with his hand, frowning.

I know his conflict. He hates seeing me hurt. But we both enjoy it too.

'You know I'd never do anything you didn't like,' he whispers.

'I know.' My eyes are still half closed.

Marc presses the sharp edge of the tongs to my unreddened breast. 'Tell me to stop.'

'Don't stop.'

'Don't stop?' Marc draws a red curve around my breast.

'Don't stop,' I gasp.

'I like to see you submitting.' Marc draws a line all the way around my breast.

'I'm not submitting,' I insist, my voice barely a whisper. 'I'm consenting.'

'Consenting, yes. To domination.' I hear a slosh of liquid, then feel coolness and let out a gasp.

The red line Marc just made around my breast – it's on fire.

My eyes spring open.

Marc's fingers come into my hair, holding me still. 'It's just alcohol. It will burn for a moment.'

I nod, my eyes watering.

'Too much?' Marc asks.

I let out a shaky breath. 'I'm okay.'

'No. It was too much.' Marc dips a napkin in water and wipes the red lines on my breast. 'Stand up.'

With some effort, I push myself up on shaky legs, and my dress falls to the floor.

I wrap my arms around my naked torso, self-conscious in the empty ballroom.

'You've come a long way Mrs Blackwell.' Marc watches me. 'You'd never have dreamed of submitting like this when we first met.'

'You know, this really isn't me *submitting*,' I say. 'I mean, we're both in this together.'

A smile plays on Marc's lips. 'It seems very important to you, all of a sudden. To define what we're doing. And who's in charge. So let me clear that up. I am in charge. Because you do as I tell you.'

I feel the familiar throb of heat between my thighs.

'Sophia. Put your arms down,' Marc instructs. 'I want to see your body.'

'Maybe we should go up to the bedroom …'

'No. Not today.' Marc is still watching me.

I hesitate, my arms still tight around my naked torso.

'Put your arms down.' Marc puts a hand to his hip, impatient. 'I want to see you. *Now* Sophia.'

Reluctantly, I let my arms drop, feeling totally exposed. And vulnerable.

Marc circles me, frowning. 'You know, you haven't *submitted* as quickly as I would have liked.'

'I haven't submitted at all.'

Marc comes behind me, twisting my hair around his hand. He gives a sharp tug so my neck snaps back, and I let out a cry of surprise.

'This isn't submitting?' he asks.

I swallow again and shake my head. 'No. Because I could say no. Any time I like.'

He leads me to the table by my hair and bends me over it.

My breasts and face find the soft cotton of the table-cloth, and I see a silver candlestick holder inches away.

'You're right,' he says again, pressing my cheek to the cotton. 'Tell me to stop, and I will. You know I will.'

I bite my lip, but don't say a word.

16

A white candle, flickering in a silver holder, swims in my vision, and I feel Marc's firm hand in my hair.

'I don't want you to make a sound,' he says, stroking my hair in his fingers.

I see him lift the candle from its holder.

'Marc. What are you—'

'Be quiet,' Marc snaps. 'And keep still.'

I know the candle is somewhere behind me, and feel a sharp sting on my back.

Ouch.

What was that?

It's hard not to cry out. But I don't.

I wait, my skin singing with electricity and anticipation.

'Marc?'

I feel the sting again, and realise it's hot wax. The heat and the sticky, pulling sensation couldn't be anything else.

I hear myself moan with pleasure.

Marc gives my buttocks a sharp slap. 'Don't make a sound.'

He presses the candle back into its holder, then paces behind me.

I try to turn, but he puts a hand to my scalp, holding me still. 'Don't move.'

'This again?' I murmur. 'Don't speak. Don't move. What next?'

'Wait.'

'Wait?' I say.

'Wait.'

Marc's hand leaves my head, and he takes a seat at the table.

I can't see his face, only his foot resting on his thigh and his wine glass lifting, then lowering.

I wait. 'Marc—'

His wine glass lowers. 'I told you to be quiet.'

I sense him watching me as he takes another sip of wine.

The wax on my back is hard now, crisping and pulling at my skin.

'This is becoming unbearable,' I moan.

Marc stands and walks behind me. 'Unbearable? Really?' He drapes a hand over my buttocks, letting his fingers lazily stroke my skin.

The effect is like an electric shock – his fingers moving back and forth, teasing, working me into an almost insatiable need for him.

'Please Marc.' I twist under his fingers. 'Please. I can't stand it.'

Marc ignores me, his fingers still sending tingles all over my body.

'*Marc.*'

A napkin is bundled up and pushed into my mouth.

I moan against the white cotton, almost delirious with pleasure as Marc's fingers continue to caress.

I want him so badly.

Just when I think I can't take anymore, when I'm about to pull the napkin out of my mouth and beg for him, Marc rests an authoritative hand on my back side.

He turns me over, lifting me onto the table so I'm staring up into intense, blue eyes.

We watch each other, chests heaving.

I know he's as desperate for me as I am for him, but the intense passion in his eyes is so *controlled*. He could walk away right now if he had to. But there's no way I could.

As I watch him, Marc frees himself from his trousers.

God.

I strain my neck to look down.

Maybe he'll make me wait again. He might make me beg for him.

But to my relief, Marc lines himself up and enters me little by little, watching with stern eyes. Then he pushes all the way inside in one, long stroke.

'Oh!'

I suck in so much air that a yelp catches in my throat, and I let out a strangulated half gasp, half cry.

'*Ooooh*. Marc. Oh *god*.' I grab his buttocks.

Marc puts firm fingers over my mouth and begins to move.

His rhythm is slow, but deep and unrelenting, his eyes holding mine.

I moan and squirm under him, unable to keep still. But then his hands come to my shoulders and I'm pinned firmly in place.

'Oh god Marc.' My eyes close as he slides into me over and over again.

I wrap my legs around him and feel the soft cotton tablecloth scrunch up under my backside.

My fingers grasp Marc's backside tight, pulling him deeper inside.

God.

I am so tense and alive and desperate for him.

Our bodies move together, over and over again, and I'm totally lost in sensation, barely able to breathe.

Warmth builds up and I find my eyes opening, searching for his.

I am so full. So complete. Our bodies fit perfectly together as Marc rocks me back and forth, building up all those good feelings.

'Oh Marc. *Marc*. I'm coming. Oh god, I'm coming.'

My legs tighten around him and warmth floods my body.

As I melt into the table, Marc takes my chin and holds me so our eyes meet.

He looks intense. Angry. Protective. But as I carry on coming, Marc's eyes flood with light, and I know he's coming too.

'Christ. Sophia. *Sophia*.'

We gaze at each other, and I see he's open to me right now. As vulnerable as I am. It's beautiful.

We watch each other for a long time. Then Marc strokes my hair and the red line on my breast.

'Does it hurt?' he asks, fingers dancing back and forth.

I shake my head.

17

As Marc carries me up to our bedroom, I try not to think about my hands being tied behind my back earlier.

I'm sure Phillipe didn't notice …

It's sort of dangerous, in a way. This obsession we have with each other. And yet I control Marc too, in my own way. We both know that.

The lobby is totally empty and the hotel's revolving front door is locked closed – both of which I suspect is Marc's doing. There's a doorman outside, but he has his back to us.

With gentle thuds, Marc carries me upstairs and into our bedroom.

'You were right,' I murmur, as Marc lowers me onto soft sheets. 'I needed to let go.'

'You mean submit to me.' Marc offers his handsome, Hollywood smile.

'No. That's not what I mean.'

'That sounds like a challenge, Mrs Blackwell.'

I shake my head against the pillow. 'It isn't.'

Marc climbs onto the bed bedside me, propping himself on his elbow. 'I take challenges very seriously.'

I roll to face him. 'Lucky it isn't a challenge then. I already told you. We're too consenting adults doing something we both enjoy. No one is submitting to anything. We're both *agreeing*.'

'Yes.' His eyes are hungry again. 'You're agreeing to submit. You did everything I told you. Absolutely everything.'

'That's not the same as submitting,' I say, holding back a yawn.

'This really *does* sound like a challenge.' Marc pulls the duvet over me. 'You want me to prove to you that you're submitting? That I'm dominating you? Taking charge of you?'

I blink at him with tired eyes. 'No. I don't want you to prove anything. There's nothing to prove anyway.'

He kisses my forehead. 'I love you. You know that, don't you?'

'I love you too.'

'Sleep now, Mrs Blackwell.' He tucks the duvet around my body. 'And tomorrow, we will show our beautiful daughter the sights of Switzerland.'

'What about our appointment?' I say, struggling to keep my eyes open.

'That's not until the afternoon.'

'Will we take Ivy with us?' I ask, watching as Marc stands and takes off his suit jacket.

'No.' Marc hangs his jacket on the chair. 'Seraphina will take care of her.'

'Are you going to tell me what this appointment is all about?'

'Sleep now.' Marc sits beside me on the bed again, slipping off his shoes. 'You need to rest.'

I wake up to bright sunshine and jerk upright.

Ivy.

It takes a moment to remember where I am, and that Ivy is with Seraphina.

Groggily, I rub my eyes and check the clock.

8am.

It feels good to sleep in.

Marc isn't beside me, so I'm guessing he's working out.

I grab a soft towelling robe from the bathroom and hurry to Seraphina's room.

18

'Hey Sophia.' Seraphina opens the door with a smile. 'How was your night?'

Ivy is on her shoulder, blinking up at the bright hotel lights.

I beam at my beautiful little baby and reach out to take her. 'Good morning, gorgeous girl.' I fold Ivy against my shoulder, scrunching up my chin so I can look at her. 'I had a great night. Did Ivy sleep okay?'

'Pretty well,' says Seraphina. 'She only woke twice. Honestly, she's been no trouble. How did you sleep?'

'Like a log,' I admit, loving Ivy's warmth and softness. 'The first full night since she was born. I feel amazing. Like a new person.'

After a breakfast of melt-in-the-mouth almond croissants and hot, fresh coffee, Marc and I walk Ivy around Montreux.

It's a pretty, chocolate-box town of wooden-beamed houses, framed by dove-coloured mountains and sparkling blue water.

We eat lunch in a seafood restaurant overlooking Lake Geneva – a simple place, where we pick our own fresh fish from a bed of ice chips. I choose lightly barbequed lobster, served with piles of French fries and a green salad.

It's easy food, cooked perfectly, and I love it.

'So can you tell me now where we're going this afternoon?' I ask Marc, taking a sip of sparkling mineral water.

'Sophia,' Marc smiles. 'I hope our daughter grows up with more self-restraint than you. I'll teach you patience if it kills me.'

After lunch, we drop Ivy back at the hotel for her nap.

I'm reluctant to leave her again. But it's ridiculous to feel guilty when she's asleep. Seraphina will take good care of her.

'I miss Ivy already,' I tell Marc, as we walk back into town.

'You may not believe this,' says Marc. 'But I miss her just as much as you do. I have no desire to be away from her more than is necessary. But *some* time *is* necessary. Especially in your case. A rested mother is a happy mother.'

I have to admit, I feel amazing today. Fantastic. But something is nagging at me. Marc was right about me needing rest. And he was right about something else too – that rest is helping me think clearly.

I really do want to act again.

For once, I don't try to push the thought back down. I'm so refreshed out here in the cool, mountain air.

Ivy is fine with a nanny. So what's stopping me from acting?

It's sounds so simple. But there's one thing that isn't so simple.

Marc.

19

'You look thoughtful, Sophia.' Marc shades his eyes from the white sunshine. 'Nothing serious, I hope?'

Automatically I shake my head. 'Just curious about this appointment. That's all.'

'You're sure?' Marc's gaze is stern.

I nod, managing a smile. But I don't meet his eye.

It's not the right time to talk about acting. Not yet. Marc's so sure I'm not ready for another movie, but I'm more grown up than he realises. I don't always need him to show me the way.

'I'm waiting,' says Marc, a smile playing on his lips.

'Honestly.' I shake my head, managing to return his smile. 'It's nothing important. So where are we going?'

We turn onto a street of grand, tall buildings.

'As a matter of fact,' says Marc, shielding his eyes from the sun, 'we're here.'

We come to a stop outside a mini castle with little yellow turrets and international flags flying.

It's funny to see a building like this sitting casually on a street corner, but here it is – a princess palace right on the street, with beautiful green and grey mountains in the background and a lake at its feet.

'It's … a school,' I say, reading the sign.

'One of the best schools in the world,' says Marc, looking over the building.

I look over the pretty, criss-cross windows. 'So what are we doing here?'

'We have an appointment with the headmistress,' says Marc. 'About Ivy's education.'

I turn to him. 'Her education? She's a baby.'

Marc takes my hand between his palms, warming my fingers with gentle strokes. 'The best schools fill up quickly. If we want Ivy to go here, we need to apply this year.'

I know my brown eyes are wide with confusion. 'But we live in the United Kingdom. Why would Ivy go to school here?'

'Ivy should have the very best.' Marc kisses the tips of my fingers.

'So we'd move to Switzerland when Ivy is school age?' I say, looking over the yellow turrets. 'How would you teach at Ivy College?'

'I was thinking of sending her here as a young woman,' says Marc, letting my hand drop. 'Twelve, possibly. Thirteen.'

'That seems an awfully long way away. So what – we'd move to Switzerland when she was twelve or something?'

'We wouldn't have to move,' says Marc. 'This is a boarding school. The girls stay here and come home in the holidays.'

I stare at him, a cool breeze stinging my cheeks. 'You're joking. Right? You think I'd send our daughter away from her family?'

'She'd be twelve years old,' says Marc, looking up at the turrets. 'This is one of the finest schools in the world. Don't you want the best for our daughter?'

'Yes I do,' I say. 'But I don't think sending her away is for the best.'

'I don't want her away from us either,' says Marc, his gaze softening. 'But I can't put my feelings first. I want what's best for her, not me. There would be no problem with security. I'd arrange the very best—'

'What's *best* for Ivy is being with her parents,' I interrupt. 'I can't believe you'd even consider something like this. You lost your mother, just like I did. Do you seriously think we should deprive our own daughter of her parents?'

'Christ.' Marc tips his head back. 'I'm trying to put Ivy first and myself second. The education she'd have here … it's second to none. And she'd make connections for life.'

I cross my arms. 'She has you as her father. I hardly think she's going to be short of connections.'

'Would you want her forever in my shadow?' he asks.

'No, but … I don't understand how you could think this would be best.'

'Sophia.' Marc turns me to him, his shoes clipping the hard pavement. 'It will hurt to send Ivy away. It will hurt both of us. But what about her? Think about the life it could give her.'

My stomach is like ice. 'You haven't thought this through.'

'On the contrary.' Marc puts a hand on my shoulder. 'I've thought this through to the point of obsession. I've been researching schools since Ivy was born.'

'I'm her mother.' I twist away from his hand. 'My say is most important.'

'And why is that?' Marc demands.

A group of laughing schoolgirls troop past us, pushing their way through wooden doors into the school.

'Because I'm with her all the time,' I tell Marc. 'I know what's best.'

Marc gives a humourless laugh. 'I think we've already established you don't always know what's best.'

I look at the pavement, considering the truth in that. I have been tired recently. I haven't been resting enough. And I've been so scared of anyone else having Ivy …

Marc was right. It's been wonderful having a nanny. More importantly, Ivy *is* fine with someone else. But this is totally different. I turn back to the school, casting my eyes over the yellow stone.

There's a brass sign by the door, gleaming in the afternoon sun.

'Work, play and good values,' I read. 'There's something missing from that statement. What about love?'

'Christ. Ivy will have love. All the love in the world.'

I shake my head. 'Not here she won't. I don't know why you think this would be best for her.'

'From an educational point of view, there's no better.'

'Please Marc.' I take his hand. 'You have to listen. This isn't just about me missing Ivy. To send her away from us … it just feels wrong.'

Marc looks down at his hand in mine. 'I fear someone will be very disappointed today, Sophia.'

20

'I won't be disappointed,' I insist. 'Because we're not sending Ivy away, and that's that.'

'It's not you who'll be disappointed.' Marc's eyes soften. 'It's the headmistress of the school. Because I'll be cancelling our appointment.'

'Oh Marc!' I smile up at him. 'Really?'

'Really.' He pulls me into a hug.

I feel relief wash over me, my cheek finding Marc's chest, warm under his white shirt. 'Thank you. I thought I'd have a fight on my hands.'

'You'd be a worthy opponent.'

I turn to the building's pretty yellow turrets. 'So what now? Since I've just ruined your afternoon plans?'

Marc holds me tight. 'Home. Back to the UK.'

I nod, liking his arms around me. I've enjoyed the break, but it will be good to get back. That silver parcel is still waiting …

I sit cross-legged on our big, squishy sofa, staring at the shiny silver box.

It lays on our coffee table, practically winking at me.

Open it.

A steaming mug of hot chocolate balances on my knee,

but I barely feel its heat.

Open it and read the script. You'll probably hate it. And then there'll be no problem.

If I open the box and love the script, a whole world of problems will rain down on me. Arguments with Marc. Guilt at leaving Ivy with a nanny. Fear of performing after a long break.

Marc is teaching. Ivy is sleeping upstairs. And I am torturing myself.

Open it.

Impulsively, I put down my hot chocolate and grab the box, pulling the lid free.

The contents are exactly as they were – a folded, silver card, which I take to be an invitation to the Riviera Film Festival, a letter printed on thick, buff-coloured paper and the weighty pages of a movie script.

I want to dive right in and read the script, but I unfold the silver card first.

Sure enough, it's an invitation to Riviera Film Festival.

I've never been one of those actresses who dreamed of awards, but the Riviera is one of my favourite ceremonies.

Oh my god.

I stare at the swirly words, eyes wide with disbelief.

The movie I made with Nadia, *Rapunzel*, has been nominated for three Silver Lotus Flowers.

Wow.

After I'm certain that I'm not hallucinating, I turn my attention to the letter.

It's from Nadia.

She writes:

Sophia,

Can you believe those nominations for Rapunzel? Pretty cool, huh? I've booked you and Marc onto my table at the Riviera Film Festival, so we can all watch the awards together. Now – onto even bigger and better things.

Read this script and promise me you'll play Violet.

I wrote her for you. Please say yes!

Nadia goes on to explain that she'll be shooting a new movie at sea, and she's hired a luxurious cruise ship for filming purposes. It will be docked at Saint-Tropez – very near the film festival. Then she talks about the other potential actors in the movie.

She signs off by saying,

When we finish filming, we'll sail to the film festival and pick up our awards. Perfect, right?

Wow.

I put the invitation and letter to one side, and slide the script free of the box, feeling its weight in my hands.

There's something magical about a new script. A whole new world.

My eyes scan the first page.

Cruise
Written by Nadia Malbeck.

Nadia *wrote* this whole script?

My lively, Spanish director comes to mind, in her leather trousers and bright-red lipstick. I can't imagine her sitting still for long enough to write a whole script. But apparently she has done.

Smiling, I think back to the film we shot together.

My very first movie.

I couldn't have asked for a better director.

Settling back into the sofa, I begin turning pages. It doesn't take long before I'm totally engrossed.

Oh shit.

I'm in big trouble.

I LOVE this script.

21

An hour later, I'm barely aware of Marc coming into the lounge.

He kisses me on the head, and I hurriedly flip the script closed.

'You were engrossed,' Marc says. 'What are you reading?'

I manage a guilty smile. 'Oh, just ... a movie script.'

Marc frowns. 'What movie script?'

I look down at my knees. 'The one in the silver box.'

He turns away from me. 'Where's Ivy?'

'Sleeping.'

Marc strides to the stairs. 'I'll go check on her.'

When Marc returns, he picks up the empty silver box from the coffee table. 'So you opened Pandora's box?'

'Is Ivy okay?' I ask.

'She's still asleep.' Marc crosses his arms. 'It must be a good script. You barely heard me come in.'

'It is,' I say, taking a distracted sip of hot chocolate and realising it's gone cold. 'Really, really good. Excellent, actually.'

'I don't see why you'd want to torture yourself.' Marc perches on the edge of the sofa.

'I ... I might not be torturing myself. Marc, I want to act again.'

'Sophia, we've already discussed that.'

'No. We haven't. You think I should study more. But I don't agree. This movie will be astonishing.'

'Look.' Marc fixes blue eyes on me. 'I know you haven't been happy at home—'

I shake my head. 'I *have* been happy. Happier than anything. I love being with Ivy.'

'Okay. That was the wrong word. You haven't been *fulfilled*. I realise that. And I know how much you love acting. You were born to it. But taking a role right now … it's not the right time. You're not ready.'

I push the script onto the coffee table. 'That's a little dramatic.'

'But true.' Marc picks up the script, frowning down at it.

'Marc, I'm just blown away by the script,' I insist. 'The emotion. I can't miss out on something like this.'

Marc turns pages. 'Nadia always makes good movies.'

'But she's never *written* one before. And do you know what? She wrote the lead female just for me.'

'Did she indeed?' He doesn't look up.

'Yes.' I put my hot chocolate on the coffee table. 'It's going to be shot partly on a cruise ship at sea. Away from the paparazzi. Could you think of anything more perfect?'

Marc taps the script in his hands. 'It's too soon, Sophia. You're not ready.'

'Oh god Marc, I'm a mother. You don't get more grown up than that.'

Marc sighs and rubs his forehead. 'What's the movie about, anyway?'

'A young girl and a dangerous man. Actually, dangerous *teacher*, to be more precise. The girl falls for her dance instructor.'

Marc raises an eyebrow. 'Nadia *has* been paying attention.'

'I want to do it, Marc.'

'You're rushing into things again,' says Marc.

'No,' I insist. 'I have to make my own choices.'

Marc shakes his head. 'Not when it concerns my daughter. I have an equal say, and I say no.'

'I'm her mother. If I thought there was anything unsafe about this—'

'Sophia, you haven't thought it through.' Marc glances down at the script again, flicking pages and frowning. 'This is too much of a challenge. The characters are interesting. I'll give you that. But the lead man is … I mean, *look* at these lines. You're not ready to play opposite such a strong character. You'll be eaten alive. Swallowed up.'

God. How patronising. I sit up straighter. 'I think I can do it.'

'No Sophia. You're trying to run before you can walk. And it's not the right time. You've just had a baby.'

I pick up Nadia's letter, waving it at him. 'If Nadia thinks I can do it, what's the problem?'

Marc takes the silver, folded card, frowning as he scans it. 'Nadia doesn't know you like I do. What's this? Your Riviera Film Festival invitation?'

'Yes.' I wiggle along the sofa so I'm sitting next to him, scanning the invitation too.

'Isn't the film festival enough for you? Look – *Rapunzel* has been nominated for three different awards. You'll have your time in the limelight.'

'This isn't about the limelight, Marc. This is about following my passion.'

'I thought motherhood was your passion.'

'It's not enough,' I blurt out. 'I need more, Marc.'

'Sophia, you rushed into movies and musicals before you were ready. And you ended up in hospital.' He kisses my head. 'I'll take you to the film festival. Okay?'

'You know, this movie shoots right down the road from the film festival.' I snatch up Nadia's letter and point to a paragraph. 'So when we finish filming in Saint-Tropez, we'll go to the award ceremony afterwards.'

'*When* you finish filming? Sophia—'

'Marc, listen. You know I haven't been … content. You were the one who said we needed a nanny. And here I am, ready to follow your advice.'

'So you could have a break. Not jump into an unsuitable movie. You'll be out of your depth—'

'It's *not* unsuitable. Nadia wrote the part for me. Ivy is happy with a nanny. And … I'm happy when I'm acting.'

I can't meet his eye. Part of me is ashamed about how I feel. I *am* happy being a mother. But I need more.

'Marc, listen.' I take his hand. 'I can handle this.'

'So you say. But I still have concerns.' Marc takes Nadia's letter, looking it over. 'Christ. *Leo* Falkirk is in this one, too? He'd better not be playing the male lead.'

'No.'

Marc scans further down the letter. '*Benjamin Van Rosen* is in the running? Sophia – I've met that man. He's a womaniser and an ego-maniac.'

'Marc.' I drop his hand. 'I want to take the part.'

'No Sophia.' Marc folds the letter into a neat little rectangle. 'I absolutely forbid it.'

I laugh. 'I don't care if you forbid it. I'm doing it anyway.'

'Fine.' Marc drops the letter and invitation on the coffee table and stands, crossing his arms. 'Have it your own way. But you will not leave the country with our daughter.'

I stand too. 'How do you intend to stop me? She's my child too.'

'Christ.' Marc runs a hand through his hair. 'I'm not happy about this Sophia. Not happy at all. It's time you grew up.'

He stalks upstairs.

'I'm already grown up,' I shout after him.

But all I hear is the slam of the study door.

22

I spend the next week phoning nanny agencies, scouring online advertisements and interviewing potential carers at our home.

This is expressively against Marc's wishes, of course, so I don't tell him.

We've barely said two words to each other since the door-slamming argument, and Marc leaves early in the mornings and comes back late at night.

The trouble is, I hate every nanny I meet.

It doesn't help that they wear stiff, starchy black uniforms and speak with plums in their mouths.

After I've interviewed twenty women with hard, grey hair and permanent frown lines, I begin to think that maybe Marc is right. This is a bad idea. If I can't find anyone like Seraphina, I should call the whole thing off.

'They're all so formal, Jen,' I complain, phone clamped to my ear as I run a pen down the 'help offered' column. 'I just want a normal person. You know?'

I'm in Marc's study, going through his business newspapers while Ivy sleeps on my lap.

'But you liked the nanny you had in Switzerland,' Jen points out. 'Why not just hire her again?'

'She doesn't work full time.' I twiddle the pen around my fingers.

'So where did *she* come from?' Jen barks. 'Maybe her agency has someone similar.'

I think about that. 'Denise recommended her.'

'Bingo,' Jen replies. 'Phone Denise and ask if she knows anyone else. It's worth a shot, right?'

'One final shot,' I say. 'But if she can't come up with anyone, then this movie isn't meant to be.'

I lay Ivy on a picnic blanket in the garden under the shade of a fruit tree, then find Denise's number in my phone contacts.

Ring, ring. Ring, ring.

The air is warm with early summer aromas – cut grass, sweet buttercups and honeysuckle.

She's not going to answer.

But then she does. On the tenth ring.

'Sophia?' Denise says, in her kind, crinkly voice.

'Denise!' I'm so happy she picked up. 'It's so good to hear your voice.'

'Are you okay, my love?' Denise's voice is full of concern.

'Um … yes.' I watch leaves sway in the trees. 'In some ways. Not so good in others.'

'Marc's been like a bear with a sore bum this week,' Denise chuckles. 'Would that have anything to do with the "not so good"?'

'Yes,' I admit, my eyes absentmindedly skimming over nanny adverts. 'I've been offered a part in Nadia Malbeck's new movie. But Marc thinks I'm rushing into things. That I should study more before I take on any acting new projects.'

'Marc's protective instinct can be a little overzealous at times,' says Denise.

'You think that's what it is?' I make a circle around an advert for 'London Nannies', and then realise I've already called them and scribble it out.

'Almost certainly,' Denise continues. 'He doesn't like letting you out of his sight. And now, of course, he has Ivy to protect too. He's being silly. You can tell him I said so.'

I look down at Ivy, lying on the picnic blanket beside me.

'I've already decided to do the movie,' I admit. 'With or without his approval.'

'Good for you,' Denise hoots.

'The trouble is, I can't find a nanny.' My eyes find the newspaper again, and all the scribbled-out numbers. 'I've been interviewing all week, but there's no one I like. I'm losing hope.'

'Childcare can be tough,' says Denise.

'Do you know anyone who could help?' I tap my pen on the newspaper.

'Mm.' Denise hesitates. 'There *is* someone who might suit you perfectly, as a matter of fact. I'll tell you what. Let me take you to the British Museum tomorrow. I'll see if my "someone" can meet us there.'

23

The British Museum café is bright with sunshine and overlooks a room of stone columns. I love it instantly. It's old London meets new, and reminds me of Marc.

Denise is already seated when Ivy and I arrive. As usual, she's flowing in colourful layers, her soft, white skin creased with smiles.

There's a three-tiered cake stand on the table, three china cups and a steaming teapot.

A black-suited lady sits opposite Denise.

I slow my step.

Oh no. Is this the potential nanny?

The woman looks just as stiff and stuck-up as every other woman I've met this week.

I feel my hands tighten on the stroller handles.

'Guess what?' I whisper to a sleeping Ivy. 'Looks like I won't be doing this movie after all.'

I park Ivy by the table and give Denise a hug. Then I turn to the suited lady.

'Hi,' I say politely. 'I'm Sophia.'

The woman gives me a tight smile, and offers her cold hand for shaking.

There is no way I want this woman as our nanny, I decide. *How could Denise think she could be right for me?*

'Sophia!' Denise gushes. 'Sit, sit. You must share these cakes with me, or I'll eat the whole lot.'

To my surprise, the black-suited lady stands and arranges her handbag on her shoulder. 'Well, I'll leave you to your luncheon,' she announces. 'If you do see Jonathan, give him my regards.'

And off she goes, striding through the tearoom.

I stare after her in surprise.

'Where's she going?' I ask.

'Who?' Denise looks around.

'The nanny.'

'Oh, you mean *Helen*?' Denise gives a little chuckle. 'God – she's not a nanny. I couldn't imagine her with children. She's one of those compulsive hand washers – can't stand dirt. No, no, she's an old acquaintance from my opera days. You didn't think I'd suggest someone like *Helen* for Ivy, did you?'

'Sort of,' I admit. 'Sorry. It's been a long week.'

Denise laughs. 'My "someone" had a class to finish, but she'll be here soon.'

'She's a student?' I take a seat.

'Yes.' Denise cuts open a scone, loading it with jam and clotted cream. 'But her studies finish this month. Perfect, don't you think?' She squints across the room. 'Ah! Speak of the devil.'

I turn, and nearly fall off my chair when I see who is weaving around tables towards us.

24

Red hair. Green-rimmed glasses. A huge grin.

'*Tanya*?' I blink at Denise. 'I don't get it. What's going on?'

Denise smiles. 'Tanya is the potential nanny I was talking about.'

Tanya strolls towards us, a huge brown-leather bag over her shoulder. She's wearing pedal-pusher jeans, red boots, a striped t-shirt and a black suit jacket. Her cheeks are flushed, and she's breathless as she reaches our table.

'Sorry I'm late,' says Tanya, throwing her bag over a Perspex chair. 'You can blame Denise for that. She forgot I had a class at ten.' Tanya pretends to strangle Denise.

Denise laughs. 'Blame my age. I used to be organised.'

'How are you doing, Soph?' Tanya puts her arms around me.

'It's so good to see you!' I hug her arms. 'But one of you is going to have to fill me in. I'm horribly confused.'

Tanya drops into a chair and fans herself with a napkin. 'Whoa! I'm sweating. Is my makeup everywhere?'

'You're wearing makeup?' I ask.

'Had to dress up, didn't I?' Tanya pulls out a little compact and checks her eyes. 'For the big interview.'

'But …' I shake my head. 'Tanya, you're an actress. Not a nanny.'

'Actually, I'm sort of neither.' Tanya snaps the compact mirror closed. 'And both. I worked in nurseries before Ivy College. I've got diplomas, first aid and all of that. And then there's my brothers and sisters. I know my way around a dirty nappy, put it that way.'

'But … why would you even want to be Ivy's nanny?' I ask. 'You're an amazing actress.'

'Well *first* off, we're not all magic like you, Sophia.' Tanya drops the compact back into her bag. 'Some of us will always need a day job. And *second*, Denise has told me all about this cruise-ship movie thing. Nadia *Malbeck*? Leo Falkirk? On a Mediterranean *cruise*? What actress wouldn't want to see that movie being made? Talk about work experience. Those cakes look amazing.'

She grabs a pink macaroon and takes a big bite. 'And taste amazing. Yum!'

'I love you being around Ivy …' I begin.

'Uh oh,' says Tanya. 'I'm sensing a "but" coming.'

'*But* I'm not sure it would be good for you. I mean, you're still an actress. Do you really want to spend the summer babysitting?'

Tanya puts a mini pecan tart on her plate, then picks up the teapot and fills our cups with steaming, caramel-coloured liquid. 'On a luxury cruise ship with some of my all-time favourite actors? YES!'

'But after that …' I take a sip of hot tea.

'Listen, I love acting.' Tanya puts the teapot down. 'But I never saw it as the only thing I'd do with my life. My plan was always to open a nursery one day.'

I hold my cup in both hands, letting the tea warm my fingers. 'But are you sure—'

'*Yes.*' Tanya cuts up her tart. 'I'd tell you if I wasn't. Really Soph. Can you imagine me signing up for something I didn't really want to do?'

'No,' I laugh.

'You need a nanny. Is that cream?' Tanya pulls the blue-china cream jug towards her. 'And I want in. What's the problem? Unless ... do you feel like I wouldn't do a good job or something?'

'No! Not at all.' I take another sip of tea. 'You love Ivy. I couldn't think of anyone better, actually.'

'So?' Tanya forks pecan tart into her mouth. 'Do I get the gig or not?'

I smile. 'Of course. I'd love you to be Ivy's nanny.'

'Hazaar!' Tanya does a little victory wiggle with her elbows. 'Now then ... is there any *clotted* cream here? Or is this place too posh for that? Wait a minute. Soph, why are you frowning?'

'Oh, just ... Marc's not keen on me doing the movie,' I admit. 'So I still have that battle to contend with.'

'He'll come around.' Tanya spoons cream onto her plate.

'I suppose he'll have to now,' I say. 'I've just found myself a nanny.'

Denise puts a warm hand over mine. 'I've known Marc a long time. When he sees how happy you are to be acting again, he'll understand. I'm sure it.'

I nod and paste on a smile. But inside, I'm not so sure.

When Marc comes home, I'm in the kitchen taking roast chicken out of the oven.

As I'm lifting the meat onto a board with a long fork, I feel Marc kiss me on the head.

'Restaurant Sophia is back open?' he asks, his voice low.

I turn to him. 'That's the most you've said to me all week.'

'I've had a lot to do in London.' He slides his hands into his pockets. 'And I thought you needed some thinking space.'

'I've definitely had time to think,' I tell him, lifting roast potatoes from the oven and pushing the door closed with my foot.

'I feared as much. Here – let me.' Marc takes the tray.

I watch him, so handsome in his black suit, putting the tray on the kitchen table.

'I found a nanny today,' I blurt out.

Marc's shoulders stiffen. He drops the oven gloves on the table and walks to the window, hands sliding back into his pockets.

'Aren't you going to say anything?' I ask.

Marc doesn't turn. 'What is there to say? You've made a decision expressly against my wishes. And involved our child in that decision.'

'Marc, please. I haven't been myself recently. You know that. This is my way of learning and growing. Of becoming myself again.'

'Three months after you've had a child?' He's still looking out at the garden.

'Yes.' I walk around the breakfast bar and stand beside him. 'If you want to put it that way. Look – Tanya has agreed to be Ivy's nanny. Could you think of anyone more perfect?'

'Tanya is an actress, not a nanny,' Marc snaps.

'She did childcare before Ivy College.' I put a tentative hand on his arm. 'She has all the qualifications. And she really wants to do it.'

Marc tips his head back, closing his eyes. 'Christ. I thought you'd have learned from your mistakes by now.'

'What mistakes?' My hand drops from his arm.

'Do I need to spell them out?' He turns to me, crossing his arms. 'Throwing yourself into a musical you weren't ready for. Taking on an *extremely* adult movie role. Before you'd even done a regular movie.'

'It was you who encouraged me to open myself up,' I say. 'You pushed me to find my passionate side in front of an audience. Or had you forgotten?'

'I hadn't forgotten. I just didn't realise you'd be playing it out so soon. And without my guidance.'

I take a step back from him. 'Why don't you admit what this is really about, Marc? You're jealous. You don't want me working with Benjamin.'

'Oh, it's Benjamin now, is it?' His eyes flash with anger. 'I didn't realise the two of you were on first name terms.'

I shake my head. 'Don't be ridiculous, Marc. I've never even met him.'

'*Yet*. Christ, you're my wife, Sophia. I'm supposed to have some say in your decisions.'

'You don't get to tell me what to do. I know what's best for me.'

'No. You don't.' His arms are still crossed. 'As you've proved on many occasions.'

I go back to the oven, kneeling to check on the vegetables. 'Are you going to dredge up every mistake I've ever made?'

'If needs be.'

'Anyway, I *am* following your advice.' I stand, turning to face him. 'You were the one who said I was being stifled. And you were the one who insisted we try out a nanny.'

Marc shakes his head. 'How silly of me.'

'There's no point arguing about this anymore.' I pick up a carving knife and start slicing the chicken, but I'm so furious I end up hacking at it. 'I want to do this movie, Marc. That's just it.'

'And what about Ivy?' Marc takes the knife from my hand. 'What if I refuse to let her go with you?'

'You wouldn't do that. She needs to be with her mother.' I look down at the shredded remains of our evening meal. 'Marc, please understand. I'm going to do this with or without your blessing. But I'd much rather have you on my side.'

'Okay Sophia.' Marc lays the knife on the wooden board. 'I'll give you my blessing.'

'Oh Marc. It means so much to me—'

'I hadn't finished. I will give you my blessing on one condition.'

'Which is?'

'I come with you on this cruise ship.'

25

I blink up at Marc. 'You want to come with me? While we're filming the movie?'

'I always want to be with you.' He watches me. 'All day and all night. You know that. And Ivy too.'

'Yes, but … this isn't some possessive thing, is it?' I duck down to lift hot vegetables from the oven, and stand to place them on a wrought-iron trivet. 'Keeping an eye on me?'

'In part.' Marc offers that half smile of his. 'I will have *two* eyes very firmly fixed on Benjamin Van Rosen. That I can promise you.'

'But what about Ivy College?' I grab a fork and prod the vegetables.

'We wrap up for the holidays a week before you start filming. Give me that.' Marc takes the fork from me. 'I don't want you massacring these too.'

'Marc, I'd love it if you were around. You know that. I just want to make sure it's for the right reasons.'

He smiles at me. 'As far as I'm concerned, it's for the very best reasons.'

'Promise you won't be jealous,' I say.

Marc leans his elbow on wooden work surface. 'I'm not going to make promises I can't keep. If you're still allowed to be stubborn, then I'm allowed a little jealousy.'

As the first day of filming approaches, I get more and more nervous.

What if Marc is right and I'm taking on more than I can handle? And what on earth should I pack for a cruise to the South of France?

I'm on my knees checking Ivy's wardrobe for 'cruise worthy' clothes, when Jen comes bursting in.

'Soph!'

I sit back onto my ankles, very aware that I'm still in my flannel pyjamas even though it's gone breakfast time.

'Jen. What are you doing here?' I try to stroke my hair into something neater than the rolled-around-in-bed look. 'Why aren't you at work?'

'It's Saturday.' Jen plops herself beside Ivy, who's laying beside me on the nursery floor. 'And that's no way to greet Aunty Jen, is it Ivy? No way at all. And you know you don't have to do your hair for me.'

My hands drop from my hair. 'Sorry. I mean, it's great to see you. It's just a surprise, that's all.'

'This is a maze of a house,' says Jen. 'Rodney said you were in the nursery, but he forgot to draw me a map. Listen. I'm here to take you into London.'

She rifles in her cream leather handbag, pulls out a small Steiff Teddy and hands it to Ivy. 'A new friend for you, Ivy. Leo thinks you should name it after him, but this Teddy doesn't look like a Leo to me.' She pretends to talk to the bear. 'Right Teddy? You're not a Leo, are you?'

Ivy reaches up to stroke the bear's tufted fur.

'London?' I look down at my pyjamas. 'I'm not even dressed yet.'

'Then get dressed. Tanya's going to take care of Ivy. Sort of a trial run before you set sail. It's all arranged. And I have some GREAT news.'

'I can't go to London, Jen,' I insist. 'I need to plan for this trip. I mean, look at all this.' I gesture to Ivy's clothes, strewn over the floor. 'It's going to take me hours to work out what Ivy needs at sea.'

'Oh rubbish.' Jen crosses her short legs. 'Rodney will do all that for you. You have to come with me. We're choosing my wedding flowers. Exciting, right?'

'Wow. Really?'

'Really. Today is a big deal and I want my friend.'

I sigh. 'Fine. I'll come.'

'That's the spirit. Come on! Hurry up and get dressed.'

26

An hour later, Keith drops us in Chelsea, under silky apple blossom trees and a sapphire blue sky.

'Just *wait* until you see the flowers this place does,' says Jen, leading me along the King's Road. 'Seriously. The owner is amazing. The royal family use her for *everything*. Kate and Wills spend a fortune here.' She grips my arm. 'Look! This is the place.'

'Here?' I see frosted glass, but nothing more. 'If this is a flower shop, where are the flowers?'

'Oh there's no window display,' says Jen airily. 'Get this. Jane Knight is so amazing that you have to be *invited* inside to see her flowers. They're too exclusive to be shown to the riff-raff on the street. What do you think about *that*?'

I laugh. 'I think these flowers will be just perfect for you.'

'The press won't leave me alone about this wedding,' says Jen, pushing open the frosted-glass door. 'Which means we get *so* much stuff for free. It's *fantastic*!'

'May I help you ladies?' A receptionist taps a pen on a frosted glass Jane Knight-emblazoned podium.

'We have an appointment,' Jen crows.

'So you're Jennifer?' The receptionist glances at her book. 'Come with me. I'll show you to the flower kitchen.'

'Oh my *god*.' Jen squeezes my arm again, as we're led into a flower-filled room. 'Flower *kitchen*. Talk about exclusive.'

I stare at giant sprays of orchids, vivid red roses and super-sized daffodils.

'These flowers are *amazing*,' I murmur.

Aproned ladies sit at a long table, cutting flower stalks and snipping ribbon amid the scented petals and freshly cut stems.

A neat, pretty Asian woman in a perfect white suit comes to greet us.

'Ladies. Welcome. I'm Jane.' She shakes our hands, her fingers soft and warm.

Everything about Jane is tidy and perfectly groomed, from her short, pixie-style hair to her flawless French manicure.

'Nice to meet you Jane,' Jen gushes. 'These flowers are in-credible.'

Jane gives a light smile. 'We do our best.' Her accent is clipped and British, but very soft. 'My ladies will bring you some refreshments in a moment. But do feel free to look around. Get a sense of what you might like.'

27

We spend the morning drinking rose tea, eating lavender and honey biscuits and admiring stunningly beautiful flowers.

At lunchtime, a special delivery arrives – a gourmet picnic of freshly-baked bread, English farm cheese, hand-cooked crisps and a patisserie of pastry desserts. There's also a chilled bottle of champagne and two iced glasses.

'Courtesy of Mr Marc Blackwell,' an aproned lady tells us, setting the wicker hamper on our table.

'He's still madly in love with you, then?' says Jen.

'So it would seem.' I pull open crisp packets. 'It hasn't been easy lately, though. He didn't want me to take this film role.'

'He's protective.' Jen pops the champagne and pours it into glasses. 'He'll come around.'

'That's what everyone else says.' I take a crisp and munch loudly on it, washing it down with a sip of champagne.

'Sophia.' Jen drums manicured fingers on her champagne glass. 'Can I tell you something?'

'You know you can tell me anything. Crisp?' I offer her the packet.

Jen shakes her head, eyes suddenly teary.

'Jen?' I drop the packet, wipe salt from my fingers and put a hand on her arm. 'What is it?'

'I'm, um … the wedding and everything.' Jen fiddles with her champagne glass. 'Recently I've been thinking … I mean, I'm not sure it's such a good idea. I'm scared. Like maybe marrying Leo isn't the right decision.'

'What's brought all this on?' I ask.

'We've been arguing a lot lately. Over stupid stuff. God – he's so messy. I feel like his mother sometimes. He can't even pick up his underwear.'

I offer a tentative smile. 'That doesn't sound so serious.'

Jen wipes a tear away, taking a gulp of champagne. 'I know. It doesn't, does it? I don't know why I'm thinking like this.'

'Probably just pre-wedding nerves.' I refill her half-empty glass.

'Did you feel nervous? Before you married Marc.' She takes another long sip.

'No, but … I mean we went through so much together.' I pull sandwiches out of the hamper. 'I think I'd got all my nerves out of the way already.'

'Oh this is silly.' Jen waves a dismissive hand. '*I'm* being silly. You're right. This is just pre-wedding nerves. Now listen – I have something to tell you about your new movie. Remember I said I had good news? You start filming next week, right?'

'Sort of.' I slide sandwiches from rustly brown-paper bags. 'Marc and I will board the cruise ship at Southampton. And then sail to Spain. Is Leo boarding at Southampton too?'

Jen picks up a cheese and pickle sourdough sandwich, takes a bite and chews thoughtfully. 'Yes. Hang on.

Why are you stopping at Spain? I thought you dock at Saint-Tropez?'

'We're picking up Nadia,' I explain, choosing a salt-beef and mustard sandwich. 'And Benjamin Van Rosen, I think. Listen, are you *sure* you're okay?'

'Honestly I'm fine.' Jen dabs her lips with a chequered napkin. 'Look. I'm being silly. Emotional. Now listen, about your little cruise ship adventure …'

'You say it like it's a holiday,' I laugh. 'I *will* be working.'

'Yeah, right.' Jen grabs a handful of crisps. 'Sailing the Mediterranean, surrounded by handsome actors. Hard work indeed.'

'God, don't remind me about the other actors,' I laugh. 'I really hope I can hold my own. I mean, Benjamin is incredible.'

'Oh I *know*. A PR girl's dream. And speaking of which …' Her eyes sparkle and she gives a delighted bounce.

'What is it, Jen?'

'Remember I said I had good news for you?'

'Um … sort of.' I take a bite of sandwich, enjoying the sharpness of the mustard and saltiness of the beef.

'Guess who's going to be Leo's plus one on the cruise ship?' Jen drops a crisp into her mouth.

'Who? You don't mean …?'

Jen jumps up and down on her stool. 'ME! Can you believe it? Nadia agreed to let me tag along.'

'Oh *Jen*.' A grin lights up my face. 'You're coming too? That's *amazing*.'

'Yes! I've blagged myself a place on the ship of dreams.' Jen claps her hands together. 'Think what this will do for my business! All those famous actors in one place. I'll do five years of sign-ups in a month. And I can see my little niece too. And you, of course.'

Jen is the best salesperson I know. Within a day, she'll probably have half the cast on her books.

'Nadia was totally cool about me coming,' Jen continues. 'She thinks I'll keep Leo happy. Little does she know, we hate each other right now.'

'Jen—'

'I'm joking,' Jen insists. 'Sort of.'

'Well this is AMAZING news, Jen.' I take a little sip of champagne. 'We can really catch up. I've hardly seen you since Ivy was born.'

'Don't.' Jen glugs from her own glass. 'I feel guilty enough about that.'

'It's fine. Honestly.' I take another bite of sandwich.

'Listen – you can't let me eat too much on the ship,' says Jen, grabbing another handful of crisps. 'I read somewhere people put on a pound a day on cruises. I have to lose weight, not gain it.'

'Jen, you don't need to lose weight.'

'Soph, you wouldn't believe how tiny designer wedding dresses are. They don't realise women have boobs.' She looks down at her chest. 'So these things are going to have to shrink down. Or I'll be flashing everyone on my wedding day.'

28

'You're sure you won't change your mind about this?' says Marc, as we drive along the coast towards Southampton.

Seagulls fly overhead and saltwater mists the limo windows.

My stomach is flipping over and over.

This is real now.

'I'm fine,' I smile. 'Really. Can't wait.'

Marc frowns out of the window.

On the horizon, a ten-storey, luxury cruise ship sparkles under the sun. It's astonishing – a floating hotel. I've never seen a boat this big before.

'Okay, I'm a little nervous,' I admit. 'Terrified, actually.'

Marc shakes his head at the window. 'If you will jump in at the deep end—'

'Thanks for your support, Marc.'

He turns to me, eyes soft. 'I'm sorry. I just think … perhaps you're being naïve.'

'This again? I'm not the child you think I am.'

'I don't think you're a child.'

The limo glides through Southampton port and into a chained-off VIP area, where two other limos are parked up.

'Tanya must have arrived already,' I say, unbuckling my seatbelt. 'God – I hope Ivy is okay. It was a long journey.'

We decided that Ivy should travel with Tanya. It matched her nap better, and there was more room for her belongings.

Marc gives a curt shake of his head. 'It's not Tanya's car. The number plate is wrong.'

Fear pricks my chest. 'So where are they? They weren't far behind us.'

Marc checks his phone. 'It's okay. They're stuck in traffic. It looks like the delay could be a long one. But Ivy's perfectly happy.'

'Will she have enough milk?'

Marc's lips twitch. 'You packed five bottles. I should think that's more than enough.'

'Okay.' My heartbeat slows, but not quite to normal. 'I hope we made the right choice.'

'We did. It's better that Ivy travel with Tanya. You're nervous.'

'I'm not,' I insist.

The driver opens my door, and I climb onto oil-stained concrete, staring up at the giant cruise ship.

Marc comes to stand by me, putting an arm around my shoulder. 'Yes *are* nervous, Sophia Blackwell. You're trying to hide it, but you are.'

I look over the enormous luxury cruise ship, as Marc's arm holds me tight to his body.

Dimly, I'm aware of our suitcases being loaded onto a golden trolley and wheeled up a huge, red-carpeted gangway lined with potted palm trees.

Marc squeezes my shoulder. 'Sure you don't want to change your mind?'

'I have to do this,' I say. 'It may sound selfish to you—'

Marc shakes his head. 'It doesn't sound selfish. It sounds immature.'

'Marc, I've thought this through. Honestly I have. I want to be a good mother to Ivy. A happy mother. A role model. Acting is who I am. I've been miserable without it.'

Marc kisses my head. 'Well we can't have that. Time to board.' He leads me towards the gangway. 'Just one more thing,' he says. 'Before we get on the ship.'

'What is it?'

'You asked me not to get jealous.' Marc's hand drops to the small of my back. 'I may have found a way to sidestep that ugly emotion.'

I laugh, taking tentative steps onto the swaying gangway. 'You? Not jealous? Impossible.'

'Right now, it's very, very possible.' He puts a hand to my arm, as I find my feet on the uncertain floor. 'I've spoken to Nadia.'

I stop walking. 'About what?'

'About the movie.'

'Marc? I'm not liking how this is sounding.'

The sea laps under our feet, grey blue and calm.

'Hear me out.' Marc's lips tilt into a smile. 'I've persuaded Nadia to consider me for the role of Nicky in her movie. I'll be playing the teacher to your student.'

I laugh in shock, not quite believing what I just heard. 'You did *what*? You can't be serious.'

Overhead, a seagull squawks.

'Deadly serious,' says Marc, leading me up the gangway. 'Benjamin Van Rosen was tolerable for the role at best. Nadia and I both agreed I'd be a better option.'

'I don't believe this.' I snatch my hand from his.

'Sophia. Think about it for a moment.'

'You *never* do movies like this one.' I grab the gangway rail. 'It's way too mainstream.'

'I'm doing it to make your life easier.' He pries my hand from metal and holds it between his.

'How will this make my life easier?' I say.

'We'll be playing out our relationship onscreen.' Marc raises a dark eyebrow. 'The worldly, dangerous man teaching the young, naïve girl. Benjamin Van Rosen would have been a bad match. Unbalanced. I'm a far better choice. I'll give you the space to blossom.'

'God Marc—'

He strokes my fingers. 'Nadia was only considering Benjamin Van Rosen for publicity. She told me so herself. He's in a high-profile relationship, and the press are desperate for interviews.'

'So what – you just had him kicked off the movie?'

'He's still in the movie,' Marc insists. 'He'll play your fiancé.' He takes my hand again. 'This isn't all about jealousy. I can protect you. Make sure you're nurtured rather than blown off the stage.'

'How patronising.' I walk away from him, up the gangway. 'You shouldn't have done this, Marc.'

He strides to catches up. 'You must admit to being curious. The two of us in a movie together. Playing out our story on the big screen.'

'Oh, so it's our story now?'

'Teacher and student. I'd say that was our story, wouldn't you?'

29

As we board the ship, two suited attendants bow to us.

'Welcome aboard, Mr and Mrs Blackwell,' says one. 'You're our very first guests.' He hands Marc two plastic, ivory-coloured cards. 'Your keys sir. For the Captain's Suite'

'No one else is here yet?' I ask.

The attendant shakes his head. 'Not yet, madam. Would you like a staff member to show you around? Help you find your suite?'

'It's fine,' says Marc, glancing at the key cards. 'Thank you. I know where it is – at the front of the ship, on this deck. We'll find our own way.'

'Taking charge as always,' I say, my words terse as we step onto the boat.

'I find it usually works out for the best.'

Marc and I walk through a circular lobby area.

'Not always,' I snap.

'I suppose you'd rather be fainting from exhaustion,' says Marc, leading me by the hand down a long, wide corridor. 'Or being knocked down by paparazzi.'

My feet feel soft, white carpet. It's incredible – to think this palace actually floats.

'I can't believe you've done this, Marc. It's beyond controlling.'

'Sophia.' Marc squeezes my fingers. 'Do you know why I took this role?'

'Because you didn't want me playing out bedroom scenes with Benjamin Van Rosen.'

'No,' says Marc. 'I read the script. Several times. I didn't see Benjamin Van Rosen as the best lead. Not with you playing Violet. As I said, the balance is wrong.'

'I'm sure he'd do a good job.'

'But *you* wouldn't, Sophia. Not beside someone like that. He'd give you no space to grow. Do you want to shoot a bad movie?'

'No,' I admit, feeling soft carpet give way to polished wood.

'The two of us … *we* fit together.' Marc squeezes my fingers for emphasis. 'I can help this movie succeed.'

'And jealousy didn't come into it?' I say, as we turn down another corridor. I'm a little disorientated now, and I have no idea how Marc knows where we're going.

'Not nearly as much as you might think,' says Marc, making another turn. 'This role wasn't even my idea. Michael suggested it.'

'Michael? You brother?'

'Yes. My scoundrel of a little brother. He cares about you, believe it or not. And he came up with a workable solution to our problem.'

We pass a marble fountain, where metallic fish blow streams of water from their mouths.

'You've been talking to Michael?' I ask, as Marc leads me around yet another turn.

Before Ivy was born, Marc promised he'd let his looka-like little brother into our lives. But from what I've seen,

Marc is still keeping Michael at arm's length, especially where Ivy is concerned. I'm surprised they've been in touch.

Michael has only been allowed to visit his new niece once, under Marc's strict supervision.

'We met up in the city last week,' says Marc. 'But I'm still not comfortable about him visiting the house.'

'You promised you'd start trusting him,' I point out.

'It's been harder than I imagined.'

'I don't think that's fair, Marc. He said he'd never see your father again.'

'And to my knowledge he hasn't.' Marc leads me down yet another corridor. 'But time will tell me everything I need to know. Honestly, Sophia, I thought you'd be pleased about me taking this part.'

'*Pleased*?' I pull him to a stop. 'That your jealousy has put another actor out of a job?'

'Benjamin's contract wasn't signed,' Marc insists. 'Nothing was written in stone. And he still has a part in the movie. You're being extremely dramatic.'

'Oh come on.' I shake my head. 'You hated me shooting those scenes with Leo Falkirk in *Rapunzel*.'

Marc's jaw goes hard. 'Be careful, Sophia. Don't say something you might regret.'

'You have to understand why I'm upset.'

'Listen,' says Marc. 'This *isn't* about jealousy. You have my word. I read the script and thought we'd be the perfect balance for one another. Come inside the suite. We'll talk.'

'I don't think we're ever going to find our suite,' I say. 'This place is a maze.'

'It's right here,' says Marc, leading me past giant vases of flowering bamboo. Ahead of us are ash-white double doors.

Marc pulls out a keycard and slides it into the door lock.

30

'Wow.' Beyond the doors is a wall of blue ocean and sky. Panoramic glass curves around the largest, most luxurious suite I could ever imagine. It's like an apartment, with its own cocktail bar and Jacuzzi pool.

'This is incredible.' I step into the room. 'We must have the whole front of the ship.'

'Not quite.' Marc slides the keycard into his pocket. 'But I made sure you had the best suite onboard.'

'*You* made sure?' I can't help grinning.

'I made sure.'

Through the panoramic glass, I see a wraparound sundeck, complete with sun beds, cube tables and an icy-blue splash pool.

Our luggage has already arrived and is stacked up by the wardrobe waiting to be unpacked.

'Is this really all for us?' I ask, going to the panoramic window and staring at our huge sundeck.

'Yes.' Marc opens bi-folding glass doors, and fresh sea air rushes into the room. 'I'm glad it's luxurious enough to make you forget our argument for a moment.'

I look out at the glistening sea. 'It's done that all right.'

'We have our own private spa too,' says Marc.

'Our own *spa*?' Oh my god.

'Only the best for my family,' Marc laughs. 'Only the best. And Ivy has her own bedroom. It leads through to the nanny suite. So no more waking in the night – you're here to work.'

I feel a glimmer of worry. 'Has Tanya sent any more messages?'

Marc checks his phone and nods. 'Yes. The traffic is very bad. They've stopped in a roadside restaurant. They'll be another few hours.'

'A few *hours*?'

'She's fine. I trust Tanya, and so do you. Don't do that.' Marc comes to me, stroking my forehead. 'She'll be here soon. You have to get used to Tanya taking care of her.'

'Yes, but—'

'But nothing. You wanted to work. This is how it's done.'

I nod, but my stomach feels unsettled.

'If you're having second thoughts, we can still leave the ship,' says Marc. 'We haven't set sail yet.'

'You know I'd never do that.' I turn to him. 'You promise you didn't take this part because you were jealous?'

'I promise.' Marc holds my hands to his chest.

'Promise, promise?' I look up at him.

'You, Mrs Blackwell, need a lesson in trusting your husband.' He smiles down at me.

'I do trust you.'

'Ah yes. It's the obeying that's the problem, isn't it?' His smile grows.

'Always has been. Call me modern, but I think a marriage should be equal.'

'Equal? Really?' Marc moves hair around my neck. 'You know, you don't look all that equal, tied to a bed with a gag in your mouth.'

'That's not fair,' I murmur, my breath quickening.

'Fair is overrated.' Marc lifts my hands above my head and presses the backs of my palms to panoramic glass. 'Have I convinced you I didn't take this role with any ill intentions?'

'I think so.'

'Good. Keep your arms up like that.'

Marc turns me around so I face calm, clear ocean, the glass cool under my fingertips.

'Stay there,' he orders. 'Don't move. Don't turn around.'

The heat of Marc leaves my body, and I hear him moving around the suite.

There is the run of a zip. The clunk of something metallic.

Then I feel Marc close again, standing behind me.

'Don't move,' he says again.

Something rough runs down my cheek.

My breathing is hot and fast on the glass.

As the roughness moves to my lips, I see a doubled-over rope against my skin.

It moves down my jaw and onto my neck.

Marc taps it against the side of my throat. 'I want you naked,' he decides. 'Turn around and take your clothes off.'

'Is this a usual way for married couples to make up after an argument?' I ask.

'Do as you're told.'

Obediently, I turn, lifting my white t-shirt over my head. Then I step out of my blue jeans and converse.

I'm wearing simple underwear – a yoga bra and g-string. It's plain. Comfortable for travel.

'And your underwear,' Marc instructs.

I pull my bra over my head and slide down my g-string, letting it fall around my ankles.

'Arms by your sides.'

Marc's fingers go to my wrists, and realise he's tying them together with the rope.

I shiver at its roughness.

'Lift your arms again,' Marc demands.

I do.

He loops the loose rope length over the curtain rail, a long, silver-blue pole that sits high above the window.

I'm suspended now. Vulnerable. My back to the water.

Marc stalks away, and I hear another zip pulled along.

When Marc returns, I see a tangle of black, knotted leather in his hands.

31

'What is that?' I murmur, mesmerised by the mess of string.

Marc runs long strands over the back of his hand. 'A flogger. They used them at sea. For disobedient shipmates. Rather fitting, don't you think?'

He drapes the flogger around my shoulder, and I see knotted leather resting over my breast.

My breathing quickens.

'If a shipmate stepped out of line,' says Marc, stroking the leather knots across my breasts, 'he'd be lashed.'

I close my eyes, waiting.

'Impatient, Mrs Blackwell?' Marc's voice is teasing.

Yes.

'Do you want to see what I can do with this?'

I nod.

SNAP!

An electric shock zips over my skin, as Marc throws the flogger against my chest.

The knots hit like fire crackers, and I'm thrown back, my wrists swinging in the rope.

The flogger comes down again, and it hurts more this time as the knotted ends finding the stings they found before.

I moan, swaying against the rope, my eyes tight shut.

'Do you want more?' Marc asks.

I nod again.

SNAP! SNAP! SNAP!

Marc delivers three quick lashes, and as my skin dances with pain, my body softens to his control.

I moan louder.

'If you can't be quiet, I'll have to gag you.' Marc runs the flogger back and forth over my breasts.

Oh god. The anticipation. I can hardly stand it …

WHACK!

Marc cracks the flogger hard against my stomach, and I can't help crying out.

It's almost unbearable. I'm desperate for him. Desperate to have him inside me.

I'm barely aware of anything now – just the intense pain and pleasure on my skin.

Marc delivers one more hard blow against my breasts, strong enough to knock me back against the glass.

Then he drops the flogger and lifts me by my buttocks, placing me around his waist. I don't notice him free himself from his trousers. Only feel the sweet relief of him sliding inside me, filling me up and making me ache with pleasure.

Oh *god*.

I'm floating on the ropes, my eyes swimming, my body on fire.

Marc is still fully dressed, and I feel the fabric of his suit as he lowers me onto him.

He holds me for a moment, hands tight on my hips. Then he moves back and forth.

I nearly faint with pleasure, feeling the hardness of him as I throb and moan.

We move together, over and over, swaying in perfect rhythm.

Pleasure comes in waves and then sweeps me away, soft and lovely.

The orgasm goes on and on as Marc moves. And then he comes too, closing his eyes and holding me tight against him.

I feel his chest, breathing against mine.

We stay for a moment, swaying together, the sea waving behind us. Then Marc kisses my lips, unhooks the rope and carries me to the circular bed. He sits me on his lap and unties my wrists, rubbing my red skin.

32

I don't mean to fall asleep, but I do.

When I wake in the cabin's luxurious round bed, I hear soft knocking at the door.

'Who is it?' I call out, rubbing my eyes and looking around for Marc.

'It's me. Tanya.'

I throw back my duvet and reach the door in half a second. On the other side, my little baby is in her stroller, blinking and smiling.

'Hello beautiful.' I grin at her big, curious eyes, then carefully unclip the stroller straps, pulling Ivy into a tight hug. 'I've missed you.'

'You would not believe the traffic,' says Tanya, wheeling the empty stroller into our suite. 'But this one slept pretty much the whole time. She's only just woken up.'

'She didn't cry?' I ask.

'A tiny bit when we pulled over,' says Tanya. 'But then she was okay. Honestly, Soph, just perfect.' Tanya, folds up the stroller with one hand and props it in the walk in wardrobe. 'She's such a good baby.'

I close the suite door. 'She can cry pretty loudly when she wants to.'

'Can't they all? Were you okay? You weren't sitting here worrying?'

I redden at the thought of what Marc and I were doing. 'Oh ... no. I hardly worried at all, actually. I was too busy ... uh, sleeping.'

'Where's Marc?' Tanya asks.

'Actually, I'm not sure,' I admit. 'I fell asleep and ... I don't see him in the suite.'

'He's probably out buying you diamonds or something. But listen – if you're missing male company, I have good news. A very fine man is on his way down here as we speak. A man I think you might be pleased to see.'

'Who?' I ask.

Tanya is grinning from ear-to-ear now. 'Don't you want to have a few guesses?'

'What man will I be pleased to see?' I say, still confused.

There's a jaunty knock at the door.

'Here he is,' says Tanya, still grinning.

A voice calls through the wood: 'Morning campers!'

Laughing, I pull the door open. 'Tom!'

'Ahoy there, shipmates!' Tom wheels into the suite, wearing a shirt with puffy sleeves, a leather waistcoat and a pirate hat. Three takeaway coffees sit on his lap, held firm in a cardboard holder.

It's so good to see my old friend from Ivy College – and also good to know he and Tanya are still going strong. Even after months together, Tom obviously cares enough to give her a personal send off.

'Good lord!' Tom looks around the suite in wonder. 'Panoramic sea view. Sundeck with pool. Bathroom bigger than my bedroom back at Ivy College. Yes, this is Mr Blackwell's room, all right. Sophia, I hope you and Marc are making good use of the space.'

Tom wiggles his eyebrows at me.

'Tom!' Tanya shouts. 'Think of the little one. You can't be talking like that in front of Ivy.'

'Oh, she's too young to understand what I'm saying,' says Tom, waving a dismissive hand. 'And it would be a crying shame not to have any hanky-panky in such a beautiful room. Right Sophia?'

'It's good to see you Tom.' I lean down to kiss his cheek.

Ivy's head drops as I lean forward, and Tom reaches up for her. 'Let's have a cuddle with this little one. She's growing so fast. I swear, she changes every time I see her.'

Tom cradles Ivy in his arms, and she looks up at him, her eyes calm and happy.

I guess she knows when someone loves her.

'There, there little one.' Tom turns her to the panoramic window. 'I think you're going to enjoy your time at sea.'

The ship horn sounds and engines begin to churn.

'Tom,' I say, my voice urgent. 'The engines are starting.'

'I hear them too, my love.' Tom gazes down at Ivy. 'My legs may be crap, but I'm not deaf.'

'Shouldn't you be heading for dry land?' I say.

Tom snorts. 'Certainly not! Hasn't Tanya told you?'

'Told me what?' I ask.

'I am *staying* onboard with you fine ladies,' Tom announces in his booming voice. 'Yes – that's right. I will be joining you both on the seven seas.'

'You're coming with us?' I squeak.

'Indeed.' Tom smiles. 'I've been a little bit cunning. You see, I have a part in the movie.'

33

'Well there's no need to stare at me like that,' says Tom. 'I'm not *that* bad an actor.'

'I'm sorry.' I snap my mouth closed. 'It's just …' I shake my head. 'This is a bit of a shock. I mean, you don't even know Nadia. And—'

'Ah ha!' Tom kisses Ivy's head. 'But I know *Marc*. And when I found out my beloved was setting sail for months on end, I had a little word in his ear. He got me an audition. Just a small role, you understand. And lo and behold, I got the part. I'm tickled pink about it. Best of all, I get to travel with this beautiful lady.'

He gives Tanya a soppy smile, which she returns – before she remembers herself and looks serious.

'You don't mind, do you Soph?' Tanya asks, with a nervous twiddle of her fingers.

'Mind?' I laugh. 'I think it's fantastic. And Tom – you're not a bad actor at all. You're a great actor, in fact.'

'Nadia offered Tanya a part too,' says Tom. 'But the silly thing turned it down.'

'You did?' I ask Tanya. 'They offered you a role in the movie?'

'I wasn't interested,' she replies. 'Not while I have little Ivy to look after. She'll keep me busy. Anyway, I'm not movie ready. Tom's been on stage since nursery school. But me – I have a lot more to learn.'

I think of Marc's words. *A lot to learn …*

'Darling, you're a *fabulous* actress,' Tom insists. 'You have to dive in at some point. It's always going to be frightening.'

'One day,' says Tanya. 'But not yet. I just know I'm not ready. Anyway. They only offered me the part because Marc Blackwell put me forward. It hardly seems fair.'

Tom bounces Ivy on his knee. 'Life is all about who you know. Especially in the movies.'

'Parts should be won on merit,' says Tanya.

'And you *do* have merit, my love,' Tom replies. 'But so do thousands of other actresses. And if there are thousands who can play a part equally well, how does one decide? Surely doing a friend a favour is no terrible thing.'

'I don't agree with it,' says Tanya, pushing her black-rimmed glasses up her nose. 'I'm here to look after Ivy. And I'd need a heck of a lot more training before I star in a movie. Slow and steady, that's my motto.'

We're so deep in conversation that I don't notice Marc in the doorway. But suddenly his voice booms, 'I only wish Sophia shared that sentiment.'

Marc leans against the doorframe, looking perfect as usual. Black suit, white shirt, dark hair – and blue eyes that are beautiful, dangerous and edgy all at once.

'Good to see you both. Tom. Tanya.' Marc stalks into the suite.

'Good to see you too, sir,' says Tom.

'Hello Mr Blackwell,' Tanya mumbles, pushing hair behind her ears.

'I see Ivy is still fond of you Tom,' says Marc, taking Ivy from his lap. 'Let's hope she hasn't forgotten who her father is.'

Ivy blinks up at Marc, then closes her eyes as he holds her against his chest.

'We should be going,' says Tanya, throwing warning glances at Tom. 'Unpack and all of that.'

'But we were just catching up,' Tom protests. 'And I had a beautiful baby to cuddle.'

'Come *on* Tom. Let's get going.' Tanya grabs his wheelchair and pushes him towards the door.

'This is quite unbelievable,' says Tom. 'Not even married yet, and you are literally pushing me around. There are breaks on this thing, you know Tanya. And I'm not afraid to use them.'

Tanya laughs, waving as she wheels Tom out the door. 'See you later.'

'Marc?' I ask. 'Where did you go?'

'I took a walk around the ship,' he replies. 'Checked the safety procedures. Security. That sort of thing.'

'Oh.'

But Marc looks distracted.

'Did you bump into anyone interesting?' I ask.

He doesn't answer my question. Instead he says, 'The staff inform me we'll be having lunch shortly. On the grand dining deck. A chance to meet the UK cast.'

'Shame Nadia's not onboard yet,' I say.

'Yes,' says Marc, holding Ivy tight to his chest. 'A great

pity. Especially since there are those onboard I'd rather not see.'

'Please tell me you're not talking about Benjamin Van Rosen.'

'No.' Marc sways Ivy back and forth. 'He'll board with Nadia.'

'We'll all be working together soon, Marc. You should give him a chance.'

'I've already given him a chance.' Marc strokes Ivy's little fingers.

'So who *is* onboard you'd rather not see?'

34

'I think Ivy would like to see the water,' Marc announces, sliding the panoramic glass apart.

He strolls onto the large sun deck, holding Ivy so she can see waves bouncing against the ship.

I follow him, feeling bright spring sunshine on my face.

'Well?' I ask Marc. 'Aren't you going to answer me?'

'Not right now.'

'This is ridiculous,' I insist. 'Whoever you're talking about … well I'm going to work it out soon, aren't I? When we all have lunch together.'

'Not necessarily,' says Marc.

'Why not?'

'He *shouldn't* be … Christ.' Marc checks his watch. 'I'm taking another walk before lunch.'

'Another one?' I ask.

'Another one.'

'How about we come with you?' I offer. 'Ivy can sleep in her stroller.'

'Best not.' Marc kisses Ivy on the head, then me on the cheek. 'I'll meet you at lunch.'

Bewildered and more than a little bit stung, I clutch Ivy to my chest.

'What's wrong with Daddy?' I whisper. 'Shall we find out? What do you think?'

Marc obviously wants to be alone. But we're supposed to be a family. A team. Whatever is bothering him, he should talk to me about it.

'Come on Ivy,' I decide. 'Let's go after him.'

I head outside, pushing Ivy's stroller over thick carpet.

We travel down cream-coloured corridors with bright art on the walls, and then out onto the main deck. Actually, I should say *one* of the main decks, because there are eight more of them below.

This ship is amazing. Dozens of restaurants, swimming pools, coffee stands and champagne bars. Real palm trees sway in pots as the ship pulls out to sea.

I don't find Marc on deck.

But I find someone else.

35

Jen is leaning over a railing, her face pale.

'Hey Jen!' I wave to her.

A dull-eyed Jen turns around. 'Soph. Hey.'

She wears a white trouser suit, nautically-striped t-shirt and headscarf-bandana with anchors all over it. The look would be amazing, if Jen didn't look so ill.

'Are you okay?' I ask.

'Sea sick.' Jen turns back to the rail. 'It's better if I watch the water.'

'When did you board?' I ask.

'Just as the engines started up.' Jen stares glassy-eyed at the water. 'We nearly missed the boat. Bloody Leo. And then, if making us late wasn't enough, Leo took off his shoes in the cabin and the smell and the motion together made me throw up.'

'Is your cabin nice?' I ask.

'It was beautiful. Before Leo arrived. Now it looks like a teenager's bedroom.'

'Have you seen Marc?' I look along the enormous deck.

'No. Why?' Jen asks.

'Just … I'm looking for him.' I push the stroller back and forth over the bumpy, wood floor.

'What happened?' Jen asks. 'You two are usually inseparable.'

'Something's up. But he's not talking to me about it.'

'Count your blessings.' Jen looks out to sea. 'Leo talks way too much. Speak of the devil …'

The tall, muscular bulk of Leo Falkirk swaggers towards us, dirty blond hair tucked behind his ears.

He's tanned as usual, with twinkling eyes and white teeth, and wears a loose surfer vest and baggy flowery shorts.

'Well look who we have here!' Leo bellows. 'Sophia Blackwell.' He throws an arm around my shoulder. 'All okay in married land?'

'Oh, you know.' I try for a smile. 'Up and down.'

Leo throws an arm around Jen's shoulder too. 'I know all about that. We're up and down, up and down every damn day. Aren't we sweetheart?'

'Leo.' Jen puts a hand to her mouth. 'You're arm is too warm. It's making me feel sick.'

Leo shrugs and drops his hand. 'Can't do anything right.' He turns to me. 'Hey – where's Prince Charming?'

'I don't know,' I reply.

'You don't *know*? How about that. I'll bet Marc knows where *you* are, though. He keeps you on a pretty short leash.'

'If you have something to say to me, Falkirk,' says Marc, appearing behind us, arms crossed, 'say it to my face.'

'Where did you spring from?' Leo looks around. 'Oh I get it. Vampires can turn invisible. Right?'

'*Leo.*' Jen's voice is full of warning.

'Take your arm off my wife,' Marc growls.

Leo lifts his arm from my shoulder. 'Jeez. I'm marrying her best friend. Relax already. Hey – is it lunchtime yet? I'm starved.'

'God Leo, show some respect,' Jen hisses, steering Leo away. 'We'll see you down there, Soph. You two have a nice talk, okay? Byeee!'

I wait until Jen and Leo are below deck, then turn to Marc. 'You have a lot of explaining to do,' I tell him.

'He had his arm around you,' Marc growls. 'It wasn't appropriate.'

'What is *up* with you?' I snap.

'You know what's up with me, where Leo is concerned.'

'Oh, come on.' I shake my head. 'There's more to this.'

'Now isn't the time.'

'Fine. If that's how you want to be, we'll see you later.' I push the stroller along the deck.

'Sophia—'

I turn back. 'I mean it Marc. Come find us when you're in a better mood.'

36

Furious, I push Ivy back to our suite and dress for lunch, choosing a loose, v-necked silk dress, brown belt and gladiator sandals.

Ivy lays on the bed, pulling soft duvet into her mouth and watching me.

As I'm tying my hair with a navy ribbon, I hear soft knocking at the door.

'Soph?' Tanya calls out. 'Are you decent? Can I come in?'

'Of course,' I shout back.

Tanya pushes open the door and lets out a low wolf whistle. 'Wowzers. You're looking pretty hot for a new mother.'

'Thanks.' I smooth the dress. 'I'm more comfortable in jeans. But … I thought I should dress up.'

'Where's Ivy?' Tanya asks.

'On the bed.' I point.

'How about I look after her while you go to lunch?' Tanya offers.

'What about *your* lunch?' I say.

'Already had it. Well. A late breakfast really. Brunch, to use Tom's word. Posh git. I don't want to eat with all those famous people anyway.'

'Tanya—'

'It's fine. Really. Ivy should be asleep by now anyway. Let me look after her. It's what I'm here for. You're supposed to be working. Right? So go meet the cast and let me take care of the baby.'

I manage a smile, but it's a weary one. 'Fine. Okay. As long as you're happy.'

'I'm more than happy,' Tanya insists. 'Off you go, Soph. Knock 'em dead.'

The dining hall is on the very top deck, and takes up the front of the ship. There are glass windbreaks and a canvas canopy for bad weather, but the tables are essentially in the warm open air.

Jen and Leo have a table already, near the cocktail bar. Leo is knocking back a beer, while Jen sips from a champagne glass.

Where's Marc? Why isn't he here already?

A suited waiter appears, a bright-white napkin folded over his arm. 'Ms Sophia Blackwell?'

'Yes?' I say, a little taken aback that he knows my name.

'Allow me to show you to your table, madam. Your husband is waiting.'

'Oh. Okay.'

So Marc is here already. Where?

The waiter leads me around glass windbreaks, to a dark-haired man with his back to me.

'Um …' I blink in surprise.

I'm about to tell the waiter there's been a mistake. That this isn't my husband. Marc would never wear a pink shirt. But then the dark-haired man turns, and I clamp my mouth shut.

'Everything okay Miss?' the waiter asks.

Oh god.

'Yes … thanks.' I take a chair opposite the man, feeling a little dazed.

'Would you care for a drink, Mrs Blackwell?' the waiter asks, tapping a pen on his pad. 'A cocktail? Your husband is enjoying a Virgin Sea Breeze. Perhaps you'd like to join him?'

I want to laugh at the word, *husband.*

'Yes, sure,' I say, barely aware of my words.

'Very good madam.'

As the waiter strides away, I lean forward and hiss at the man across the table, 'Is this some kind of joke? What are you doing here?'

37

Michael sits across from me, grinning as he butters a bread roll.

Marc's brother.

He wears a dark blue suit and pink shirt, his brown hair loose and windswept.

'Is that any way to greet your brother-in-law?'

Michael looks so like Marc that I'm not surprised he had the waiter fooled. But I would know Marc anywhere.

It all makes sense now. Marc's dark mood, and his strange comments earlier.

'I thought Ivy would be with you.' Michael looks disappointed. 'What – is she sleeping or something?'

'Never mind that,' I snap. 'Does Marc know you've taken his place at lunch?'

'Not yet.' Michaels takes a mouthful of buttered roll. 'God, he nearly killed me when he found out I was onboard.'

'What are you *doing* here? You shouldn't even be on this ship.'

'I know! Funny, isn't it?' He chews his bread.

'It's not funny at all,' I say. 'What happens when Marc turns up?'

'He won't.' Michael pops the last of the roll into his mouth. 'Not for a while. I sent him to the other side of the boat. He's waiting for you there. By the time he works it out, I'll be long gone.'

'Michael!' I pull my chair closer to the table.

'Look, he's furious with me anyway, so why not have some fun? What are little brothers for? Bread?' He grabs the last bread roll from the basket and drops it on my side plate.

'He really *is* going to kill you—' I snap my mouth closed as the waiter appears and places a bright-blue cocktail on my glass coaster.

'Señor.' Michael taps his arm. 'More bread rolls. There's a lad.'

'Very good sir.' The waiter strides off.

'What are you *doing* here, Michael?' I ask.

'I wanted to see my niece,' he replies. 'So I stowed away.'

The way he's talking – it's like this is all some big joke. But it's serious. If people realise there's someone else who looks like Marc, he won't be able to help us evade the paparazzi anymore.

The waiter reappears with a bowl of bread rolls, brightly coloured in saffron yellow and beetroot pink.

'Thanks,' we both say in unison.

'Never seen a bread roll like this before, have you?' says Michael, as the waiter walks away. 'I love all this fancy stuff. You know, once in London—'

'*Michael!* What happens when you get found out?'

'I won't get found out,' he insists, tearing a roll open. 'Everyone thinks I'm Marc. The eye sees what the head believes.'

'I think you're sailing pretty close to the wind, don't you? Taking his place at lunch?'

'I thought you'd be bringing my niece here.' Michael liberally butters his roll. 'I wanted to see her. You have to understand, nothing like this has ever happened to me before.'

'Nothing like what?' I ask.

'Like love.'

I laugh, but Michael stays serious.

'It's not funny,' he replies, eyes flashing with hurt. 'I am madly in love with that little baby of yours. I've hardly seen her all year. She's growing every day.'

'Oh god.' My smile falls away. 'You mean it, don't you?'

'I'm an uncle now,' says Michael. 'I take the job seriously. Ivy is my family and I want to be with her whenever I can.'

'But this is such a massive risk. Marc will kill you.'

'She's worth it.' Michael looks at his bread roll. 'You know, I never had much of a family. But then Marc came into my life. And you. And Ivy. I finally feel I have something worth bettering myself for. You know? I will look out for that little baby of yours as long as I live.'

I sigh. 'Marc's going to be so furious.'

'What else could I do?' Michael insists. 'It could take him years to trust me again. By that time, Ivy could be all grown up.'

'We can figure out a plan,' I decide. 'But listen. You can't stay here. Marc isn't stupid. He's going to work out where I am, sooner or later. And if he knows you took his place at lunch—'

'Too late.' Michael's face turns pale. 'I think I've been rumbled.'

Marc strides across the dining deck, a thunderous look on his face.

Our waiter notices Marc, then looks back at our table. Bewildered, he turns his head back and forth between the two men like he's watching tennis.

Marc reaches our table in five long strides. 'Michael. Come with me. Right now.'

Michael manages a weak smile. 'You're sure you won't stay for a drink?'

'Don't be too angry with him, Marc,' I insist. 'He was just—'

'I don't want to hear it,' Marc barks. 'Get up, Michael. *Now.*'

Reluctantly, Michael stands. He takes a last hasty sip of his cocktail.

'Sophia, stay here,' says Marc. 'I'll be back soon.'

With Marc and Michael gone, the eyes of the dining room turn to me.

I want to hide behind a napkin.

Dimly, I notice Jen hurrying around tables.

'You okay, Soph?' she says, as she reaches my table.

I can't manage much of a reply. 'Um …'

'Come with me.' She grabs my arm and clicks her fingers at a waiter. 'Have our lunches brought to Leo Falkirk's cabin,' she tells him. 'Okay?'

38

Jen and Leo's suite is lovely.

If I hadn't seen my own, I would guess it was the best onboard.

There's a cocktail bar, and real fish swim under the bathroom floor.

'Leo loves those fish,' says Jen, stooping to pick up a trail of towels. 'God, he's such a messy bastard.'

'I can tell which side of the bed you sleep on,' I remark.

On one bedside table sits a gleaming Kindle and neatly folded eye mask. The other has tangles of wires, loose script pages and a stray sock.

'Bloody Leo,' Jen moans, grabbing a crumpled pair of cargo shorts from the floor. 'Can't he behave like an adult, just once in his life? How can it be so messy already? We've been here like, half an hour.'

I laugh. 'He's good for you, Jen. He balances you out. You're sensible, he's childlike. And somewhere in the middle, you get magic.'

Jen's eyes look faraway. 'He *can* be magic sometimes.' Her gaze falls on a pair of underpants. 'But oh my GOD, why can't he be tidier?'

'No one's perfect,' I say.

'Marc is perfect.'

'No.' I shake my head. 'He isn't. He's controlling.'

Jen falls backwards onto the soft bed, hands behind her head. 'So how come Michael's onboard anyway?'

'He snuck on without anyone knowing,' I tell her.

'But why?' Jen asks.

'He wanted to see Ivy.'

'That's sweet.' She throws pants into the open wardrobe.

'I know,' I agree. 'If only Marc could see'

There's a sharp knock on the door.

'Sophia?' Marc's voice cuts through the wood.

Jen and I glance at each other.

'I'll get it,' I tell Jen, opening the door. I find Marc in the doorway, frowning and serious, hands on hips.

'You didn't throw Michael overboard, did you?' I say, trying for a joke.

'The thought had occurred to me.' Marc stalks into the suite, closing the door behind him.

'I hope you listened to what Michael had to say.' I sit on the bed. 'He just wants to be a good brother and uncle—'

Marc paces back and forth. 'My brother needs no one's sympathy. He has too much of our father in him.'

'But he didn't mean to—'

'Oh, he never means to.' Marc throws his hands up. 'But here we are, yet again. Another mess to sort out, thanks to Michael's dazzling sense of humour. Jen – I'll be needing your skills. The waiter on that dining deck needs a reason to keep quiet. I don't care what it costs.'

'I'm on it. Wait.' She puts a hand to her mouth and runs to the bathroom. 'Just … let me throw up quickly.'

'Christ.' Marc runs a hand through his hair. 'Jen – it's okay. You can't work if you're sick.'

'It's FINE!' Jen shouts through the bathroom door. 'I can do it. Just give me a minute.'

'You don't sound fine at all,' Marc barks.

'I'LL DO IT!' Jen shouts, crashing out of the bathroom, drinking from a toothbrush mug. 'I've just taken three sea-sickness tablets and gargled with Listerine. I'll be fine. I *am* fine.'

Marc raises an eyebrow. 'The indomitable Jen.'

'You've got that right. Now excuse me, I have diners to talk to.' Jen drops an iPad in her beige Chanel bag, fluffs her hair and clip clops out of the suite.

Marc's smile grows. 'She's quite a girl, that friend of yours.'

'I know. But listen. About Michael —'

'It's already done.' Marc sits beside me on the bed. 'He'll leave the boat when we reach Spain. And stay out of sight until we get there. I've had a cabin arranged. All his meals will be below deck from now on.'

'Sounds like you're throwing him into prison,' I say. 'All he wanted to do was spend time with his family.'

'And he did so in the most careless, thoughtless way.'

'Not everyone is as logical as you, Marc. He just went with his heart.'

'Well maybe he'll learn to go with his head in future.'

'You're not being fair. He wants to see Ivy. And *I* want him to see her too. The more love she has, the better.'

Marc is still frowning. 'Michael can give her all the love he likes back in the UK.'

'But you hardly ever let him visit,' I point out.

'Trust takes time.'

'What else can he do? He's trying, Marc,' I say, taking his hand.

'And so am I. You have to understand, Sophia. I'm doing my best to protect you and our daughter.'

'I just think Michael deserves a break,' I say.

Marc's frown deepens. 'In time.'

39

The ship ploughs on through clear waters, and with Ivy looked after by Tanya, Marc and I have a chance to explore our luxurious transportation.

'This is like a floating paradise,' I say, as we stroll past real flowerbeds and swaying palm trees, the sea churning below us.

On the top deck, we discover three salt-water swimming pools and various cocktail and champagne bars. On the deck below, we found a Turkish bath, cinema and massage room.

Marc and I dine alone that night, enjoying a champagne and seafood supper on our private balcony as we watch the pink sun set over sparkling water.

The sun fades, stars come out and I ask Marc if we'll reach Spain by morning.

He leans back in his chair, watching the water. 'Yes. Ms Malbeck's luxury floating taxi service.' His lips twitch. 'And Benjamin Van Rosen's too.'

I feel my stomach skip over.

Benjamin Van Rosen.

He's an incredible actor, and almost as famous as Marc. Certainly as infamous.

'Something the matter, Sophia?' Marc turns to me, eyebrow raised.

I shake my head. 'I'm fine.'

'Not nervous at all?' He refills my champagne glass.

'Of course not. I'm ready and raring to go.'

'Sophia—'

'Look, if I tell you the truth, you'll just say "I told you so".' I pick up my glass.

'Why don't you try me?' Marc asks.

I take a sip of champagne, letting the bubbles swill around my mouth.

'Okay, fine. I'm incredibly scared. The nearer we get to filming, the more I feel … like maybe I'm not ready for this. Especially acting with someone of Benjamin Van Rosen's calibre. And reputation. Happy now?'

'Not in the slightest.' He refills his own glass. 'But you can't back out.'

'Of course not.'

Marc taps thoughtful fingers on the table. 'So how about accepting some tuition?'

'Tuition?'

Marc nods.

'You'd teach me again? Out here?' I ask, gesturing to the huge, dark ocean churning around us.

'Why not?' says Marc. 'A classroom can be anywhere.'

'You don't want to rub it in?' I say. 'How right you were about me jumping in the deep end?'

'I don't see the purpose of humiliating you. At least, not outside the bedroom.' Marc raises an eyebrow.

'But there's no time to teach me, Marc. We start filming tomorrow.'

Marc checks his watch. 'There's time. We can start right now.'

'Now? It's nine at night. Actually – ten o'clock Spanish time.'

'There's no time like the present.' Marc pulls his sleeve cuff back in place. 'But don't expect me to go easy on you, just because it's late.'

I laugh. 'I'd forgotten how strict you could be.'

'It gets results.' Marc takes a neat sip of champagne, then examines his glass in the moonlight.

'It certainly does.'

'What are you struggling with, so far?' Marc asks, placing his glass on the table.

'The dialogue,' I admit. 'It's so different to how we talk these days. The lines aren't going in.'

Marc frowns. 'You've been studying the script too hard.'

'But you *always* memorise the whole script before you film,' I insist.

'True.' Marc nods. 'But you don't need to hold on to it too tight.'

I grab the script from a sun lounger. 'These sorts of lines – you can't mess around with them too much. Or it'll sound too modern.'

'You can still ad lib,' says Marc. 'You'll see. Once you relax.'

I turn pages. 'You know, I'm supposed to hate you for a good part of this movie.'

'I'm sure you have plenty of real life experiences to draw upon.' Marc takes the script from my hand. 'You don't need that. Not right now.'

'I do.' I try to take my script back, but Marc holds it away from me.

'Feeling contempt yet?' he asks.

'Beginning too.'

'Good.' Marc picks me up and throws me over one shoulder, the script still in his fingers.

I yell in surprise as he carries me into the suite and throws me on the bed.

'Marc!'

'Just getting into character,' he says.

'Hey.' I sit up and push hair from my face. 'Give me my script.'

'I already told you. It's not going to help you right now. You want to learn how to own this movie? You want to really *feel* the lines?'

'Yes,' I mutter.

'Then listen to your teacher.'

I shake my head. 'I can't adlib. It won't sound right. The words just aren't there. They're all jumbled up and in the wrong order.'

'Let's try.' He throws the script onto the study desk.

'Marc—'

Suddenly, Marc flashes into character. 'This is bullshit,' he yells, his eyes furious and intense. 'You don't care about me. What am I to you? Nothing more than a half-time show. Grow up and go back to your boyfriend.'

Whoa.

They're lines from the script. Sort of. Although Marc has put his own spin on them.

Sometimes I forget what an amazing actor Marc is. He's just mesmerising.

I catch my breath.

For a moment, my mind trips over 1930s phrases. But then words begin to flow.

'Why are you pretending?' I snap back. 'That dance *meant* something. You know it did.'

I try to stand again, but Marc pins my shoulders.

God, he is incredible. His conflict, loving my character, but hating her too … I can feel it all in his stare. I know of no other actor who can do that. Marc was so right to take this part. Benjamin Van Rosen would be nothing in comparison.

'Go live your life, princess,' says Marc.

'That's what I'm trying to do,' I shout, pleased that the words sound okay. Not too out of place.

Marc's eyes are filled with pain. 'Live it with him, not with me.'

'I don't want *him*,' I yell. 'I never wanted him. It wasn't real. The way I feel about you … *this* is real. *You're* real.'

I'm surprising myself. Okay, my words are a little modern. But the emotion is there, and I get what Marc's trying to do. Find the emotion first. Worry about the words later.

Marc watches me for a moment, his blue eyes stormy and thoughtful. He holds the pause for just long enough. Long enough for the audience to lift themselves off their seats and scream, *kiss her*!

DEVOTED BOOKS

I am SO happy you're still reading!

Want to chat with me on Facebook? You can here:

http://www.facebook.com/suzykquinn

If you look like my sort of person, I'll accept your friendship.

Be quick though – I've nearly at my Facebook Friend limit :).

Also, here's a little window into my writer's world – the Pintrest board I used whilst writing this series.

https://uk.pinterest.com/suzykquinn/ivy-lessons/

No more interruptions I promise.
See you at the end, lovely lady.

Suzy K Quinn xx

40

Then Marc kisses me.

His lips are firm on mine, and he is so passionate – uninhibited and uncontrolled.

I kiss him back just as fiercely, and our bodies tangle up.

Marc is Nicky – in love, but too proud to admit it. And I am Violet – the girl who wants him, but knows there is no future.

Marc pulls back and stares at me, breath rising and falling in his chest, his eyes intense and in love.

'This can go nowhere,' he says, his words panting and desperate.

'I know,' I gasp.

'But I can't stop.' Marc pulls my top over my head and moves his lips down my chest and onto my breasts.

My body tightens and I grab his hair.

'Tell me you don't love him,' says Marc, his mouth on my skin.

'Nicky—'

'Tell me.' Marc moves back up my body, cupping my face in his hands.

'I don't love him,' I say softly. 'I love you.'

Marc leans back onto his elbows, watching me with soft hurt in his eyes.

'You don't mean that, rich girl.'

'Yes. I do.'

Marc shakes his head, and I see his sorrow. 'This can go nowhere.'

'Kiss me,' I beg. 'Please just kiss me.'

Marc stands, and suddenly he is himself again – cool and in control. 'That's not the line.'

'I thought you wanted adlibbing,' I say.

'Don't play games, Sophia. You know what's supposed to happen in this scene. Nicky says there's no future. And you are hurt. Frustrated. Rejected. And run back to your fiancé. If you can't differentiate between your professional and private life, you have no business being an actress.'

'I just wanted—'

'I know want you wanted,' says Marc. 'I wanted it too. But an actor should stay in control. Always. Even in rehearsal. That's what makes the difference between a great actor and someone who fades into the background. Control. Discipline and concentration. You're the leading lady, Sophia. I expect more from you.'

I grab my top, holding it against my body. 'I'd forgotten you could be like this.'

'You need tuition,' Marc barks. 'You'll have to take it how it comes. Strictness is necessary, because you obviously still haven't learned to control yourself.'

'I just lost it for a moment. I wanted to—'

Marc puts hands to his hips. 'Acting isn't about you. In this scene, Violet decides to go with her head.'

My body is still warm from Marc, and I want him so badly.

'Maybe we could talk about this another time,' I murmur. 'And give into the moment …'

'Oh no.' Marc smiles. 'You, young lady, need a lesson in self control. There are three more scenes like this one. If you can't control yourself, there'll be problems.'

I scoot to the edge of the bed. 'It'll be different when the cameras are rolling.'

'How so?'

I pull the sleeves of my top the right way around. 'Well I'm hardly going to … you know, lose control when other people are around.'

'So what are you planning on doing?' Marc demands. 'Acting by numbers? The audience want real passion, not cardboard.'

'Then how can I do it?'

Marc stalks back and forth. 'You practise. You listen to your teacher. Do you remember what happens after this scene?'

'Yes.'

'Tell me.'

I think for a moment. 'Nicky refuses to teach her unless she follows his exact instructions and doesn't question him.'

'Exactly right.'

'And he asks her to do weird things,' I continue. 'Like dancing in the dark. But she can't ask why.'

Marc strides right up to me, looming over the bed. 'In the bedside drawer there are two sets of handcuffs. I want you to take them out.'

I laugh. 'Now who's losing control?'

'This isn't a joke, Sophia.' He takes the top from my hands and throws it to the floor. 'You won't be needing that.'

'Really?' I raise an eyebrow. 'Because it sounds like you're not thinking about the movie anymore. There are no handcuffs in any scene I remember.'

'Trust me.' His lips flicker.

I consider arguing with him. But the truth is, I want Marc so badly. And handcuffs sound pretty good.

Turning around, I crawl over the bed and towards the bedside table. 'This drawer?'

'Yes.'

Inside, I find two gleaming sets of handcuffs, both silver and heavyweight.

'Take them out,' Marc instructs.

I lift the clanking handcuffs, feeling their weight as I pass them to Marc.

'Lie on your stomach,' Marc demands. 'Face on the pillow.'

I do, my cheek finding soft cotton, my arms stretched up in anticipation.

'Well, well, Sophia.' I hear the smile in Marc's voice. 'You certainly *have* learned a lot since we first met.'

Marc dangles the handcuffs along my back, letting cool metal stroke my skin.

I gasp, then stammer, 'I thought I was always a good pupil.'

'You've certainly learned how to position yourself ready for restraint,' Marc remarks. He clicks the cold handcuffs on my bare wrists, cuffing me to the bedpost.

I moan, my eyes already half closed.

If I wasn't certain, to the very bottom of my heart, that Marc loved me, I would hate this side of him. But the truth is, I love being his captive, bound and ready.

I wait, listening to Marc moving around the room.

A lock clicks and the wardrobe door slides back and forth.

I turn my head, trying to catch a glimpse of what's happening. But I can't see much.

Then Marc's hips come into view. He's naked, except for black jockey shorts. One hand resting on my naked back, he says, 'I want you to stay in character,' he says. 'Understood?'

I would never guess, from the quiet command of his voice, that he is rock hard.

'I'll try,' I stammer.

His hand leaves my back, and a swish of blue and green waves near my face.

What is that?

41

It's a peacock feather, I realise, blue and purple strands coming into focus. *Where did he get that?*

I moan, as Marc strokes the feather down my back.

'You are Violet,' Marc orders. 'And you will react as she would react. Or I won't let you come.'

The feather reaches my backside.

A moan catches in my throat, but I give Marc a hard look, knowing that Violet would stay strong.

'You're being an excellent pupil.' Marc strokes the feather back and forth over my buttocks.

It's a struggle to stay in character, but I manage to say, 'You won't break me, Nicky. I'm stronger than you think.'

A firm hand parts my legs, and Marc lowers the feather inside my thighs.

I keep firm eyes on Marc.

'Very good,' Marc remarks. 'There's hope for you yet.'

The feather is right between my legs now – into the heat that's begging for him.

Marc swishes the feather around.

I bite my teeth together and glare at him.

But I don't moan.

Marc swirls the feather, lazily stroking it between my legs and over my buttocks. Then he rests it on the small of my back.

There's a clicking sound as a vibrator whirs to life.

You've got to be kidding …

'Marc. You can't be serious,' I say. 'How can I possibly stay in character if you use that on me?'

Marc stands right by my face.

I see his hardness, straining against the thin material of his jockey shorts.

God, I want him so much.

He's holding the vibrator – a long, metallic one with studded bumps all over it.

'Try harder, Sophia.'

I feel pressure on the mattress as Marc climbs on the bed, kneeling behind me.

It's torture – hearing the whirring of the vibrator and feeling the heat of Marc's body.

I try to turn, but Marc puts a firm hand to my cheek, holding me against the pillow. 'Don't move.'

He lowers the vibrating cylinder to my back, rolling it back and forth.

I stay rigid, thinking of Violet and her strength.

Oh god.

The vibrations roll down, down, over my buttocks and then to my legs.

I feel the heat and movement as Marc pushes vibrating metal between my thighs.

As he slides the vibrator inside me, I can't hold back anymore. I moan, and squirm against the bed.

Marc holds me firm, sliding the vibrator in and out.

Oh *god.*

Then he slides the vibrator right out and along, over the sensitive, burning heat between my legs.

Back and forth, back and forth.

Dimly I think, *I want him inside me.* But it's too late.

I come, throbbing against the vibrations and pulling against the handcuffs.

'You weren't supposed to do that,' Marc says, his voice deep and authoritative.

Sliding the vibrator free, he brings his other hand down to grasp my buttock.

He holds me like that for a moment.

Then he slides the vibrator into my backside.

God!

I nearly leap off the bed again, feeling vibrations thrum inside me.

Marc squeezes my buttock hard – hard enough to leave a mark. But I barely notice. All I can feel is the heat of the vibrator.

It's uncomfortable, and I'm sensitive after my orgasm, but Marc is merciless, holding me in place and sliding the vibrator further, up and up.

I gasp as he pushes it deeper, gritting my teeth against the achy pleasure pain as he slides it free and pushes it in again.

Marc pulls me onto my knees, and my wrists catch in the handcuffs, suspending my arms in midair.

I can barely see straight, but I don't moan like Sophia would.

God, this is too much.

Marc knocks my legs further open with his knuckles, and I sense his hips getting into position.

I nearly shout, '*No. Please Marc, I can't do it …*'

But thank god, he slides the vibrator free and gives me a moment – just a moment – before he pushes himself inside me, all the way in.

After the vibrator, I'm uncomfortable. But as he starts to move, the good feelings build up again. All I know now is him pounding in and out, lighting me up inside.

When I come a second time I can hardly breath.

'Oh Marc. *Marc.*'

The orgasm goes on and on, becoming another and then another. I can't tell the sensations apart – my body floats along on one long wave of pleasure.

Dimly, I feel Marc pull back. And then with one last thrust, he comes, pulling my hips onto him and moaning, '*Sophia.*'

We stay together for a moment, the handcuffs biting my wrists, Marc's arms tight around my waist, holding me against his body.

Then he gently unlocks the handcuffs and carries me to the bathroom.

Marc sits me on his lap while he runs a hot bath. Then he slides me into the water and washes my body.

When I'm clean, he wraps me in a soft bathrobe, towels my hair dry and carries me to the bed.

He kisses my forehead. 'Rest now. Tomorrow will be hard work. I'll teach you more when I can.'

'Will I rehearse with Benjamin Van Rosen tomorrow?' I ask.

Marc's face darkens. 'You and I should rehearse in the morning. I'm not sure of Nadia's schedule, but I don't want you rehearsing with that man alone. He's not to be trusted.'

'So what do you suggest?' I ask. 'Bring the husband along?'

'If needs be.'

I blink sleepily. 'I hope you're joking.'

Marc frowns. 'I'm not joking. There are some things you're not ready for yet. But you will be. With practise. Benjamin is well known where women are concerned. *Very* well known. If he tries anything with you, I'll kill him.'

'You can't possibly be jealous,' I insist, stifling a yawn. 'I haven't even met him yet.'

'Not jealous. Protective.'

'Well you don't need to be protective.'

But through sleepy eyes, I sense Marc is still frowning.

42

The next morning, I wake to bright sunshine as our automatic curtains whirr open.

Blue ocean glimmers all around, and in the distance I see a hazy, colourful line – the coast of Spain.

I sit up.

Whoa. We're at Spain already.

Marc isn't beside me, but that's no surprise.

I know his habits by now – he'll be at the gym, and back when he *thinks* I'll wake up. I guess he didn't account for the automatic curtains.

Tanya took care of Ivy last night, and I have to admit it was amazing getting another full eight-hours sleep.

Wandering onto the sundeck, I watch the colours of Spain get clearer and brighter.

It's *hot*.

Enjoying the sun, I pick up the deck phone and order an early breakfast – orange juice, sliced avocado, roasted seeds and poached eggs on toast. Ivy won't wake up for a while, and it'll be good to eat without any distractions.

My food arrives within ten minutes, and I have it outside, watching Spain get sharper.

As I finish my last bite, I hear Marc's voice behind me, low and soft.

'You're awake.' He kisses the top of my head.

I smile. 'Good morning to you too.'

Marc is wearing grey jogging bottoms, the cord tied tight along his muscular abdomen. He's not wearing a shirt, and I find myself breathing in his amazing smell.

'The curtains opened on their own,' I tell him.

'Looks like you're not the only one up early,' says Marc, pointing to the horizon.

A gleaming white motorboat skips and jumps over the water.

'That boat is a long way from land,' I note.

'Because they're headed for our ship.'

'How do you know?' I ask.

Marc smiles. 'Nadia always likes to make an entrance.'

'Nadia's on that boat?'

'Among others.' Marc grabs a bottle of mineral water from the deck mini bar, and takes a long gulp.

Together, we watch the motorboat. It hops nearer and nearer, and soon a floating jetty is lowered.

I shield my eyes against the sun, watching as Nadia is helped onto the jetty.

She looks great in tight, leather trousers, a fur gillet and long, black hair full of volume.

'Isn't she overheating?' I remark, thinking of her fur and leather.

'Nadia is Spanish,' says Marc. 'She's probably freezing. Ah … just as I thought. She has company.'

Marc's right – Nadia isn't alone.

A blond man steps onto the jetty too. He wears Ray-Ban sunglasses, white shorts and a polo shirt. His skin is smooth and tanned, and his hair slicked back like a 1940s gangster.

Benjamin Van Rosen.

I have to admit, he is extremely good looking off screen, as well as on.

'Christ – I thought Nadia had more sense,' Marc growls. 'Arriving with him like this … his ego will get even bigger.'

'It's going to be weird,' I hear myself say. 'Acting with someone so famous.'

I watch, as Benjamin saunters onto the boat.

'So famous?' Marc raises an eyebrow. 'And here I was thinking you cared about calibre, not sidewalk stars.'

'You know what I mean.'

'The man has an ego the size of a planet,' Marc snaps. 'It would have been better he'd stayed a z-lister.'

I shield my eyes.

Benjamin is shorter than I'd imagined he would be – but then most movie stars are. Marc is the exception to that rule.

A bunch of paparazzi line the port, all snapping and flashing away.

'You'd better get dressed, Mrs Blackwell,' says Marc. 'You'll be meeting your new cast member soon. I hope he lives up to your expectations.'

I dress in a light vest and flowery shorts – a little girly for me, but I team the outfit with my traditional converse.

As I'm pulling on my shoes, a crew member arrives with a message – we're to meet Nadia and Benjamin immediately, at the top-deck amphitheatre.

'Quite a sense of occasion Nadia has,' Marc remarks, as he reads the message.

'I thought you liked theatres,' I reply, lacing up my trainers.

'Since meeting you, I've liked them more and more.' Marc gives me that half-smile of his.

I grin back. 'I hope you're not planning on repeating what we did at the Globe.'

Marc folds the message and slots it in his desk drawer. 'Not with Benjamin Van Rosen looking on.'

'You really don't like him, do you?' I say.

'No. I really don't.' Marc reaches for my hand.

43

By the time we reach the top deck, the ship's engines have started again and we're slicing through the water, away from the Spanish coast.

'So will Michael get taken to shore?' I ask Marc.

Marc checks his watch. 'He should already be on dry land now. I gave orders for the whole thing to be handled discreetly.'

I look across the water to Spain, wondering what Michael will be up to. 'You know, Marc, Michael was just trying to be a good uncle.'

'He needs to try harder.' Marc quickens his pace.

The air is fresh and warm, but brisk as the ship's motion pulls us through the breeze.

'Oh come on,' I say, making quick steps to stay by his side. 'Stowing away on a ship? I think that's trying pretty hard, don't you?'

'Yes. But in the wrong way. Look – I'm not ruling out what you're saying. I appreciate Michael has a good heart. Perhaps we'll work out a plan back in England. As long as he can prove to be responsible.'

We continue along the deck until we reach the back of the boat, where a full-sized, open-air amphitheatre is nestled around the curved stern of the ship. It's like a sunken wedding cake – tiered rings graduate down to a circular stage.

Nadia sits within the theatre on a graduated seat, ankles crossed, takeaway coffee in her hand. She's gesturing animatedly and talking loudly.

Benjamin stands beside her, hands in his cream shorts pockets, looking serious in black sunglasses.

'Hey guys.' Nadia calls, waving us over. 'Come and meet Benjamin.'

Marc and I walk along the seat row, single file, me in front.

Benjamin shields his eyes from the sun, his gaze lingering on me unapologetically.

I reach back to take Marc's hand.

'Good to see you.' Nadia jumps up to kiss me enthusiastically on both cheeks. 'Of course, you've heard of Benjamin. Right?'

Beside her, Benjamin drops sunglasses on his eyes. 'A pleasure to meet my fiancée in person.' He reaches out to shake my hand. 'My word, you're beautiful aren't you? Quietly so, but beautiful. Childlike. Is that the word? Definitely marriage material.'

I manage an uncomfortable laugh, sensing Marc's anger behind me.

'Marc Blackwell.' Benjamin lets his fingers slip from mine. 'When did I see you last? Somewhere in Hollywood?'

Marc's grip on my hand tightens. 'Something like that.'

'I hear you stole my part.' Benjamin raises a blond eyebrow.

'You heard wrong,' Marc growls.

Nadia puts a hand to her forehead. 'Guys. Come on. Let's start friendly. Okay? So listen – today you all need to get a suntan. And rehearse the hell out of these scenes. I'm expecting magic when we reach Saint-Tropez.'

Benjamin turns to me. 'Can you make magic, Sophia?'

'Um …' I glance at Marc.

'Let's find out,' Benjamin continues. 'Meet me here at 11am and we'll try out the wedding rehearsal scene. Okay?'

Marc pulls me back, so I'm almost behind him. 'Sophia is rehearsing with me this morning.'

Benjamin laughs. 'Well when you're done, I'll take my turn.' He reaches to grab a schedule from Nadia.

I sense Marc's rage simmering.

'Hey,' I whisper, putting a hand on Marc's chest. 'Don't.'

'He needs to be careful,' Marc growls back. 'Or he's going to find himself swimming home.'

44

Marc and I decide to go for coffee before we rehearse, so we can talk over the script.

We stop at the third-deck coffee bar, and Marc orders us espresso shots and Spanish nougat.

'So how about this script, Mrs Blackwell?' Marc stirs his espresso. 'You've hardly said a word about it. Usually you're full of opinions.'

I flip pages. 'There's not much to say.'

Marc watches me. 'Nothing you'd change?'

'No.' I take a sip of sharp, strong espresso. ' I just want to do it justice.'

Marc drinks his own coffee. 'You don't have to be perfect.'

'But I *do* want to be perfect.' My hair is blowing in the sea breeze, and I push it behind my ears.

Marc smiles. 'Imperfections are what make movies interesting. You're over-thinking things. Take a walk. Clear your head.'

I look around the deck. 'Now?'

'Yes. Now.'

'Don't you think my time would be better spent rehearsing?' I set my cup back on its saucer.

Marc shakes his head. 'There's no sense rehearsing when you're nervous like this. You'll just end up frustrated.'

'Do you want to come with me?'

'Better not. Less distractions.'

I smile. 'You were planning on distracting me, were you?'

Marc's lips tilt up. 'Always.'

Walking over polished wood, I take in deep breaths of cool sea air.

The ocean froths and foams beside me, and the breeze whips my hair.

Is this really helping? I wonder.

I'm tempted to go back and tell Marc we should start right away and stop wasting time.

But after a lap of the upper deck, I feel looser. Calmer.

Walking past a cool-blue swimming pool, I fight down a smile.

As usual, Marc knows what I need better than I do.

The script dances around my head, and for the first time I'm able to play around with the words and make them my own.

As I'm mouthing lines to myself, I notice someone sprawled on a wooden sun lounger, a sheaf of script papers in hand.

Benjamin.

He's frowning at the script through sunglasses, his white clothing immaculate.

I hesitate, then walk past quickly, hoping he won't notice me. I'm not fast enough, though.

'Sophia.' Benjamin's voice is crisp and clear, upper-class American and authoritative.

I stop, turning back. 'Hi Benjamin.'

'Well if it isn't the girl who got away.' Benjamin sits up, pushing sunglasses into his hair. 'Where's your ball and chain?'

'Are you referring to Marc?' I reply coolly.

Benjamin laughs. 'Unless you have another husband.'

'He's on the top deck.' I tuck hair behind my ears, ill at ease and wanting to walk away.

'I thought you two were supposed to be rehearsing,' says Benjamin. 'Marc can't steal you away from me and then not even make use of you.'

'I was getting frustrated.' My feet move awkwardly. 'So a walk seemed like a good idea. My head feels much clearer now.'

'Frustrated, huh?' Benjamin sits up on his lounger.

I take a step back. 'I don't mean to be unfriendly. But I have to get back now, and—'

'Don't be like that. Talk to me. I won't bite.' Benjamin pats his wooden sun lounger. 'We should have some rapport, don't you think?'

I hesitate. 'So long as you know I'm happily married.'

Benjamin laughs. 'That's what's bothering you? My reputation? You shouldn't believe everything you read in the newspapers. Besides. You can't get pregnant just by sitting next to a guy.'

I laugh without meaning to. Well … it was pretty funny.

'That's better.' Benjamin grins, showing Hollywood white teeth. 'So who's *really* worried about my reputation? You or your husband?'

I perch on a sun lounger near him. 'I won't pretend Marc's happy about me acting with you. But he'll have to get used to it.'

'What's his problem?' Benjamin's light-blue eyes find mine. 'You're a professional. So am I. And you're married. I respect married women.'

Not what I heard, I think, remembering the many press articles about Benjamin Van Rosen's affairs with married actresses.

'You know, you and I have some pretty hot scenes together.' Benjamin lies back on the sun lounger again. 'Is your husband okay with that?'

'We only kiss once,' I reply. 'And it's sort of forced. I wouldn't call that hot.'

'Don't you like it *sort of forced*?' He jerks upright. 'Well, if the rumours about Marc are true.'

My stomach goes cold. 'I really should be going.'

I get up, my cheeks burning.

'Wait.' Benjamin jumps to his feet. 'I'm an idiot. I didn't mean it. I just like to joke, okay? You know, you're pretty in real life.'

'Your jokes aren't funny.' I start walking.

'Come on – at least give me a minute.' He catches up with me. 'I'm still nursing a loss.'

'What are you talking about?' I snap. 'What loss?'

'For the part I should have had. It should have been me playing Nicky. I'm not used to having parts stolen from me.'

I slow down. 'Marc didn't steal your part. Nadia never confirmed it was yours. Everything was still up in the air.'

'Bullshit. It was in the bag until Marc swooped in from on high.'

'I guess that's for you and Marc to discuss,' I say, quickening my pace.

Benjamin grabs my hand. 'Hey. Look, I know I'm acting like an idiot. I'm not used to being out-powered. I'm always the big name on set. That's all it is. It'll bring out the best in me. I just hope you're open to it.'

I yank my hand away and walk faster.

'I can see why Marc's crazy about you,' Benjamin calls out. 'You've got that child-woman thing going on. Are you going to drive me crazy too?'

God!

How am I ever going to act with this man?

I can't tell Marc what just happened, I decide. *Or he'll be even more jealous.*

I can handle Benjamin by myself.

I think.

45

After dinner that night, Jen invites me for drinks and dessert in her luxurious suite. She invites Tom and Tanya too, and orders chocolate brownie ice cream, crème brulee and Veuve Clicquot from the room service menu.

I arrive first, and find Jen lying on the bed, skimming Google images on her iPad. 'You brought my little niece! Just like I asked you to,' she exclaims, seeing Ivy in her stroller. 'Oh goody!'

'Where's everyone else?' I ask, rolling Ivy into the suite. I could have left Ivy with Marc, but I haven't seen her all day and just wanted her with me.

'Not here yet,' says Jen. 'I banished Leo to the ship's movie theatre. We had another row.'

'Uh oh.'

Jen shakes her head, exasperated. 'He's just so messy, you know? I mean, look at this place. Do you want some champagne?'

She reaches into an ice bucket at the foot of the bed, and pours out a glass, passing it to me.

'Thanks.' I balance the flute on Jen's tower of marketing books, while I unstrap Ivy and lay her beside Jen. 'This place doesn't look too bad. Who's on your iPad?'

'Benjamin Van Rosen,' says Jen, tickling Ivy's feet. 'I had to find out more. I mean, look at this shot. He's totally ignoring his girlfriend and chatting up a *married* super-model. So brazen! Oh, I forgot to tell you. We're having a mystery guest.'

'A what? Who?' I sit beside Jen on the bed.

'Then it wouldn't be a mystery.'

I think of the cast and crew I've met so far, and can't imagine who Jen would invite.

'As long as it's not Benjamin Van Rosen,' I say.

Jen laughs. 'No. It's not him. Hey. I have an idea. We should make cocktails.' She heads to the leather-padded bar circling a corner of her suite.

'With champagne?' I ask, looking at my full flute. 'Are you sure that's a good idea? We're both working tomorrow.'

'Oh it'll be fine.' Jen grabs a stainless steel cocktail shaker from the drinks bar. 'Maybe we'll come up with a famous new invention.'

I notice Jen's iPad on the bed, still lit and showing a flickering picture of Benjamin Van Rosen.

The headline says, 'WIFE STEALER, BENJAMIN VAN ROSEN, SETS HIS EYES ON A NEW TARGET'.

Benjamin is looking seductively at a long-legged blonde model in a skin-tight dress. A model famously married to a movie producer.

In the background is another girl – a scowling blonde wearing a high bun and swooping black eye shadow.

'We should definitely put fresh fruit in this cocktail of ours,' says Jen, muddling ice and strawberries. 'And *lots* of vodka.'

'I'm in trouble, Jen,' I say, rolling Ivy onto her stomach so she can enjoy the soft duvet and laying beside her. 'I have to act with Benjamin Van Rosen tomorrow. But I can't stand him.'

'Does it matter if you like him?' Jen asks. 'I mean, you're an actress. Your job is to fake feelings.'

'It's not going to be easy.'

'Do you have any bedroom scenes with him?' Jen asks, pouring chocolate sauce into the shaker.

'Not exactly,' I admit. 'In the movie, we have an arranged marriage. It's supposed to be sort of formal. I'm a girl from a rich family, who's promised to Benjamin's character. And then Marc comes along and rocks the boat.'

'Well I can't give you acting advice,' says Jen. 'But plenty of actors hate their co-stars and still make fabulous movies. Have you talked to Marc about this?'

'No. And I'm not going to.'

'Good idea.' Jen cracks ice into the shaker. 'He'd probably throw Benjamin off the boat.'

'Exactly. Michael only narrowly escaped going overboard.'

'Speaking of which.' Jen clips the lid on the shaker and gives it a rattle. 'You remember that mystery guest I was talking about?'

46

'*Michael's* here?' My eyes widen.

Jen nods. 'Perfect, don't you think? He can see Ivy, and Marc will be none the wiser.'

I sit up on the bed. 'But he should have left the boat at Spain. Marc will be *furious*.'

'Marc needs to chill out,' says Jen, rattling the cocktail shaker. 'Michael's a good guy. And he's so desperate to see Ivy. This evening was his idea.'

'I don't like sneaking around behind Marc's back.'

'Oh nonsense. Marc shouldn't be so protective. Although …' Jen sighs. 'I wish Leo was the sort of man who'd throw someone off the boat for me.'

I notice Jen is blinking quickly, not smiling.

'Jen?' I scoot across the bed so I'm nearer to her.

She tips vodka into the cocktail shaker. 'Tell me the truth. Should I really marry someone so messy?'

I laugh. 'If messy is your only problem, then yes.'

'It's not our only problem.' Jen pours chocolaty liquid into a conical glass. 'He hates me bossing him around. But I can't help it.' She manages a smile, but it's a forced smile. 'I suppose we're fine.'

'Come on Jen. You can't hide things from me either, remember? Are things still not right with you and Leo?'

Jen lowers the cocktail shaker to the bar. A single tear rolls down her cheek.

'Oh *Jen*.' I leap off the bed and throw my arms around her. 'What's happening?'

'It's okay,' says Jen, wiping the tear and smoothing her hair. 'We just had another fight, and … I always say, what will be will be. Right?'

'What does *that* mean?' I put my hands on her shoulders. 'You and Leo are supposed to be getting married. Jen, if you're really not sure about this—'

'No, I am. I mean, everything's all arranged. I can't back out now.' She gives a light laugh.

'Of course you can.'

'I don't want to, though.' Jen's eyes fix on the shaker.

'Are you sure about that?'

She nods. 'Yes. I do love him.' Then she frowns. 'I think I hear someone coming.'

There's a sharp knock on the door.

'That'll be Michael,' says Jen, calling out, 'Come on in!'

'*Michael*.' I turn to the door, and see Marc's brother shouldering his way into the suite, arms full of gifts. He has a stuffed toy rainbow fish, a kaleidoscope, a Teddy bear and a giant fluffy shark.

Michael grins at me. 'Where's my little niece, then?'

I can't help smiling. 'She's here.'

Michael's eyes go soppy and soft when he notices Ivy. 'Look at that gorgeous little thing. Did you ever see anything more beautiful? You won't tell Marc I'm still here, will you Sophia? I know this against all the rules.

But love will make a man do crazy things.'

'Do you want to hold her?' I offer, lifting her off the bed.

'I can't think of anything I'd like more.' Michael takes Ivy, cradling her head. 'I've been reading up on babies. How to change them. Do up those babygros. All sorts.'

'Champagne?' Jen offers. 'Chocolate cocktail?'

Michael shakes his head. 'With the little one here? No way. I need to be on top form. Best behaviour.'

'Sophia's having a drink,' says Jen. 'One won't hurt.'

'Nope.' Michael is adamant. 'I will be a responsible uncle, through and through. How are you, little one?' He smiles down at Ivy.

'I wish Marc could see how you are with her,' I say.

Michael nods. 'He never gives me a chance. This year was supposed to be a fresh start.'

'Marc's just being protective,' I say. 'It's nothing personal. But Michael – he really is going to be furious when he finds out you're still onboard. How can he trust you if you keep going behind his back?'

'I honestly meant to leave.' Michael strokes Ivy's downy head. 'But I found I couldn't.'

'You *have* to fly back to London when we reach Saint-Tropez,' I insist. 'Marc isn't stupid. You can hide on a cruise ship, but not in a villa. And if he knows you stayed, he'll never trust you again.'

'There'll be two motor boats taking us ashore at Saint-Tropez,' Jen pipes up. 'Michael – I'll get you on the list for the one Marc isn't on. We'll dress you up as security. Okay?'

'Promise me you'll do it, Michael.' I put a hand on his arm. 'This is serious. If Marc finds out you went against his wishes, it'll take years to build up the trust again.'

'He doesn't trust me as it is,' says Michael. 'What's the difference?'

'I'll keep working on him,' I promise. 'You deserve to see your niece. And *I* trust you. Marc just needs to see things the way I do.'

Michael snorts. 'I've never seen anyone change Marc's mind before.'

47

When I wake the next morning, I wonder how I can persuade Marc to let Michael back into our lives.

Michael's not perfect. But I believe he's good for our daughter, and that's all that matters. He really wants to be a good uncle. I just have to convince Marc that he can be trusted.

'Ivy?' I whisper, poking my head into her bedroom. 'Are you sleeping?'

Ivy stirs a little, but doesn't cry out.

It's only 6.30am. She'll probably sleep until 7am.

Carefully, I close the bedroom door and look around for Marc.

I find him on the sundeck in his training sweatpants, looking out to sea.

He's holding a script and black fountain pen.

'You've been training already,' I say, putting my arms around his waist.

Marc drops an arm around me, pulling me close. 'I wondered when you'd wake up. You were back late last night.'

'Not as late as I could have been,' I say, enjoying the smell of his bare skin. 'What are you doing? Making changes?'

'A few,' says Marc, clipping the pen onto the script and throwing them both onto a sun lounger. 'But all in all, it's a good script.'

'I like it too,' I say.

'It's challenging, though.' He turns, wrapping his arms around my shoulders.

'I have you to help me.' I grin up at him. 'How about you? You must have *some* challenge?'

'For me, the biggest challenge is how to play this part without dumbing down. How to add depth.'

I laugh. 'That's a little snobby, don't you think?'

'I choose movies for good reasons. I wouldn't have chosen this. But since my beautiful wife is in it—'

'You didn't have to do it. There were others ready to take the part.' I notice the script pages fluttering in the breeze, and think of what Benjamin said yesterday. 'You ... you sort of swooped in.'

Marc raises an eyebrow. 'That's not how I'd put it.'

'You just said you wouldn't have chosen this movie.'

Marc touches his forehead to mine. 'And ordinarily I wouldn't. It's not my sort of thing. Nadia knows that.'

'Why not?' I look into his deep, blue eyes. 'It's got emotion. Depth.'

'My films aren't known for their happy endings.' Marc's lips twitch. 'Who'd have thought? The two of us together. In a film about dangerous love. The world really does have a sense of humour.'

My eyes wander from his, out to sea. 'You didn't take this part from Benjamin, did you?'

'Sophia, I'm surprised you even need to ask that question.'

'You're right. I'm sorry.' I find his eyes again.

Of course Marc wouldn't do that.

Yet that's how Benjamin sees it. And something tells me it's going to be hard to convince him otherwise.

'Marc, I wanted to talk to you about something.'

Marc raises an eyebrow. 'Not Benjamin Van Rosen, I hope?'

I shake my head. 'No. About Michael, actually.'

'What about him?' Marc holds me tight, and we sway a little as the ship moves.

'He … he loves Ivy so much. You must see that.'

'I see it,' Marc agrees.

'It's not fair to shut him out of Ivy's life.'

Marc kisses my lips. 'Trust is earned over time.'

'At this rate, there'll be no time left,' I insist. 'Ivy's growing so fast, and Michael's missing all of it.'

'He has some growing up to do himself, Sophia,' says Marc, now frowning slightly. 'That latest stunt he pulled, sneaking onboard this ship, showed me how irresponsible he can be.'

'It was just desperation,' I insist. 'He wanted to see Ivy. Surely you can understand. You've done some desperate things yourself for love. Climbing up my balcony – I'd call that pretty risky.'

'A calculated risk.' Marc puts a hand to my cheek. 'You're not letting this go, are you?'

'No.' I give him a determined stare. 'Not until you're fair to your brother.'

Marc smiles. 'You think of me as so unfair?'

'In this case, yes. I think you're holding onto past fears.

And what about Ivy? Are you going to deprive her of a loving uncle because you're afraid?'

The frown appears again. 'This has nothing to do with being afraid.'

'It does,' I say, my fingers finding Marc's frown lines and smoothing them away. 'Please, Marc. Just give Michael a chance. When we get back to England, will you let him visit? And take it from there?'

'One visit?' says Marc.

'That's all I ask.'

'I can do that.'

'Thank you.' I can't help grinning, because one visit will become more. I'm sure of it. As soon as Marc sees how Michael is with Ivy, all his trust issues will be gone.

48

After a morning of rehearsals, Marc and I have a quick lunch on our private sun deck. We eat Serrano ham, Manchego cheese and salsa potatoes, washed down with ice-cold Coca Cola.

Ivy lies beside us on a nest of blankets, drinking milk and watching the blue sky.

Tanya insists on being around to help with Ivy, rushing out every five minutes to apply sun cream and adjust Ivy's umbrella.

'Sorry, sorry,' she says each time. 'Don't mean to interrupt.'

'It's really fine,' I tell her, the third time she comes out. 'Honestly. Come join us.'

'Oh, I wouldn't want to intrude,' she says.

'You'll come back out in five minutes anyway,' I point out.

'Oh … okay.' Tanya plops herself on a chair beside me, her eyes fixed on Tanya. 'So what's happening this afternoon?'

'I have a rehearsal with Benjamin,' I say, handing Tanya an icy cold can of Coca Cola.

'*Benjamin*. Ooo,' Tanya teases, cracking open her can.

Beside me, I sense Marc stiffen.

'Are you nervous?' Tanya asks. 'He's a big star.'

'A little nervous,' I admit. 'I mean … it's all new.'

'Where are you meeting him?'

'In the show theatre,' I say. 'On the fourth deck. It'll just be the two of us.'

Marc bangs his water bottle down and gets to his feet, stalking to the deck rail and staring out to sea.

'If it were me, I'd be bricking it,' says Tanya, barely noticing Marc's anger. 'I mean – *Benjamin* Van Rosen. I know everyone says he's a dickhead, but he is *amazing*. He's in two of my top ten favourite films. And he's fucking gorgeous. He's—' She glances at Marc. 'I mean, he's supposed to be a bit of a ladies man, isn't he? Lucky Marc's here. So he knows you're off limits.'

'Um …' I glance at Marc too. 'Yes.'

The show theatre is still and quiet when I arrive.

I love that about theatres – the way they sleep and wake up.

At first, I think I'm all alone. But then I see Benjamin by the stage in a white polo shirt and cream-coloured shorts.

He's watching me, hands in pockets, pale blue eyes on me like a laser.

I try for a smile. 'Nice choice of venue.'

'You like it?' Benjamin watches me, the predatory look still in his eyes.

'I love empty theatres.' I walk down the steps towards him.

'Me too.' Benjamin pats the edge of the stage. 'Sometimes, I wish I could go back to those days. When I acted in theatres and no one knew who I was.'

'Really?' I reach him. 'You strike me as someone who enjoys being famous.'

'Not at all.' He smiles. 'Be careful what you wish for. Fame is a deal with the devil. You can never go back.' He gestures to the stage. 'Theatre is where my heart is. I was discovered in a theatre. In New York.'

'New York? Really? Is that where you're from?' I ask.

'Brooklyn. Once upon a time.' He offers me his hand. 'Shall we?'

I hesitate. 'Where's best? On stage?'

'Of course on stage.'

When I don't take his hand, he gestures to the steps. 'Okay. After you then.'

I climb the steps, and Benjamin hops up after me.

'Where do you want to start?' he asks, when we're both on stage.

'Um … how about the fight scene?' I suggest.

'With you?' He raises a blond eyebrow. 'I'd rather save that for Marc.'

Oh god. 'Benjamin—'

'Joke, joke.' Benjamin holds up his hands. 'So you're ready for a fight, are you?'

I laugh. 'Definitely.'

49

I shake my arms out and roll my head around my shoulders.

'Jonathan,' I begin, my words faltering. 'You're … here.'

'Where else did you expect me to be?' says Benjamin.

'With the men. Playing cards.'

'I have a better question,' Benjamin demands. 'Where were *you*?'

'My dance lesson overran, is all,' I say, acting flustered. 'Dorothy had lots of extra steps—'

'That's a damned *lie*.' Benjamin circles me. 'You were with *him*. Now you listen here.' He wags his finger. 'I'm your fiancé. You will do as I tell you. There will be no more dancing—'

'Jonathan, please.'

'It's utterly ridiculous,' Benjamin shouts. 'And *you* look ridiculous. No wife of mine will behave this way, Violet. If you ever do anything like this again, God help me …' He balls up his fists.

I take a deep breath. 'Jonathan, I don't love you anymore.'

Benjamin runs a hand through blond hair. 'What does love have to do with anything?'

'I can't marry you,' I blurt out.

Benjamin grabs my arm. 'Violet, don't be so stupid. You don't know what you're saying. Think of everything you'd be throwing away.'

'Let go of me!' I pretend to struggle. His grasp looks hard, but it's an actor's hold and doesn't hurt.

'Damnation, Violet! What is all this for? Some stray dog dancer who'll be gone in a week.'

'Please.' I whirl around. 'Jonathan, let go.'

'You *will* marry me Violet,' Benjamin insists. 'And you will behave like my fiancée.' He pushes his lips against mine, and I struggle against him. Really struggle, actually.

I push him away and stumble back. 'Benjamin.' I shake my head, breathless. 'That wasn't in the script.'

'So?' He shrugs. 'Go with what works. You can't tell me a kiss doesn't add drama.'

I hesitate, playing out the scene in my mind.

He sort of has a point.

'What's the problem?' Benjamin asks. 'Mr Marc Blackwell won't like it?'

'It's not that …' I insist.

'Isn't it?'

I think about that. Maybe I *am* worrying about Marc. I'm certainly very aware of Benjamin's reputation.

'Sophia.' Benjamin puts a hand on my shoulder. 'Give me a chance, okay? I want to make the best movie. Think about it. That scene will work *so* much better if I kiss you. Play it out with me, honey. Please—'

'I'm not your honey.'

'Okay, okay. Would baby be better?' He gives me a cute boy band smile, all dimples and smouldering eyebrows.

I laugh.

'Come on.' Benjamin gestures me towards him. 'Let's act the shit out of this scene. Look, I'm an idiot, okay. Everyone knows it. But I sure can act. I know what I'm doing. Trust me. Okay honey baby?'

I roll my eyes, but I'm smiling.

Benjamin laughs. 'That's better. Things got a little serious there. Hey listen. How about we make our own scene where Violet hits Jonathan on the nose. Would that work for you right now?'

'Yes. Definitely.'

'Just go easy on me.' Benjamin shakes out his arms. 'I guess being with someone like Marc—' He stops himself. 'I mean … just don't punch me too hard. This face has got to stay pretty.'

I smooth my hair down and loosen my body. 'Shall we start again?'

'Sure. From where we left off?' Benjamin asks.

I nod, launching straight into it. 'Jonathan, how dare you kiss me like that! We're not even married—'

'You're my fiancée,' Benjamin shouts. 'You let that mongrel put his hands all over you—'

'How did you know, Jonathan?' I shout back. 'That I was with Nicky? You tell me that.'

'I had you followed. I don't apologise for it.'

'*Spying* on me?' I yell. 'You had no right—'

'Oh I had *every* right.' Benjamin puts his hands on his hips.

'We were *dancing*,' I insist. 'That's all.'

'Is that the name for it?' Benjamin growls. 'You know Violet, I swear you're the best call girl on the block.'

I slap him around the face – an actor's slap, and he reacts convincingly, turning away, hand springing to his cheek.

'Do that again,' his voice is menacing, 'and I'll forget you're a lady and fight you like a man.' He rubs his skin. 'I saw plenty today. You with your leg over his shoulder. Being dragged across the dance floor.'

'Jonathan—'

'Enough.' He grabs my shoulders, shaking me a little. 'This ends today. Do you hear me? This nonsense ends. You are not a dancer. You never will be a dancer. You will be my wife and behave with decency.'

I feel tears in my eyes. 'I've never felt so alive as—'

'As *what*?' He stops shaking me, his eyes boring down.

I turn away from him. 'When I'm dancing. I feel alive.'

'That's not what you were going to say.' His hands drop from my shoulders. 'You were going to say you've never felt so alive as when you're with *him*! That gutter rat. Do you love him?'

'Jonathan, don't ...' I look to the floor.

'Tell me the truth.' Benjamin grabs my arm.

'This is a ridiculous conversation.' I try to pull back from him.

'Answer me.' Benjamin pulls me closer.

'Jonathan, stop!'

He raises a hand and I cower, sobbing.

In the script, the scene ends there. And I run away to Nicky, covered in bruises.

I wipe my eyes and stand up straight, a little shy to find myself under Benjamin's soft gaze.

'Are you okay?'

I nod, feeling damp on the backs of my hand.

'Seriously?'

'Fine.' Although in truth, I'm still getting my feelings together. Not everyone acts like I do, by feeling every single thing. But it's the only way I know how to do it.

'Hey, come here.' He opens his arms.

I shake my head. 'Honestly. I'm fine. Just give me a minute.'

'You're not fine. I act the same way you do. With feelings. To tell the truth, I still feel pretty angry at you.' He grins, and I see his perfect white canines.

'Oh come on,' I say, picking up on his humour. 'It's not my fault I'm in love with somebody else.'

'That guy doesn't deserve someone as perfect as you.' Benjamin is still grinning. 'And speaking of which, how *did* Marc Blackwell win you over?'

I feel my features soften. 'By being the most amazing man I've ever met.'

'Amazing. Really? You know, I read the newspapers, same as everybody else.'

'Newspapers are full of rubbish,' I say, hoping to change the subject.

'Sometimes,' says Benjamin. 'But usually there's a grain of truth in there. I sure have heard about Marc on the grapevine. He likes to be in charge.'

I shrug. 'I like that he knows his own mind.'

'Really? Because the way I heard it, he wasn't even in this movie when we started out. He jumped onboard when he discovered you were taking the role. Sounds a little jealous to me. And controlling.'

'He … he's protective,' I admit.

Benjamin grins. 'Am I being an idiot again?'

'A little bit.'

'See? I'm learning?' He puts a friendly arm around my shoulder. 'Hey, how about we take a break together tonight? There's a movie theatre onboard. We could watch a black-and-white classic. I promise I won't try and steal your popcorn.'

I duck out from under his arm. 'Maybe another time.'

'Won't daddy let you stay out late?'

'It's not like that. I have a baby.' I check my watch. 'She'll wake up soon.'

'And she has a nanny, right? I've seen her. Red hair. Nice ass.' Benjamin winks. 'Come spend time with me. A movie works best when the cast get along.'

'We can get along without spending time together.'

50

Marc is working at his desk when I get back to our suite, dressed in his black suit, tieless with his shirt collar open.

I put my arms around his shoulders. 'Where's Ivy?'

'Still with Tanya.' Marc frowns at his laptop. 'She's taken her swimming in one of the many pools.'

'Everything okay?'

He turns to me, frown softening. 'A dispute over planning permission in London. It's … frustrating. But nothing that can't be fixed.' Pulling me onto his lap, he says, 'How was the rehearsal?'

'Emotional,' I admit. 'But good.'

'Not too emotional I hope?'

'How could it not be?' I enjoy the warmth of Marc's body. 'Acting is all about emotion.'

'And control.' His arms tighten around me. 'Don't forget the control.'

I smile. 'How could I when you're around?'

'Are you calling me controlling, Mrs Blackwell?'

'I wasn't. Someone else did.' I regret the words as soon as they come out of my mouth.

'Let me guess.' Marc's eyebrows pull together again. 'Benjamin.'

'He was just joking,' I say.

'I'm failing to see the funny side.' Marc slots his fingers into my hair. 'Control is a very serious matter. What man wouldn't want to protect someone as beautiful as you?'

'You know, some people would say that control and protection are two different things.' I let my head follow his fingers. 'You don't *control* me. You do realise that, don't you?'

Marc is smiling now, still running fingers throw my hair. 'And I wouldn't even try.'

I move so I'm straddling him, looking into his intense blue eyes.

Marc spins the computer chair around, so my back is against the hard edge of the desk. He closes his laptop, pushes it to one side and says, 'Once upon a time, the law said a husband owned his wife.'

'Thank goodness that law has changed,' I say, my hands reaching up to find Marc's thick, brown hair.

'A husband ruled the household,' says Marc, pushing my summer dress up my hips and over my head. 'And his wife would obey his every command. And if she didn't, he'd punish her.'

'I don't want you to control me,' I murmur.

Marc's blue eyes are on fire, as he lays me back on the desk. 'You're quite sure?'

I nod, my head bumping hard wood.

'Because I'm certain that you do,' says Marc. 'Absolutely certain.'

'You're wrong.' I look up at him.

'Am I?' He pulls my legs around his hips.

I can feel his hardness pressing against me, and give a little moan.

'We don't have long,' I whisper. 'Tanya could be back any minute.'

Marc nods, his eyes holding mine. His hands leave my hips for a moment, and I hear the zip of his trousers. Then he slides inside me, and I let out a cry.

'Oh *Marc.*'

He begins to move, slow and steady, one hand pressing firmly between my breasts, pinning me to the table.

I soften beneath him, hearing ocean spray as the ship ploughs through the water, and feel the whip of sea breeze from the sun deck.

My eyes squeeze shut as I feel and enjoy Marc thrusting his hips back and forth with unrelenting precision and focus.

He's not usually this kind to me. He hardly ever enters me straight away.

I feel warmth growing, as his firm hand keeps pressure on my body.

Then, as suddenly as he started, he pulls back.

'Don't stop! *Please,*' I beg.

'So who is in control in this scenario?' Marc asks.

Oh *god.* I swallow.

'Sophia?' he demands. 'I asked you a question.'

This again?

'Please Marc,' I say. 'I don't want you to stop.'

'You don't sound very in control.'

'Can't we just—'

Marc gives me a sharp smack between my legs, and I yelp. 'You, Mrs Blackwell, will learn self control if it kills me.'

He pushes himself back into his trousers.

I sit up on the desk. 'Marc. You can't just ... this isn't fair!'

'It's perfectly fair. And a valuable lesson. If I can control myself, why can't you?'

'You're ... you're *you*,' I say. 'You're not like other people.'

'Anyone can learn self-control,' says Marc. 'As long as the mind is willing, the body will follow. But your mind isn't willing.'

'You never said that you were going to—'

He frowns at me. 'Do you think real life comes with warnings? Will you always know what the other actor is going to do?'

I think of Benjamin earlier, and that unexpected kiss.

'Okay, okay. I get it,' I say. 'But for today, can't we just—'

'No Sophia, we cannot.' Marc pulls a script from his inside suit pocket. 'Time to rehearse.'

'*What?*' I sit bolt upright.

'Hurry up.' He taps the script on the desk. 'Do you remember page 51? Quickly now.'

'I can't rehearse *now*,' I say. 'I'm all ... well ... you know.' I redden.

'Well Mrs Blackwell. Let's see what we can do to distract you. Remember the script. And say your line. Here. Maybe this will help.' He throws my dress at me.

I catch it. 'Marc—'

'Say your line.'

I glare at him. But reluctantly, I climb into my dress and push my hair behind my ears.

'If you can't remember your lines ...' Marc offers me the script.

'I don't need it,' I snap, pushing the pages away. 'I know it by heart. Page numbers included.'

'Very good.' He drops the script on the desk beside me. 'So let's get started.'

'Page 51 starts with *your* line.' I drop down from the desk, my feet finding soft carpet. 'Not mine.'

'Don't get all preachy on me, lady,' Marc yells, strolling around the suite, waving his hands around, 'I don't even like you.' He turns to me, smiling that handsome Hollywood smile of his. 'That's the line, I believe.'

'Your memory is as sharp as ever.'

'I hope you're not going to have an attitude,' Marc raises an eyebrow. 'You know how I handle things when you don't do as you're told.'

'I don't always do as I'm told,' I say. 'And you don't always handle things like … like you just did.'

'You seemed to enjoy it.'

I nod. 'Until you stopped.'

'Control, Sophia. Control, control, control. Now give me your line.'

I take in a deep breath and let it out. 'And if ever there was a man I despised, it's you,' I say. And right at this moment, I mean it.

'Very good,' says Marc. 'Almost a little too good. If I didn't know better, I'd say you were angry at me.'

'Furious.'

'You despise me, lady?' Marc marches right up to me. 'You know what they say. Love and hate – two sides of the same coin.'

'Then I must be madly in love with you.'

'You wouldn't be the first girl.' His face is inches away now, and I see the fury in his eyes.

'God help anyone who fell in love with you,' I fire back. 'You're so unbelievably arrogant.'

'That's what you think of me? That's who you think I am?'

'What else can I think?' I say.

He turns away. 'Things aren't always as they seem.'

'Oh really?' I demand. 'Then tell me. Tell me how they are.'

I catch my breath, knowing what's coming next. And I'm not disappointed.

Marc grabs me and kisses me with such force and passion that I can barely breathe.

He pushes me against the wall, arms wrapped tight around my body.

I kiss him back, tears stinging my eyes, my hands going into his thick, brown hair.

'You want to know how things are?' says Marc, carrying me to the bed. 'You're a rich girl and I'm a dance teacher. *That's* how they are.'

He throws me onto the bed. 'You stay in this fancy first-class suite. I'm below deck. *That's* how things are.'

Marc climbs on top of me. 'I love you, and it's killing me. *That's* how things are.'

'You … you love me?' I stammer.

'Stupid, ain't it?' Marc replies.

'No.'

We kiss again, more passionately this time, and Marc pulls my dress over my head.

I help him by lifting my arms. Then Marc flings off my bra and puts his mouth to my breasts.

I know one day soon we're going to have to do all of this on camera. And it's going to be tough.

It's funny – thinking about acting with Marc like this.

When Leo and I did a bedroom scene, it was a little bit awkward. I had to really concentrate to stay relaxed. But this is the most natural thing in the world.

Marc is between my legs now, simulating sex, moving his body back and forth.

He is rock hard and pressing on all the right places, and I let my head fall back and moan – a real one.

I roll on top of him and make delicious circles over his hips.

Marc's hands come to my ribs, and he looks up – eyes soft and full of love.

It's funny, seeing him in character like this when we're halfway making love.

How can he do it?

I'm barely holding it together and I know it. But I'm getting better at this.

Looking into his soft eyes, I try to feel the relief my character would feel – finally giving in to her feelings.

I manage it for a moment, but then having Marc between my legs is just too much.

'Oh *god*.' I lean forward, falling against his hard chest, still moving my hips against him.

'Well done, Sophia,' Marc murmurs into my ear. 'We're making progress. Would you like me to put you out of your misery?'

I manage a laugh and nod.

Marc reaches down and frees himself from his trousers. Then he lifts me by my buttocks and lowers me gently onto him.

I close my eyes as my hips sink down.

'*Oooooh.*' I begin to move. Back and forth, up and down, hands in my hair, desperate for him.

Marc clamps his hands on my hips and moves me more precisely.

'Oh Marc. Oh god, oh god.'

I move and move and move.

Marc's hips come up to meet mine, and he watches me, fierce and intense – the Marc I know and am obsessed with.

His thumb comes between my legs, moving in warm circles.

Outside, I hear seagulls call and the waves wash against the ship. But soon I'm barely aware of anything – only Marc's body under mine.

I close my eyes and let the feelings wash over me, my hips moving automatically.

I feel a hot circle where his thumb is, and it gets hotter and hotter until I'm crying out, calling his name, thrusting my hips.

Marc moves his body up to meet mine, staring deeply into my eyes.

We move and move, and soft moans leave my lips as a deep orgasm builds up and sweeps over me. It starts between my legs and spins up through my stomach and chest.

'Oh god. Oh Marc. Marc.' My eyes close as my body is dipped in warmth. 'I love you,' I murmur, falling against his chest.

Marc's arms come around me, holding me tight.

After a long time, I open my eyes.

Marc watches me, protective as ever.

'You didn't come,' I whisper.

'No.'

'Why not?' I ask.

Marc's lips twitch. 'I wanted to show you what self control is all about.' He rolls me over, sliding out. 'Rest there for a moment. Then get dressed.' He shields his eyes and looks out of the window. 'I see Saint-Tropez on the horizon.'

51

The ship rolls on through blue water, and Saint-Tropez grows bigger, glowing white and orange in the afternoon sun.

Luxury motorboats sail us ashore, and Ivy loves zipping through the water, bundled against the breeze. But as the waves get choppier, Marc takes her from me.

'She's getting soaked through,' he says. 'I'll bring her into the cabin.'

I nod, watching the shoreline. 'Is it okay if I stay up here? I want to take in every bit of Saint-Tropez.'

Marc strokes salty, wet hair from my face. 'You don't need to ask.'

I smile, turning back to the cruise ship giant on the horizon, and see a second motorboat whizzing behind us. Jen is on the deck, talking to what appears to be a security guard. But I know better ...

Michael.

I smile.

He's actually doing as he's told for once. Heading back to London.

As I lean on the rail, enjoying the cool ocean spray, Benjamin crosses the boat to join me.

'You're soaking.'

I shuffle my hands along the rail, away from him. 'I don't mind. I'm just enjoying the view.'

'Aren't you worried about your hair getting messed up?' Benjamin asks.

I laugh. 'I couldn't care less.'

'You shouldn't.' He edges his hands closer to mine. 'You look beautiful either way. Hey – I've been thinking about our last scene. You know, where I sort of beat you up. It's a bit heavy.'

'I know,' I agree, 'but it has to happen. There has to be a good reason for Violet to run away. Otherwise, she'd just be selfish.'

'Maybe we could tone it down a bit.' Benjamin looks out to sea. 'Couldn't he just slap her or something?'

'It's not enough.' I feel saltwater spray on my face. 'The audience needs to be in no doubt that she can't stay with him.'

'You think a woman should stay with a guy who slaps her?' Benjamin asks, wiping seawater from his forehead.

'Of course not,' I say. 'But things were different years ago. A husband had more right to keep his wife in line that way.'

Benjamin points to the shoreline. 'You see those houses over there? I own one of those.'

I look to where he's pointing. 'Do you?'

'Yup.' He puts his hand back on the rail. 'I usually rent it. But I made sure it was empty this time around. In case I needed some privacy. Or … someone else wanted privacy with me.'

'Oh,' I say, not really knowing how to answer. 'Benjamin? What's making you want to change this scene?'

'Can't you guess?'

'No.'

'Well.' His blue eyes go soft. 'I can't stand the idea of hitting you.'

I laugh, sure he must be making another joke.

'I'm serious,' he insists,' I just—'

'Hey party people!' Nadia comes clattering over in her tall boots, black sunglasses wrapped around her face. 'So. Saint-Tropez is beautiful, right? But listen – wait until you see the villa.'

'Is the security good?' Benjamin asks. 'Sophia is new to all this. We don't want her bothered.'

'Of course,' says Nadia. 'The best. Hey – this is Saint-Tropez. They live for good security around here. Why do you think the rich and famous love it so much? Oh!' She grabs the rail, as the boat shakes a little. 'Time to dock. Saint-Tropez – watch out!'

52

White limousines pick us up from the port, driving us through the town and up the coast.

Marc and I take a limousine together. Ivy travels with Tanya to avoid the paparazzi.

'I have fond memories of travelling in cars with you,' says Marc, as we glide past pretty white houses with orange-tiled roofs. 'Especially cars with tinted windows.'

'Me too,' I murmur, staring at the French countryside.

'You seem preoccupied,' says Marc. 'What's on your mind?'

'It's nothing.' I turn to him, managing a smile. 'Just something Benjamin said earlier. That's all.'

'Benjamin?' Marc's eyes darken. 'Why would he be talking to you?'

'We're on a movie together, Marc. It's good to talk. Make friends, even. Acting is all about rapport. You've said so yourself.'

Marc turns to the window. 'Rapport can be faked.'

'You're being jealous.' I reach across the white leather seat and take his hand.

'Perhaps.' Marc squeezes my fingers. 'You know these limousines come with all sorts of built in pleasures, don't you?' He opens what I assume to be an armrest, and I see a mini fridge inside, chilling a half-bottle of Veuve Clicquot champagne and two tall, frosted wine glasses.

'Perfect.' Marc pulls the bottle free and unravels gold metal foil. 'I think we should celebrate our arrival.'

'You really think we should be celebrating just yet?' I ask, watching his fingers untwist the cork cage. 'It's not even lunchtime.'

'Think of this as a relaxation for your rehearsal later.' Marc pops the champagne cork and pours me a glass.

I take the bubbling glass. 'Here's to us. And our beautiful baby.' I turn to the car behind, where Ivy travels with Tanya. 'Who I wish was here with us.'

'You know it's safer this way.' Marc pours his own glass. 'The paparazzi have already tried for pictures.'

I see the pair of us reflected in the smoky-black driver's partition glass.

'How did someone like you end up with me?' I wonder, seeing Marc's strong jaw, thick brown hair and intense blue eyes. He suits this car. He belongs in this sort of vehicle.

Me, in my light summer dress, hair all loose, barely any makeup – I only belong here if I'm with Marc.

'I rather thought I was the lucky one,' says Marc.

'Oh come on,' I insist. 'You're amazing. I'm just … normal.'

Marc smiles. 'I don't think anyone could ever refer to you as normal. You're astonishingly beautiful. And an incredible actress.'

I shake my head, loose hair spilling around my shoulders. 'I'm not *astonishingly* beautiful. And my acting … I just do what I've always done. Act with my heart.'

'You'd be surprised how many people can't do that.' Marc arranges my hair over one shoulder. 'And surely by now, you've noticed how men look at you.'

'Men don't look at me,' I say, watching Marc in the glass.

'They do. Believe me. I hate it.' He strokes my hair.

I watch Marc's handsome profile and strong fingers. 'I thought you were working on that jealousy of yours.'

'I'm trying.' He twists my hair around his fingers. 'Especially when there are men like Benjamin Van Rosen around.'

'Oh … I think he's harmless.' But in our reflection, I find myself unable to meet Marc's eye.

'How does it make you feel?' Marc asks. 'When men look at you?'

'They don't look at me, Marc.'

'They do. Drink your champagne.'

'I am drinking it.' I take another sip, feeling delicious, sharp bubbles on my tongue.

'Drink it faster,' says Marc.

'Why?'

He fixes me with intense eyes. 'So I can make you come in this car.'

53

Oh god.

'Marc.' I shake my head. 'Not here.'

Marc leans back against soft, white leather. 'I'd have thought you'd be familiar with the inside of a car by now.'

'Yes but ... *your* cars. This is ... no, we just can't.'

Placing his champagne glass in a pull-out holder, Marc opens another compartment – a freezer drawer. There's a gold ice-cube tray inside, and he cracks a cube into his hand.

'If you're having a problem following orders,' says Marc, 'we'll take things one step at a time. Put this into your mouth.'

I look at the hard, sharp-edged cube. 'It's cold.'

'Do as you're told.' Marc holds the ice cube to my lips and moves it back and forth.

My heart flutters and a blush spreads to my cheeks.

'Why do I do these things with you?' I ask, my lips burning. 'I'm just a normal girl.'

'Obviously not as normal as you think.' Marc moves the ice cube to my lower lip, dancing it over my skin.

'Meaning?' I stammer.

He holds the cube still for a moment, reaching for his champagne glass and taking a thoughtful sip. 'Meaning ... I brought out what was already inside.'

'You're saying that inside I want to be … um …'

Marc puts his champagne glass back into the holder. Then he reaches to take mine. 'The word you're searching for is dominated.'

'You're wrong,' I say, letting him take my glass and clip it beside his.

'Your body says different.' Marc moves the ice cube from my lips and slips it under my dress.

'Oh!' I practically jump out of the seat as the cold hits my skin.

Marc moves the ice cube down, down …

'Marc!' I gasp as the cold ice finds its way into my panties.

With deft fingers, Marc moves it around. Around. Up. Then inside me.

'OH!'

Marc takes another ice cube.

I shake my head. 'You're not going to—'

'I am.' He pushes the second ice cube into my panties, and then inside me.

A pleasurable achy cold feeling swells between my legs, and I find myself holding on to the car seat.

Marc watches me. Then he unbuckles his seatbelt and parts my knees.

Pulling my panties over my thighs, he lifts each foot free.

'Marc, I don't think this is a good idea.'

'I didn't ask for your opinion.' Marc runs a hand between my legs, and I stifle a moan.

'*Marc.*'

'Careful,' he warns. 'Or the driver will hear.'

I nod, pushing my lips together.

He lifts my dress, looking at me. 'How can you say you're not astonishingly beautiful?'

'Down there I'm *definitely* not.'

'Good god, you are. So, so beautiful.' Putting an ice cube between his teeth, Marc ducks under my dress and presses it between my legs.

I close my eyes and hold back a moan as he guides the ice cube back and forth, back and forth, building up a gentle rhythm.

The hard, coolness does things to me I can't believe, and I squirm against the leather.

Marc clamps firm hands on my hips, holding me still.

I try not to cry out, but it's hard.

Marc moves up and down, over and over, the ice chilling and warming me all at once. It's melting – I can feel cool water between my legs.

My eyes close. My body tenses and releases, and the ice cubes move around inside me.

Suddenly, I feel Marc's warm tongue.

It's too much. I can't stop myself.

Pushing my lips tight together, I come with a low, silent moan.

My whole body shudders and tenses, and Marc's movements become softer.

'Oh Marc,' I whisper.

Marc takes a white, cloth napkin from the armrest and folds it up, then places it into my panties.

'The ice cubes stay there,' he instructs. 'Until they melt. Husband's orders.'

'And if I take them out?' I ask.

He raises an eyebrow. 'Then I'll deal with you in my usual way.'

The car pulls to a stop by tall wrought-iron gates, shiny under bright sun.

Marc turns to the window. 'Well here we are, Mrs Blackwell. Our little French Chateaux.'

54

The giant gates swing open, and our car moves over gravel.

'Whoa.'

Marc follows my gaze. 'Nadia certainly knows how to find sensational locations.'

'It's beautiful.' I press my face to the glass, noticing a limousine crawling ahead of us. There are none behind though – Tanya, Tom and Ivy must have got caught at some lights or something.

Our car drives past a fountain, green lawns, a bright-blue infinity pool and several mini-villas. Then it pulls to a stop outside an enormous orange-and-white villa with tall pillars and sweeping mosaic steps. Stone snakes guard the entrance.

Across the crisp lawn is a private beach, patrolled by marine security.

Marc takes my hand. 'May I help you out of the car, Mrs Blackwell? You look a little uncomfortable.'

I glare at him. 'I can't believe you've done this to me.'

'You mean, you can't believe you didn't say no.'

'Something like that,' I admit.

Nadia leaps out of the limousine in front, hands on hips as she surveys the magnificent complex. 'What a place, huh?' she calls to us. 'Built in the 1930s. Totally authentic.'

I smile, moving my legs awkwardly as Marc and I cross the gravel.

'Marc?' Nadia drops black sunglasses on her nose. 'What do you think?'

'I'll tell you when I've seen inside,' says Marc, looking over the building.

'You'll like it,' Nadia insists. 'And guess what? You two have the whole top floor.'

'The whole top floor?' I say, my legs still not sure what to do with themselves.

'What else for my star couple?' says Nadia. 'Go right on in. Take a look around. Freshen up if you want. Then come down to the swimming pool – the whole cast and crew are meeting, okay?'

I glance at Marc, wondering exactly how I'm going to manage the staircase.

Without saying a word, Marc lifts me into his arms.

'You're carrying your wife over the threshold, huh?' Nadia observes. 'How romantic.'

'I never miss an opportunity to carry my wife,' says Marc.

'Thanks a lot Marc,' I laugh, as he carries me up the stairs. 'Now Nadia's going to think I'm some 1950s wife, carried around by my husband.'

'I couldn't stand another moment of you shifting your legs back and forth,' says Marc, a half smile on his face.

'It's *your* fault!' I laugh.

'And my correction.'

55

The top floor is incredible – sloped ceilings, regal antique furniture, fur rugs and a fantastic view of the whole complex and the beach in the distance.

It's decorated in 1930s French country style, with light, chiffon curtains and lavender-coloured bed linen.

A housemaid unpacks our luggage, while I wash my hands and face in the ensuite under a gushing gold tap.

Marc watches me from the bedroom area, a half smile on his face.

'Are those ice cubes still giving you a hard time, Mrs Blackwell?' he asks, as I dab my face with a towel.

I glare at him, nodding my head towards the housemaid.

'It's okay,' says Marc. 'She doesn't speak English.'

'Even so …'

'How *are* those ice cubes?' he asks again.

'If you must know,' I snap, 'they've melted.'

'Shame.' He raises an eyebrow at me. 'I was enjoying the thought of them.'

'Listen up everyone!' Standing on concrete diving board steps by the crystal-clear, perfectly square swimming pool, Nadia shouts through a mini megaphone.

The entire cast and crew are arranged around the still, blue water, whilst waiters hand out glasses of ice-cold orange juice.

Benjamin leans against a fish statue, Ray-Bans on his nose.

Leo has positioned himself on a sun lounger, flip-flopped feet dangling off the end.

I stand between Marc and Tom.

Tanya and Jen are investigating the villa with Ivy.

'Welcome to Saint-Tropez,' shouts Nadia. 'There's been a *small* set back – we're still waiting for one more person to show up. The drive from Paris … there's been some traffic issue. Sophia – I won't need you until this afternoon. But you can stay and listen to the briefing if you want. All right?'

'Pardon me, Nadia.' Tom raises a hand. 'I hope you don't mind the question, but who are we waiting for?'

Nadia looks down at her clipboard. 'Didn't you get memos about this?'

'Never got one,' says Benjamin.

'Huh.' Nadia flips pages. 'Oh wait, they're still here. Hey – sorry gang. I can't believe this didn't get passed on. We got ourselves another big name, last minute. Cassandra Kilburn.'

Cassandra Kilburn.

Something in my stomach turns over.

Marc was in a movie with her. Years ago. When he was a teenager.

I turn to him, and notice his expression is stormy.

Tom leans over and whispers, 'Just when I thought the cast couldn't get any more famous.'

'I've only ever seen one of her movies,' I whisper back. 'The one Marc was in.'

'Oh yes, I remember,' Tom nods. 'She was a Mrs Robinson, wasn't she?'

Beside me, Marc clears his throat. 'Nadia?' he calls out. 'Cassandra Kilburn wasn't part of the original line up. Why the change?'

Nadia shields her eyes. 'Meredith pulled out. So we got Cassandra. Thank god. I couldn't believe she was free. You worked with her before, right?'

Marc's frowning. 'A long time ago.'

'What's the problem?' says Nadia. 'Is she a bitch or something?'

Murmurs of laughter float around the group.

'I wouldn't know.' Marc turns to the ocean. 'I haven't seen her in years.'

Nadia holds up her hand. 'Wait guys, I hear the gates. This could be her.' She checks her watch. 'Great. Let's give her a warm welcome, okay? She's good news for this movie.'

At the end of the gravel path, the villa gates swing open and a black Cadillac rolls into the complex, pulling to a stop by the main house.

The passenger door opens, and red shoes step onto the gravel.

A tall, slender woman steps out. She wears a fitted grey dress, and long black hair tumbles down her back.

Nadia motions to her assistant. 'Go up to the house. Tell Cassandra to get down here – we're already running behind.'

56

The meeting continues, but I get the sense that most of us aren't really listening to Nadia. We're all waiting for our mysterious new co-star.

Eventually, Cassandra saunters along the white, stone path towards us. She's in no particular hurry, as her heels click along. Thick, black lashes line her eyes, matching her hair.

'Bonjour.' Cassandra walks right up to Nadia and kisses her on both cheeks. 'Good to see you chica.' Then she scans the group, her eyes holding when they reach Marc. 'Marc Blackwell. Of all the movies in all the world.'

'Who'd have thought?' Marc says humourlessly, sliding hands into his pockets.

Cassandra's red lips stretch into a smile. 'My, haven't you grown?'

'In lots of ways,' Marc replies.

'Not a boy anymore,' Cassandra coos.

'Not young and stupid.'

Cassandra raises a black eyebrow. 'I wouldn't say stupid.'

'I would,' Marc fires back.

The hairs on the back of my neck stand up.

Cassandra glances at me. Then her dark eyes find Marc again. 'So you got married.'

'Best thing I ever did,' says Marc.

'Listen guys,' Nadia lifts the megaphone. 'Catch up some other time – we have work to do. Cassandra, I need you and Benjamin.'

'Shame. I was hoping for Marc first.' Cassandra grins, but Marc looks away.

I swallow tightly.

'Um … Nadia?' I call out.

'Yes honey?'

'You don't need me right now, do you?'

'Not until this afternoon.'

'Would it be okay … I just think I should check on Ivy,' I say.

'Sure. No problem,' Nadia replies.

I turn to go.

Marc frowns. 'Sophia?'

'I need to be alone for a minute.' I whisper.

I expect Marc to ask me more. But he doesn't.

'Sophia, are you okay my love?' Tom asks, as I hurry past him.

'Fine,' I murmur.

But I'm not.

57

I find Tanya reading *Jane Eyre* on our comfy velvet sofa, while Ivy sleeps in the travel cot.

Our floor is lit by bright sunlight, and smells of lavender and lemons.

'You all right Soph?' Tanya asks. 'What's up?'

I slump onto the wooden bed, falling back to stare at the ceiling. 'I'm not sure. But something.'

Tanya closes her book. 'Tell Aunty Tanya all about it.'

I roll over onto my elbows. 'I think I just met another of Marc's ex-girlfriends.'

'Really?'

I nod. 'Cassandra Kilburn.'

'*Cassandra* Kilburn?' Tanya closes her book and places it on the sofa arm. 'Since when was she in this movie?'

'Since now. A last minute addition.'

'You think she and Marc had something?' Tanya asks.

I nod. 'I think so.'

'But she's like … forty.'

I sit up on the bed, crossing my legs. 'Did you ever just know something?'

'Is it such a big deal?' Tanya comes to sit beside me. 'You knew he had sex before.'

'Yes but … something about this feels different,' I say. 'I mean, he hasn't even told me anything happened. But I just … know.' I look down at Ivy, her eyes lightly closed, her breath soft.

'Oh shit.'

'I'll look after Ivy this morning,' I tell Tanya. 'Why don't you enjoy the villa. Or explore Saint-Tropez?'

'Aren't you supposed to be working?' Tanya asks.

'They don't need me until this afternoon. And I could do with some baby time.'

Tanya gets to her feet. 'Okay. I'll be back by lunchtime. That'll give you and Marc a chance to eat together.'

I frown. 'I don't want to go to lunch with Marc. Not right now.'

'You know, Soph.' Tanya's hand lingers on the side of the travel cot. 'Some stones are best left unturned. Keep the past in the past. It's the best place for it.'

'I can't ignore this.' I go to the window. The cast have dispersed now, and cameramen are setting up around the swimming pool.

'Why not?'

'He didn't come after me,' I murmur. 'That's not like him. What if he's still in love with her, Tanya?'

'Don't be daft.' She grins. 'That man is smitten with you. And now little Ivy has come along, he can barely take his eyes off the pair of you. Honestly Soph, you have nothing to worry about.'

But I'm not so sure.

58

Half an hour later, there's a knock at the door.

It's not Marc. I know his knock.

Ivy is still sleeping, but she stirs at the noise. I resettle the blanket over her, and creak the door open.

'Oh!' I take a step back. 'Benjamin.'

Benjamin Van Rosen leans against the doorframe. 'We're filming in half an hour,' he tells me. 'By the pool. Did you know?'

I shake my head, heading back into the bedroom. 'Did they change the schedule?'

Benjamin follows me inside. 'Yup. Nadia sent me to tell you. Well, sort of. I offered.'

'Why didn't Marc offer to come?' The words come out hard.

Benjamin shrugs. 'He wasn't there.'

I lean down to smooth the blanket over Ivy again. 'Where did he go?'

'I'm not sure,' Benjamin replies. 'He just left. What's up?'

'Nothing.'

'Uh oh.' Benjamin sits on the velvet sofa. 'Marc and Cassandra were in a movie together once, right?'

'So?'

He looks at me with light-blue eyes. 'Sometimes people hook up in movies, right?'

I turn in circles, looking for my phone. 'I should call Tanya.'

Benjamin smiles. 'Are you trying to get rid of me?'

'No, I just …' I shake my head. 'I don't know what I'm doing.'

'You might not believe this.' He leans back on the sofa, arms spread along the back. 'But I'm a good listener.'

'Thanks, but honestly – there's nothing to say.'

'She's got a reputation, you know.' He crosses his ankles. 'Cassandra. Is that what you're worried about?'

The churning in my stomach whips into a frenzy.

I know I shouldn't ask. It'll just make everything worse. But I can't help it.

I sit on the sofa arm. 'What do you mean by that, Benjamin?'

'I can tell you haven't hung out in Hollywood much.'

'I haven't hung out in Hollywood at all,' I tell him.

'Lucky you.' He pats the seat beside him. 'Come sit here. With me.'

'I'm fine here,' I say. 'And I know all about Marc. I know he has … a past.'

Benjamin drums his fingers on the sofa back. 'So you know about Cassandra?'

'No,' I admit.

He meets my eye. 'Do you want to know?'

'Okay.' I nod. 'Tell me. What is it?'

'You're sure?'

'No.' I slide down into the seat beside him. 'But tell me anyway.'

'You've heard of Jessica Goldberg, right?' says Benjamin.

'Yes.'

'Jessica. Cassandra. They used to have fun together, if you know what I mean. At least, that's what the Hollywood rumour mill says. And sometimes they'd invite guys to join in.'

I think I get where he's going with this … and I want to be sick.

'Hey.' Benjamin slides his arm around my shoulder. 'I don't know if Marc got involved. Seriously. I didn't want to hurt you.'

I nod, so numb I barely know where I am.

Benjamin squeezes my shoulder, pulling me against his body. 'You've got nothing to worry about from Cassandra. She's fucking forty something.'

I give a humourless laugh.

'You're a zillion times better.' Benjamin kisses my nose.

I swipe at tears.

'A trillion, zillion times better.' He kisses my lips. It feels friendly. But …

Blinking away tears, I suddenly notice Tanya in the doorway, her mouth open.

59

I pull back from Benjamin.

'Um … Soph?' Tanya calls. 'They're saying they need you for filming. Want me to take Ivy?'

I feel myself nodding, as Benjamin drops his arm from my shoulder.

He gets to his feet. 'I'll see you down there, okay?' Benjamin heads for the stairs.

'What was all that about?' Tanya whispers, glancing back at the doorway. 'Watch out for him. He has a reputation.'

'He was just being nice.' I lean back against the sofa, my mind whirling.

'Very nice,' Tanya remarks, coming into the room.

'Do you know what?' I say. 'Right now, I couldn't care less. Marc is hiding something from me.'

'Is there something you want to talk about?' Tanya sits beside me.

I shake my head. 'No. They want me down there right now?'

'But Soph, are you sure you're okay to—'

'I'll be fine.' I get to my feet. 'I'm an actress. We spend our lives pretending things aren't true.'

I walk back to the swimming pool, still feeling sick to my stomach.

Nadia is chattering about lighting and angles. She says something to me, but I don't take in a word of it.

I watch Cassandra.

She's sitting on a sun bed wearing 1940s-style loose shorts and polka dot blouse, having her makeup done.

'Where is everyone?' I hear myself ask.

And where's Marc?

'Resting. Rehearsing.' Nadia signals a runner and grabs papers. 'I only need you and Cassandra right now.'

I swallow. 'I thought Benjamin and I—'

Nadia cuts me off with a shake of her head. 'Change of plan.'

'Have you seen Marc?' I blurt out.

'I think he went for a walk.' Nadia flips through papers.

Did he indeed …

'You okay, honey?' Nadia asks distractedly.

I swallow again. 'Actually Nadia, I'm not feeling so good.'

'You look fine to me.' Nadia lowers her sunglasses, brown eyes full of concern. 'Is Ivy okay?'

'Yes. God yes. She's fine.'

'Then it's nothing.' Nadia gives my waist a playful squeeze. 'Run over there and get dressed for me, okay?'

A wardrobe assistant appears with a black and white polka dot bikini, thrusting it into my hands.

'Perfect!' Nadia shouts. 'Sophia. Put that on, okay? Then we'll get you in makeup.'

I'm shown into a makeshift changing room of canvas and tent poles, and the world becomes a blur of mirrors, makeup and hairspray.

Before I know what's happening, I'm being led out to the pool.

From a sun lounger, Cassandra watches me.

'I need you here,' says Nadia, steering me beside Cassandra. 'Hey – you two haven't been introduced yet, right?' She waves at a crew member in the distance. 'Not *there*. Oh Christ.'

Nadia marches around the pool to berate a cameraman.

I stand awkwardly by Cassandra, not quite knowing what to say.

'I'm Sophia,' I manage. 'Um … hi.'

'I know who you are.' Cassandra's gaze turns to the calm, blue swimming pool. 'You're the wife. Did Marc ever tell you? What he and I had?'

A lizard runs along the white stone rim of the pool, right by Cassandra's sun lounger.

'Marc is my husband,' I say. 'If you and he had a past, I don't want to know about it.'

Cassandra laughs. 'I have to admit, I am a little fascinated by you. He never would have changed. Not for me.'

'I don't think this conversation is appropriate,' I say, my voice shaky.

'Movies are funny, aren't they?' Cassandra continues. 'Here I am playing your mother. And yet in real life, I fucked your husband.'

Oh *god*.

I stare at her, my stomach spinning round and round.

'What's the matter?' Cassandra asks, hitting me with dark eyes.

'I …' My mouth is dry, and I try to swallow but can't. 'Excuse me for a moment.'

I turn left and right, nearly tripping over my feet. Then I decide on a direction and walk away.

Past the pool. Past the bungalow villas and across the lawn.

I run towards the beach.

She's won. Marc's gone, and she's won.

60

I stare at the waves, crashing over each other under an orange sun.

Yachts are scattered far out to sea, waving on the water.

I put hands to my face, sink to the sand and let the tears come.

I cry and cry, hot tears turning to salt in the sun.

When I'm all cried out, I take off my socks and trainers and walk along the beach.

My toes sink into the soft, wet sand as the bad thoughts and feelings tumble around.

This is so humiliating … how can I stay with a man who has this sort of past?

Why didn't he come for me?

I guess I must have walked a few miles before I realise running away isn't the answer.

I have a movie to shoot and a baby to look after.

This isn't solving anything.

As I turn to go back, I see a swimmer far out at sea.

I shield my eyes, watching strong arms tear through the water, following the waves towards shore.

It's …

Marc.

I watch, frozen to the spot.

Marc is getting nearer, his lean body sparkling in the sunshine.

I want to leave. But my legs stay locked.

When Marc is a few feet away, he stands in the waves and strides towards me, flicking water from his hair.

His body is incredible – a perfect male specimen. Toned and muscular, long limbs, strong arms. An iron jaw below piercing blue eyes.

'Sophia,' he growls. 'What are you doing out here? There could be photographers—'

'I don't *care* about photographers,' I shout. 'Where have you been? How could you just leave me like that?'

His feet reach dry sand. 'I didn't leave you. It was you who left.'

I put hands on my hips. 'You could have come after me.'

He marches towards me. 'I thought you needed space.'

'I needed *you*.' I wipe away angry tears.

'No.' He reaches the pile of clothes, inches from me. 'You didn't. I was the last thing you needed.'

'What happened between you and Cassandra?' My eyes search his.

'Sophia –'

'Tell me everything,' I insist. 'Every nasty, dirty disgusting detail.'

Marc grabs a crumpled grey t-shirt from the sand and pulls it over his head. 'That's not a good idea.'

'You don't think I deserve to know about my own *husband*?'

'There's no sense in talking about this.' Marc pulls his shirt over his chest. 'My past is … my past. I've told you many times. I'm not proud of who I was. There's nothing I can do about it.' He strides back along the beach.

'Well I *want* to know,' I say, taking big strides to keep pace with him. 'So tell me. Even Benjamin knows more than I do. He said Cassandra had a friend. Jessica. And … and …'

I can't finish that sentence.

Marc stops. 'I was very young when I met Cassandra. Young and stupid.' He turns to me. 'She fulfilled a need I thought I had. But that need only grew. It was never fulfilled. I was never whole. Not until I met you. You want me to be totally honest? She was probably the closest thing I had to a relationship. Until you came along.'

'Did you love her?'

Marc gives a humourless laugh. 'No. I didn't love her. I didn't even like her half the time.'

'Then how could you—'

'Sleep with her?' He looks out to sea. 'I've slept with many women I didn't care about.'

'No. I mean have a relationship with her.' My insides are churning.

'She saw things in me.' He flicks water from his hair. 'Showed me … I suppose, how to be the way I am.'

'She made you—'

'Yes. She made me dominate her.' He turns to me. 'And yes, at times there was another woman involved too. With Cassandra, there were no inhibitions. Nothing was off limits. Is that what you want to hear? I did things to her I would never, *could* never, do to you. Things I'm ashamed to think about.'

I feel sick. 'She still wants you.'

'I doubt that. I was one of her many play things. A sixteen-year old toy to fuck around with. I'm all grown up now.'

'If you hadn't met her—' I insist.

'I still would be the way I am.' His eyes are softer now, and he puts a hand on my shoulder. 'She just made it acceptable. Without her ... Christ, I don't know. It always would have come out one way or another.'

I put my hand over his. 'I can't be in a movie with her, Marc. I just can't.'

He nods. 'I'll talk to Nadia.'

'Oh god.' I close my eyes. 'If you do that, and Cassandra gets thrown off the movie because of me ... that isn't right either.'

'It's your call, Sophia.' His thumb strokes my shoulder. 'I'm happy to talk to Nadia as soon as we get back. Believe it or not, I'm not all that happy about acting with Cassandra either.'

I realise something. 'This isn't all of your past, is it?'

'What do you mean?'

'I mean, there'll always be girls coming out of the wood-work. Sigourney ... God knows who else.'

'Probably.'

I drop my hand from his. 'I'm not sure I can handle it.'

'Sophia, I thought you understood. I've been honest with you from the start about the man I used to be.'

'Everything's different now. We have Ivy.' I step back from him, forcing his hand to leave my shoulder. 'I don't know, Marc. I don't know if I can live with this pain. Not knowing when it's going to come. It's torture.'

244

'Sophia—'

'I need some time alone.' I turn away.

'That's what I was trying to give you.'

'No, I mean real space. I … I want you to move out of our room. Until I figure things out.'

Marc's jaw tightens. 'If that's what you feel you need.'

61

That evening, Marc's things are moved out of the main villa and into a luxury mini-villa near the beach.

I watch from the top floor window as his luggage is ported through the complex.

It's not that I want to punish him. It feels terrible that he'll miss time with Ivy. But I have a lot to think about.

No inhibitions.

No limits

Jessica ....

I've watched Jessica Goldberg on TV for years. She's pretty. Fresh-faced. America's sweetheart.

I thought there was nothing more in Marc's past that could hurt me. But it just keeps on coming.

Can I cope with this? A husband with so many skeletons? And how can he be content with me?

I sway Ivy in my arms, tears running down my cheeks.

Ivy is awake, blinking at me, and I have an overwhelming urge to keep her safe, protected from all these bad things.

Does that mean leaving her father?

That thought hurts most of all – the realisation that maybe I *should* leave Marc. For Ivy's sake.

There's a soft knocking at the door, and I will whoever it is to go away.

'Now listen to me, Sophia Rose.' Tom's voice is muffled through wood. 'I've crammed myself into a tiny elevator to get up here and talk to you. So you just jolly well open up.'

Usually, Tom makes me smile. But I'm not much in the mood for smiling today.

'*You're* complaining, Tom?' I hear Tanya's equally muffled voice fire back. 'I had to squash into that elevator too. You had a comfy seat the whole way up.'

'Some people would pay good money to be squashed against the famous Tom Davenport,' Tom replies. 'Now LISTEN HERE SOPHIA. This wheelchair makes an excellent battering ram. Let us in or I'll break the door down.'

Reluctantly, I walk to the door and click open the lock.

'At long last!' Tom wheels himself into the room. 'You're not dead. That's something, at least.'

'How's Ivy doing?' Tanya asks, concern on her pale face.

'Fine,' I say.

'And how are *you*?' Tom booms.

'Not so good,' I admit, putting a hand on Ivy's cot.

Tom wheels himself beside me, touching my arm. 'Love. What's happening? Tanya thinks this is all to do with some ex-girlfriend of Marc's, but I told her you'd never get upset over something so silly.'

'When you're thinking of divorcing the father of your child … there's nothing silly about that.' I stare down at Ivy, sadness gripping my chest.

'Oh come now, Sophia,' says Tom. 'Surely you can't be serious? You and Marc are made for each other.'

'I love him.' My fingers stroke the travel-cot fabric. 'But … I'm frightened. What else is going to come out of the woodwork? How much more can I take? And what about when Ivy grows up? I don't want her tainted by any of this.'

'I don't mean to pry,' says Tom. 'But I've missed a page in the script, somewhere. Would someone fill me in?'

'Marc … had a thing with Cassandra Kilburn,' says Tanya, sitting on the bed.

'*No*! He did?' Tom turns to her in surprise. 'She's … you know, *old*.'

'She's not that old,' says Tanya. 'She's only forty something. And she wears it well.'

'Thanks for reminding me,' I mumble.

'Sorry,' Tanya replies. 'You know me. Say what I see.'

'But surely that was years ago?' says Tom. 'Ancient history.'

'It's not ancient history when it turns up at your villa,' says Tanya.

'And you have to act alongside her,' I add.

'Look. I don't want to say the wrong thing.' Tom takes my hand. 'But I'd hazard a guess that any extremely attractive, famous man has his share of past women. Surely you never thought you were the only one?'

'I knew I wasn't the only one,' I say. 'But this is … I don't know. There's more too it. Cassandra brought out his dark side.'

'Ah,' says Tom, with a playful waggle of his eyebrows. 'Like Tanya does with me.'

'More like the other way around,' Tanya laughs. 'But listen, Soph. Tom is right. Marc has been with plenty of women. I'm sure he's got up to all sorts. I know it's horrible. But the past is the past.'

'These women keep appearing in my life,' I say. 'And not just my life – my movies.'

'You could stop making movies?' Tom offers.

'She can't do that!' says Tanya. 'Acting is her life.'

'Ivy is my life,' I correct her. 'Closely followed by Marc. At least, that's how I thought things were. But I can't keep doing this. I can't keep going through this pain. It's humiliating. And I feel like everyone is talking about me.'

'Well I didn't know anything,' says Tom.

'And I only knew because you told me,' Tanya adds.

'Benjamin was up here earlier,' I say. 'He told me. About stuff with Marc. And Cassandra. And another woman too.'

'Oh, that's horrible,' says Tanya. 'Benjamin should have kept his mouth shut.'

'Maybe,' I admit. 'But I'm glad he said something.'

'Are you?' says Tom. 'It seems to me some things are best kept quiet.'

'You have a baby with Marc,' says Tanya. 'You'll work things out. I know you will. Just give yourself a bit of space and time. You've had a shock. But you'll get over it. I'll tell you what. Why don't you hit the town tonight? Have a few drinks. Forget your worries.'

'I'm really not in the mood. Anyway, I have Ivy to look after.'

'I'll look after Ivy,' says Tanya, coming over to the cot. 'You can go out with Jen and Tom. I'd be happy to—'

I shake my head. 'I'm just too miserable.'

'Tanya's right, Soph,' says Tom. 'It will do you good to get out. You've got some big decisions to make. It's going to be hard to make them if you stay here, brooding.'

I sigh. 'Maybe some other time.'

62

When Tom and Tanya leave, I draw the curtains, even though it's still light outside.

I put Ivy in her cot and lay on my bed, willing sleep to come.

All I can think about is Marc and Cassandra.

As I'm considering getting a glass of water, I hear footsteps on the stairs.

Marc?

But it's not him. I know his footsteps, just like I know his knock.

'Who is it?' I call.

The door falls open and Jen appears, one hand on her hip. Over her arm, she's holding a dry-cleaning bag.

'You're in *bed*?' she demands.

I rub my eyes. 'So?'

'You *can't* be in bed.' She marches into the room. 'It's barely even nine o'clock.'

I sit up. 'I didn't really feel like doing anything else.'

'Tanya told me everything.' Jen throws the dry-cleaning bag on the bed. 'You and I are going out for cocktails. Look – I brought you a dress. It's free, as long as I take one photo of you in it. Chop chop! Let's hit the town.'

'No, Jen.' I pull the duvet up around me. 'I'm really not in the mood.'

'Of course you're not in the mood.' She sits heavily on the bed beside me. 'You're miserable. But we're going to change that. You're in Saint-Tropez, for crying out loud! With your good friend, Jen. And I'm going to show you a good time.'

'Jen—'

She puts an arm around my shoulder. 'Look, I know you're hurting. But Ivy doesn't need a moping mother. Come out with me. We'll have a few drinks. And work out what to do. Okay? Tanya is ready and waiting to take over.'

'I don't know.' I rub tear-tired eyes.

'I'm not taking no for an answer,' says Jen. 'So just save time and say yes.'

Dressed in fluttery, strapless grey silk, I step out of the limousine onto the hot pavements of Saint-Tropez.

Beside me, Jen is polished and perfect in a fitted cream shift.

'I can't believe you talked me into this,' I say, as we join the moving street party of young, rich and elegantly dressed.

'And I can't believe how amazing you look in that outfit,' says Jen. 'The designer is going to be *so* happy with the pictures.'

In the evening heat, loud voices ring out and champagne and cocktails are knocked back.

Jen arranges my hair around my shoulders. 'Look at you. The perfect Saint-Tropez princess. I'll bet you get mistaken for a Chloe model or something. You'll probably get signed by some French agency.'

I fiddle shyly with my hair. 'Hardly.'

'Come on.' Jen grabs my arm and leads me down hot, crowded streets. 'The best party is with a client friend of mine. It's this way.'

63

At the harbour, it's easy to see where the party is.

A giant, 200-foot luxury yacht flashes with lights and trembles with beats.

Beautiful, bronzed girls swim around the boat, laughing and screeching as men pour champagne over them from the deck.

Jen links her arm through mine and walks us confidently up the gangplank, waving away the security man.

'If this party doesn't cheer you up, nothing will,' says Jen, grabbing us each a glass of pink champagne from a passing bikini waitress.

'I don't know, Jen.' I feel noise and chaos on all sides. 'I'm not sure this is for me right now.'

'It will be when you get drunk. Trust me.' She thrusts a glass at me.

'I can't get drunk,' I insist, taking the glass. 'I'm filming tomorrow.'

'Don't be ridiculous,' Jen snorts. 'Plenty of actors party before filming. And you need to let loose. Come on – down in one.' She necks her champagne. 'Your turn,' she urges.

I look at my glass reluctantly. 'I'm a mother now. I can't be downing drinks.'

'Yes you can,' Jen barks. 'It's just one night. You need to take your mind off things. This is your psychological health we're talking about.'

'Oh, fine.' Some hedonist part of me clicks into place, and I find myself knocking back the glass.

'That's my girl!' says Jen. 'Okay – let's go dance.'

She pulls me towards the back of the yacht.

'Oh my god.' I see a cocktail bar, Jacuzzi and mini swimming pool. 'This is a *yacht*?'

Tanned men and women sip cocktails on white-leather sofas and dance on varnished wood.

'Yes,' says Jen. 'Well, if you're a billionaire.'

Half an hour later, Jen and I are dancing back-to-back, downing champagne and singing along to dance tracks.

'You're right,' I shout over the thumping music, 'I did need to loosen up.'

'Told you,' says Jen. 'Are you feeling better?'

'A little,' I decide. 'There's light at the end of the tunnel.'

'Time heals all, right?' Jen replies.

'Maybe.' I accept another glass of pink champagne from a man in a Ralph Lauren v-neck.

'Pardon me,' the man asks me, with a hopeful smile. 'Are you a model?'

He has sun-bleached brown hair, a dark tan and an upper-class West London accent. The yacht suits him perfectly.

I laugh. 'No.'

'She should be,' Jen interrupts. 'Hey, I know you, don't I? You're Sebastian Blatch, right?'

The man shakes his head. 'That's my brother.'

'So you must be Tobias.' Jen gives him her mega-watt smile. 'I'm Jen. You own the Wahu chain, right? Is business good?'

'We're getting there.' Tobias glances at me. 'Jen. Would you be kind enough to introduce me to your friend?'

'Of course!' Jen's face lights up. 'Tobias. Meet Sophia. My very best friend.'

'And the most beautiful girl on this boat,' says Tobias, not taking his eyes off me.

I twiddle my hair, feeling awkward.

'Would you girls like to join us in the cabin?' Tobias asks.

'Oh, no thank you,' I say, turning back to dance. But then I see someone at the yacht bar who makes me lose my footing.

Cassandra.

64

Cassandra Kilburn stands by the cocktail bar, sipping from a martini glass and elegantly puffing a gold-tipped cigarette.

Jen follows my gaze. 'Oh my God! That bitch.'

'I want to go,' I say.

'Sophia, you're not going anywhere,' says Jen. 'Don't you dare leave a party because of that old cow. You can't run away. Why not face your fears? You'll have to act with her tomorrow.'

'That's tomorrow,' I say.

'Sophia Rose.' Jen puts a hand on her curvy hip. 'You are not going to leave a great party just because some tarted-up old woman slept with your husband.'

'Jen!' I hiss. 'Keep your voice down. And she didn't just sleep with him. I wish it were that simple.'

'You're the one wearing the ring,' says Jen.

Across the boat, Cassandra notices me and smiles an actress's smile.

I'm startled, not knowing where to look.

'What is she looking at?' Jen snaps.

'Me,' I say.

'Hey. HEY!' Jen shouts, marching across the boat.

'Oh god. Jen, no!' I call out, hurrying after her. 'Don't say anything. *Please.*'

But Jen strides right up to Cassandra. 'I'd like a word with you,' she demands, slamming her champagne glass down on the bar.

I wince.

Cassandra blinks languidly. 'Who are you?'

Jen glares up at her. 'My name is Jen. I'm Sophia's friend.'

'Can't Sophia talk for herself?' says Cassandra, with a cat-like smile.

'Jen,' I say, grabbing her arm. 'It's fine. Honestly.'

'You had a thing with Marc Blackwell once upon a time. Right?' Jen yells.

Oh god. I want to cover my eyes.

'Right,' says Cassandra.

'When you meet his *wife*,' says Jen, 'the polite thing to do is keep quiet about it.'

Cassandra shrugs. 'The word wife means nothing to me. No one will ever have what Marc and I had.'

Ouch.

Music still pounds, but half the crowd have stopped dancing. I feel their eyes on us.

'Come on Jen,' I say, pulling her arm. 'Let's go.'

But Jen isn't budging.

'Are you fucking kidding me?' Jen shouts. 'That's my friend's husband. You put your claws away.'

'I don't need to use claws.' Cassandra puts her drink down. 'Marc's always been mine. It's only a matter of time before he comes home. Now if you'll excuse me.'

She waves at a waiter, and he hurries over with a white fur coat.

Cassandra slips her arms into the fur. 'Tell Marc to wait up for me. I'll be home soon.'

She smiles graciously and strides away.

I put a hand to my mouth, feeling tears coming.

'Don't listen to a word of it,' says Jen, glaring after Cassandra. 'Marc *loves* you. *That's* the real Marc. Everything before was just an experiment. Come on – you were just saying it's time to forgive and forget.'

I clutch my champagne glass. 'I feel like I've been hit by a bus.'

'Marc was a *teenager* when he met Cassandra,' says Jen. 'Too young to know better.'

'I need to go back,' I say, pushing my glass on the bar. 'I need to talk to Marc.'

65

Back at the villa, I creep upstairs to check on Ivy, while Jen uses the bathroom.

The bedroom is dark, and I expect to see Tanya sleeping on the daybed.

But Tanya is nowhere in the room.

Oh my god.

Ivy!

I nearly trip over my feet, hurrying to the cot.

Thank heavens.

My baby is sleeping soundly on a crisp, white sheet, her thumb pushed into her mouth.

But where on earth is Tanya? I know she wouldn't just leave Ivy like this.

'Sophia.' Marc's voice rings through the darkness, and I see the shadow of him, rigid in a Chesterfield chair.

Moonlight shines across one sharp cheekbone.

'Marc.' I grasp the cot in surprise. 'What are you doing here?'

'Waiting for you.'

'You didn't need to do that. Where's Tanya?'

'I relieved her.' Marc stands. 'A better question is, where were you?'

'Out with Jen.'

'Just Jen?' I feel his glare in the darkness.

'No,' I say. 'A whole lot of people.'

'Cassandra told me,' says Marc.

I feel sick. 'You talked to her?'

'She came to see me.'

I grab a pillow and throw it at him.

Marc catches it and places it on his chair. 'I want to know what happened tonight.'

'This was my first night out since Ivy was born,' I say. 'It's barely even midnight. Given what you've brought into my life recently, I'd have thought you'd be happy for me to be letting loose. I can't *believe*—'

'There were drugs at that party.' Marc stalks towards me. 'You put yourself in danger. If you're not old enough to choose your company wisely, then you should stay home.'

'We had nothing more than cocktails,' I say, meeting his glare. 'And who are you to tell me to stay home?'

'I'm your husband.'

'How dare you tell me what to do,' I snap, 'after you've been entertaining your ex-girlfriend—'

'There was no entertaining,' says Marc. 'She had something to tell me. We talked briefly. And that was that.'

He says the words coolly. As if there's nothing wrong at all. But fireworks explode in my chest.

I shake my head, furious. 'I came back willing to forgive you. To move on.'

'Cassandra was concerned,' Marc growls.

'Oh, like hell she was,' I say, barely holding back my rage. 'She wants you back.'

Marc turns to the moon, shining through the latticed window. 'I already told her. I have no intention of revisiting the past.'

Ivy stirs in her cot.

'And why would you say something like that?' I hiss.

'It was … necessary.' He turns back to me. 'We're moving off the point. Right now, it's your behaviour I'm concerned about.'

'Don't talk to me like I'm a child.'

'Then don't act like a child.' He walks around the bed and pulls back the duvet. 'It's late. You've been drinking. Get some sleep. Maybe you'll see sense in the morning.'

'Don't tell me what to do.' I sit on the velvet sofa and cross my arms. 'I'll go to bed when I'm good and ready. You can go now. I don't want you here.'

'I'll leave you to your temper tantrum.' Marc goes to the cot, places a gentle hand on Ivy's chest, then stalks out of the room.

When the door closes, I climb into bed and burst into tears.

A few minutes later, I hear Jen's voice.

'Soph?' she says softly, and I know she's standing right by the bed. 'I heard … a bit of that. I didn't mean to listen in. I just came up to check on you. Do you want me to stay?'

I shake my head at the duvet. 'I just want to be alone.'

66

I don't sleep well that night, and wake at Ivy's every murmur and movement.

My furious conversation with Marc keeps running around my mind.

How dare he lecture me about going out, when his ex-girlfriend visited him late at night?

Oh god. I am so angry I can barely think straight.

Images of Cassandra, with her fur coat and red fingernails, at the door of Marc's villa ...

How could he even *speak* to her? Doesn't he know how much pain she's caused me?

I was ready to forgive and forget. But now I'm not so sure.

Letting go of Marc ... could I do it?

Surely anything is better than this pain. Jealousy is eating me up inside.

Ivy gives a little murmur, and I rest a hand on her back, watching her sleep.

Marc is the love of my life. There will never be anyone like him, ever again. But if he wants Cassandra ...

Stop thinking like that. It's crazy.

But I can't help it.

What if Marc does have unfinished business? What if she can give him things I can't?

'Sophia, wake up.' A hand shakes my shoulder.

Through sleep-softened eyelids, I see Tanya's anxious face.

'Is it late?' I say, pulling myself up in bed. I look around for Ivy, and to my relief see her still sleeping in the cot.

'No. It's still early.' Tanya perches on the edge of my bed. 'But you have to see this before everyone else does.'

'See what?' I blink at the sunlight.

Tanya waves a newspaper in front of my face.

'What is it?' I ask, my mouth feeling dry.

'A French tabloid.' Tanya drops the paper on my lap.

I try to focus on the blurred front-page image.

Oh god.

'It's—'

67

'It's you,' says Tanya. 'And Cassandra.'

The front page is split into two pictures.

One is a beautiful, posed red-carpet shot of Cassandra, all red lips and glossy hair. The other is me, talking to Jen and Tobias on the yacht deck.

My face is blurred, and Tobias is leaning attentively towards me.

I scan the article, trying to make sense of it.

'Do you know any French?' I ask Tanya.

'A bit,' she says. 'I did it for A-level.'

'Do you know what the article says?' I ask.

Tanya hesitates. 'Sort of. It says Cassandra was comforting Marc last night. While you were out partying.'

I close my eyes. 'Oh god.'

Turning the page, I see a grainy, night-time shot of Cassandra at the door of Marc's villa.

She's wearing lacy underwear, sheer enough to show her nipples. Around her shoulders hangs the white fur coat she wore last night.

'What happened to her dress?' I spit.

'God knows,' says Tanya.

I throw back the duvet. 'I need to talk to Marc. Right now. Will you watch Ivy?'

My feet are bare as I run across the complex towards Marc's beach villa.

As lawn turns to soft sand, I imagine Cassandra taking this same walk last night, high heels sinking into the ground.

Did she take her dress off before she got to Marc's villa? Or did she come inside and …

The villa feels silent as I approach folding glass doors, but I sense Marc is awake.

I take deep breaths and lift my fist to knock. But before my knuckles hit the glass, Marc appears. He's wearing grey sweatpants and nothing else, his toned torso long and muscular.

'Sophia.' Marc pulls the door open.

I see white tape wrapped around his knuckles, torn in places with blood showing through.

'You've been boxing,' I say.

He nods. 'For some reason, I felt the urge to punch something.'

'You saw the newspaper?' I ask.

'Come inside.'

68

The beach villa is made of white wood, with two walls of bi-folding glass.

Breakfast is laid out on the wooden veranda outside, and I see an untouched basket of croissants.

'Did you eat?' Marc asks.

'Not yet.' I scuff my bare foot back and forth on bare wood floorboards. 'I'm not really hungry.'

'Sophia—' Marc crosses his arms.

'Please Marc.' I look up at him, knowing my eyes are brimming with tears. 'There are more important things to talk about. I couldn't eat, even if I wanted to.'

Marc pulls open the veranda doors and strolls out into the morning sun. He pours coffee and offers me a cup.

'Take this, at least,' he insists, as I walk outside to join him.

'Thank you.' The warm cup feels comforting.

'Would you sit down?' he asks.

I shake my head. 'I'm fine standing.'

'Good god, must you always be so headstrong?' Marc pulls out a white-wood chair. 'Just sit down. Please.'

Reluctantly, I take a seat.

Marc picks up his own coffee and takes a sip. 'I already told you Cassandra came to see me.'

I give a curt laugh. 'You didn't tell me what she was wearing. Or what she wasn't wearing.'

Marc eyes fix on me. 'I have no idea what she was wearing.'

'Oh come on. You didn't notice she was in her underwear?'

'I'm telling the truth, Sophia.' He puts his cup down, placing both palms flat on the table. 'I was far more interested in what she was telling *me*. About you. I didn't even let her inside. You, on the other hand, were looking extremely friendly with Tobias Blatch.'

I look away from him. 'Nothing happened.'

'Oh yes.' He takes a seat opposite me. 'I could see how innocent things were. By the way he was looking at you.'

'You can hardly complain,' I say. 'There's a picture of a half-naked woman coming to your room.'

'She came *to* my room,' says Marc. 'Not inside. Christ – when she told me what was going on at that party, I nearly marched straight out and carried you home over my shoulder.'

'So why didn't you?' My words are softer now.

'You were already on your way back,' he says, taking my hand across the table. I feel the soft, cotton bandage wrapped around Marc's hand, and the angry blood smattering his knuckles.

'How could you have known that?' I ask.

'Does it matter?'

'Yes. It matters,' I say.

He grips my hand tight. 'I had security follow you.'

Waves crash, and the sky overhead turns ominously grey.

I blink at Marc, not quite believing what I'm hearing. When it sinks in, I snatch my hand from his.'

'You had me *followed*?' I shout.

'What did you expect me to do, Sophia?' Marc crosses his arms. 'You were upset. Not in a sound frame of mind. Anything could have happened.'

I get to my feet. 'When are you going to realise I'm a grown up?'

'When are you going to stop acting like a child?' Marc stands too, palms back on the table.

'Oh, so it's grown up to have me followed?' I shout. 'I thought we were supposed to love each other. Trust each other.'

'This isn't about trust,' Marc growls. 'It's about safety.'

'Oh really?' My eyes drop to his bloodied, bound fists. 'Because from the state of your knuckles, this is about jealousy.'

'You're jealous too,' says Marc darkly.

'Any wife would be jealous if a half-naked ex-girlfriend visited her husband late at night. It's just disrespectful,' I shout back.

Marc's eyes drop to his knuckles. 'Cassandra doesn't have a lot of boundaries. There's no sense making an issue of it. I told you – I didn't even let her in.'

'That's not what the papers think,' I snap.

'Since when did papers tell the truth?' His eyes find mine, and they're suddenly soft, blue and light. 'Look, I had no idea Cassandra was going to pay me that late night visit. But I'm glad she did. You could have got yourself in some serious trouble.'

My throat feels thick and tight. 'She told me last night that I could never have what you and she had. That you would come back to her. Did you know that?'

Marc comes towards me. 'Look, for what it's worth, I told Cassandra her visit wasn't appropriate. But I appreciated the information she brought. God knows, security didn't know you were getting into that sort of trouble.'

'I wasn't.' I'm caught in his eyes now.

'You might not have meant to do anything,' Marc continues, 'but Tobias could have had other ideas. You've had your drink spiked before. You can hardly expect me not to worry.' He takes both my hands, swinging them, toying them back and forth. 'For what it's worth, I'm sorry.'

'For what?'

'For having you followed,' says Marc, his eyes still light and holding mine. 'And – I'm sorry about this article. Christ, I should know by now how Cassandra works.'

'Do you think she set up the photo?' I blink up at him.

'Who else could have done it?' He squeezes my hands.

'How can you not hate her for doing that?' I ask.

'I wouldn't waste my energy.' He takes a step closer, pulling me against him and stroking my hair. 'Cassandra has enough of her own demons, believe me.'

'I have to shoot a scene with her this morning,' I murmur into his chest.

'No. You don't.' His hand carries on rhythmically stroking. 'I want her off the movie.'

'If that happens, she'll have won,' I say. 'You were right Marc. This movie is a challenge. I need to learn. Test myself.'

'This is a test too far,' Marc growls, and I feel the words in his chest.

'No. I signed up for this movie. I made a promise to Nadia.'

'This isn't about winning, Sophia.' He takes my hand.

'Of course not. It's about being a professional.' I step back, looking up at him. 'Marc, I don't want you there. When I shoot my first scene with Cassandra. I want to handle this myself.'

He frowns. 'Cassandra is a strong character.'

'So am I.'

69

'So where the fuck is she?' Nadia paces by the swimming pool, hands on leather-clad hips.

Cassandra is late. Very late. And no one knows where she is.

The crew have assembled by the swimming pool, and I've been bronzed and buffed and bikini dressed, all ready to play the out-of-control daughter.

My stomach has been twisting itself over since I met Marc earlier.

Nadia checks her rose-gold watch. 'Jesus!' she shouts. 'This isn't anything to do with the newspapers this morning, is it? Sophia?'

'I doubt it,' I say, thinking, *because Cassandra set up that article.*

Nadia grabs a glass of fresh orange juice and hands it to me. 'Here. Drink this. You look pale. Out until the early hours last night. Right?'

'Not quite,' I laugh. 'I was home by midnight. Don't believe everything you read in the papers.'

'I know, I know honey.' Nadia puts a friendly arm around my shoulder. 'We all know it's nonsense. As if Marc and Cassandra could have a history! I mean, come on. Marc was *sixteen* when they worked together.'

I look away. *Don't remind me.*

Nadia turns to the main villa. 'Okay, enough is enough. Cassandra must still be in bed or something. I'll send a runner.'

'I'll check the villa,' I say.

'What?' Nadia's arm drops from my shoulder.

'I'll go find Cassandra,' I say. 'Tell her it's time for the scene.'

'After the article this morning?' Nadia shakes her head. 'Why would you do that?'

Because it's the perfect way to show Cassandra I'm not scared of her.

'Um ... I should talk to her,' I tell Nadia. 'About the newspaper. Smooth things over.'

'Well ... if you're sure.' Nadia looks like she's about to say something else. But then she gets distracted by a cameraman lugging a big projection screen behind the pool. 'Not like that, Phil! Jesus – move it five metres left. Oh my goodness! If you want something done right, do it yourself.'

My thoughts exactly.

70

Cassandra's bedroom is on the first floor, towards the back of the villa.

The door looks innocent enough. Thick, polished wood with a wrought iron handle. But my hand is shaking as I go to knock.

Maybe this is a bad idea …

Then I hear a noise.

My knuckles hesitate.

The sound is kind of like someone coughing or choking. I step back.

Then I hear the noise again – a sort of choking sound. And something else.

Thump, thump, thump.

Now I'm worried.

What's happening in there?

I take the handle and push the door open.

Oh. My. God.

Cassandra is lying completely naked on the bed, ankles and wrists bound with white rope and a velvet blindfold over her eyes.

I see the long, muscular bronzed back of a man, moving back and forth between her legs.

He has her bound ankles resting over his shoulder, and holds them in place as he moves.

'You want it, baby?' says the man, moving back and forth.

Neither Cassandra nor the man are aware of me.

'That's it,' the man says. 'You're mine. You want it harder?'

Oh god. That *voice*.

With a shudder, I realise I know it. More than know it, actually.

Suddenly, the man spins into focus. His long, tanned back. His blond hair. His muscular arms.

Leo.

I hear rhythmic slapping, and Cassandra moans.

'That's it baby, that's it,' says Leo.

Oh my god. Oh my *god*.

Leo and Cassandra.

I close the door quickly, leaning against it, my heart pounding.

What am I going to do?

I need to speak to Marc.

71

Marc's head snaps up, as I charge into the beach villa.

He's sitting on the veranda, our baby on his lap.

'Sophia.' Marc puts Ivy to his chest and reaches me in three strides. 'What happened?'

I swallow, willing the tears to stay back. How do I describe what I just saw?

'It's okay.' Marc reaches an arm around my shoulders and pulls me close. 'Whatever it is, it's okay. Ivy's safe. You're safe. Just tell me.'

I take in a deep breath, feeling the hardness of Marc's chest and softness of Ivy's little body. 'Cassandra and Leo. I just saw them in bed together.'

'Christ. Oh Christ.'

'I need to tell Jen.' I wipe tears from my eyes.

'Slow down.' Marc puts a hand to my shoulder. 'What did you see?'

'Enough.' I swallow. 'Believe me.'

'Fucking Leo. I'll kill him.' He clutches Ivy tight to him. 'The man is an idiot. A complete idiot.'

'Jen won't forgive him,' I say, feeling hardness in my chest. 'It'll be over between them. But she has to know.'

'Where is she?' Marc turns to the door.

'I suppose … town or something. She can't be in the villa or Leo would never have … Oh god. Here – let me take her.'

Marc passes Ivy to me, gently supporting her head. 'Think carefully about this, Sophia.'

'What other option is there?' I sway back and forth with Ivy.

'Have Leo tell her.' Marc crosses his arms.

Across the beach, waves rip into each other and foam sprays up.

'I think Cassandra wanted to get caught,' I say, kissing Ivy's head. 'She must have known someone would come and get her.'

'I wouldn't put it past her.' Marc growls. 'This is a whole new world of fucked up. She's trying to hurt you through your friend.'

'It takes two, Marc' I say, cuddling Ivy close. 'Leo isn't an innocent victim.'

'I beg to differ on that,' says Marc. 'Certainly an innocent idiot. At any rate, this has already gone too far. I want Cassandra gone.'

'Won't she be under contract?' I ask.

'There are ways around contracts.' He turns and looks out to sea. 'Money, usually.'

'So you're going to buy her off the film?' I ask.

He gives a swift nod. 'If I have to.'

'The papers will have a field day,' I say, turning Ivy so she can see the water. 'I can just imagine the articles …'

'There are ways around that too,' Marc replies.

I feel myself nodding. 'Okay. Do what you have to do.'

'Take Ivy for a walk on the beach,' says Marc, grabbing a t-shirt and pulling it over his head. 'I'll take care of everything.'

It's warm, almost sticky hot, as I push Ivy by the lapping waves.

The stroller won't move in the sand, but there's a path of old railway sleepers leading right along our private stretch of coast. I bump Ivy along them, and she falls asleep straight away.

I'm ten minutes or so down the beach, when I hear the soft thuds of a jogger behind me.

I turn, knowing it must be someone from the villa, and am surprised to see Benjamin Van Rosen pounding over the sand.

He's wearing loose, white shorts and a navy runner's t-shirt.

'I didn't know you ran,' I call out.

Benjamin slows as he reaches me. 'I didn't know you walked.'

'I do.' I try for a smile. 'All the time.'

Despite our tensions, it's good to see Benjamin. Right now, he feels like a friendly face.

'So what are you doing out here, all alone?' Benjamin asks, falling into my pace.

'I'm … Marc is sorting something out on set.' My hands grip the stroller handles. 'I'm giving him space.'

Benjamin laughs. 'Daddy didn't want you around while he was doing grown-up business?'

'You don't need to put it like that. So what are *you* doing out here?'

'Running off the pain.' He stops walking for a moment, picking up his foot to do a calf stretch.

I stop too. 'What pain?'

'I've gone and done something stupid.' He picks up his other foot, gritting his teeth as he pulls it to the back of his thigh. 'I've fallen in love with somebody.'

I laugh. 'How will all those married women feel about that?'

'You shouldn't joke.' He drops his foot. 'Love is painful.'

'Wow, Benjamin,' I tease. 'You're using the past tense. That means you've been in love more than once. I'd never have picked you as the type.'

He cocks his head. 'Of course I've been in love before. But that was nothing compared to this. This is real, grown-up love. Have you ever felt like you'd just die if you didn't have somebody?' His eyes are on mine now.

I start walking again, feeling uncomfortable. 'Of course,' I say lightly. 'When I met Marc. Nice weather this morning, isn't it? Nadia was worried about rain, but … it looks fine.'

Benjamin walks alongside me. 'So Nadia let you leave the set, huh?'

'I *should* be shooting a scene,' I say. 'But … stuff is happening.'

'Stuff?' He keeps pace. 'Here – let me take the stroller.'

'It's fine,' I say, keeping a firm grip on the handles. 'Thanks, but … Ivy can sense if someone else pushes her. She'll wake up.'

'So what *stuff?*' Benjamin asks.

I bite my lip. Everyone is going to know this sooner or later. I may as well tell him. 'If you must know,' I say, 'Marc is … well he's talking to Nadia about Cassandra.'

'Oh?'

'Cassandra has betrayed a trust,' I stammer, 'and … it's best if she's not in the movie anymore.'

Benjamin laughs. 'Could I have that in English please?'

'I just saw Cassandra and Leo … well you're an adult. You can work out the rest.'

'You're kidding me.' Benjamin puts a hand on the stroller handle, forcing me to stop. 'The two of them?'

I nod.

'Jesus.' He lets out a low whistle. 'I thought Falkirk was getting married to that friend of yours. Nice girl, too. Why would he screw it up?'

'I have no idea,' I say, feeling stupid tears well up again. 'But Jen's going to be devastated.'

Benjamin watches me for a moment, cocking his head. Then he turns abruptly, and jogs back down the path towards the villa.

'Benjamin?' I call. 'Where are you going?'

'To punch Leo Falkirk in the face,' he shouts back, not slowing his pace.

I turn the stroller around, racing to catch up with him. 'What?' I shout, as the pram wheels bump over sleepers. 'Wait. *Please*. Why would you do that?'

Benjamin slows, but still doesn't turn.

'Because he hurt your friend.' The words float back to me on the breeze.

'Why does that matter to you?' I call out, still hurrying to catch up with him.

When I finally reach him, Benjamin turns and says, 'Because I love you, Sophia. I love you.'

72

Oh god.

'Benjamin …' I shake my head.

There's hurt in his light-blue eyes.

'Me and my big mouth, huh?' says Benjamin, managing a laugh.

'You love me?' I say. 'You hardly know me. Are you making a joke?'

The hurt doesn't leave his eyes. 'I've never been more serious about anything in my life.'

My hands squeeze the foam stroller handles. 'Look, if this is some sort of chat up line—'

Benjamin slips hands into his pockets. 'It isn't. I know it's hopeless.'

'Listen.' I let out a long breath. 'Is this because I'm married? Like some married-woman conquest thing?'

Benjamin gives a harsh laugh. 'None of the above. I just … think about you. I dream about you. I can hardly stand knowing I can't have you. You're the woman I want to have kids with. I don't even *want* you to leave your husband. Not if it would make you unhappy. How about that? But then again … maybe you could be happier with me. Someone who isn't so controlling. I hate that he might hurt you. That you might not know what making love really is.'

'I love Marc.'

'Pretty fucked up kind of love, if you ask me,' says Benjamin. 'I mean, Jesus. Is he your husband or your father? But if you're happy …'

'Benjamin. You're … great. But …' I put a hand on his arm.

'You know, this is karma.' He puts his hand over mine, clasping it tight to his arm. 'All those girls I messed around. Some of them even left their husbands for me. And here you are. In love with some other guy.' He looks at my hand under his, eyes sad. 'I didn't mean to tell you. It just came out.'

My hand slides from his arm. 'Thank you. I'm flattered. But there's another girl out there for you.'

'I'm not so sure about that. I've met a lot of girls. Believe me.'

I nod. 'I believe you. Can we still be friends?'

'Good friends?' He raises a flirtatious eyebrow.

'Just friends.'

'I still want to knock Leo Falkirk's teeth out,' he insists.

'That's sweet,' I say. 'But I have a feeling Jen will do it for you.'

'I'll see you on set, okay?' Benjamin turns and jogs away.

I watch him, thinking, *Wow. Today really is the day for broken hearts.*

There's an awkward atmosphere back at the villa. I can sense it even as I push Ivy across the lawns. By the time I reach the swimming pool, I can almost touch it.

Crew members quieten as I approach.

'Where's Nadia?' I ask a cameraman.

'She went inside.' He doesn't look at me.

'And Cassandra?' I ask.

The cameraman still doesn't look up. 'You'd have to ask Nadia about that.'

73

I find Nadia inside the main villa, pacing around the light, airy lounge area.

Behind her, bright tropical fish swim in a crystal clear aquarium. They dart in and around as she shouts, 'I mean, *Jesus* Christ. You don't shit where you eat.'

Nadia takes a fierce sip from a blue espresso cup, and rolls her eyes to the heavens.

I see Marc by the window, dressed in a black suit and frowning.

'Hi,' I say tentatively, parking up the stroller. 'Um … anyone want to fill me in?'

Nadia gives me a tired smile. 'Sure. You want to sit down?'

I sit on the edge of the sofa, looking towards Marc.

His eyes find mine, silently asking if I'm okay.

I give a weary smile and tiny nod. But I'm not really okay. Not until I know what's going on.

'So what's happening?' I ask.

'Upheaval.' Nadia tips her head back. 'Movies would be so much simpler without actors. It's like one big soap opera sometimes. Trying to keep one person happy. And then someone else …'

'Where's Cassandra?' I ask.

'Gone,' says Nadia.

I should feel warm relief sink into my stomach. But I don't.

'And … she was okay about leaving?' I ask.

Marc lets out a harsh laugh.

'No,' Nadia admits. 'She was … not okay. But she made her bed. I couldn't keep her on. I'm a family woman. The whole set is my family. We work together. You don't do that to your sisters.'

'What about Leo?' I ask.

'He's still on the movie,' says Nadia, taking a seat beside me.

I turn to her. 'But he was just as much to blame.'

Nadia smiles. 'I love you for your fairness. But he did nothing malicious. Just stupid. Cassandra … I don't believe she did anything by accident.'

'Leo was the one in the relationship,' I say.

'He is a silly boy,' says Nadia, slapping her knees for emphasis. 'But I've decided he can stay. For now.' She stands and goes to the fish tank, sending yellow fish swimming in different directions. 'Now we have a decision to make. Do we tell Leo's girlfriend, or hope he has the balls to do it himself?'

'Leo won't say a word,' Marc growls, striding to the sofa. 'You can count on that. Not unless someone forces his hand.'

'I'm going to tell her,' I announce, standing.

'Are you sure?' says Nadia.

'I can't keep a secret from Jen, even if I wanted to.' I head for Ivy's stroller. 'She'll have it out of me. Anyway, this is going to get out, isn't it? Cassandra clearly knows her way around a tabloid. Someone has to tell Jen before she reads about it in the newspaper.'

'Sophia is right,' says Marc. 'It will come out.'

'Listen,' says Nadia. 'You two take the afternoon off, okay? I need to rejig some things. Work out how we'll move forward. There'll be no more filming today.'

I blink at her. 'But we're already behind –'

'It's okay.' She waves a hand. 'Movies always run behind. And we always catch up.'

'Well whatever happens with filming, I need to find Jen right now,' I decide.

'She's … with Leo,' says Nadia. 'They're both in town. I sent them away before I talked to Cassandra. Leo has no idea what's going on.'

Marc frowns. 'Yet.'

74

The villa complex has a collection of sports cars for guest use, so Marc drives me into town in a red Venturi.

Ivy stays with Tanya, sleeping soundly in her stroller.

'Jen's shopping,' I tell Marc, as we zoom past a field of plump, purple grapes, then swerve around a white-washed vineyard.

It's hard to read my phone while we're driving so fast, but I'm just about managing it. 'She's ditched Leo,' I continue. 'He's looking for surfer gear. And she's in Saint Eves, or something. Do you know it?'

'You mean Yves Saint Laurent?' says Marc, giving the wheel a sharp turn. 'The extremely famous French designer?'

I laugh. 'You know your way around designers.'

He eases the car around a corner. 'I'm offered a lot of free clothes.'

The pavements become wider, and I see clutches of beautiful, tanned men and women swinging shopping bags.

As I'm watching the handsome crowd, I see a familiar face amid the shoppers.

Leo.

His tanned, muscular body is decorated casually in a faded surfer t-shirt and cargo shorts.

In London, Leo would be mobbed. But in Saint-Tropez

there are too many rich, famous people for him to stand out.

'Wait!' I point to the busy pavement. 'There's Leo.'

Marc skids the car to a halt.

'Wait here.' He leaps out.

Before I know what's happening, Marc is striding towards Leo, jaw hard, eyes furious.

'Oh god.' I struggle with the seat buckle. But I'm too late. By the time I've jumped out of the car, Marc has already knocked Leo to the ground.

Leo lies on the pavement, rubbing his jaw.

'Get up,' Marc barks, fists clenched.

'*Man*.' Leo's eyes swim in and out of focus. He tries to stand, but falls back onto his elbow. '*Jesus*! Blackwell. What the hell is wrong with you?'

A crowd have gathered and cameras flash.

'Marc.' I run to him. 'You've done enough.'

Marc massages his fist. 'No. Not nearly enough.'

Leo clambers to his feet, and spits blood on the pavement. 'I haven't been *near* Sophia. I swear it.'

'We should go,' I mutter, aware of the ever growing crowd. 'I want to find Jen.'

Marc is still glowering at Leo. 'I thought you were a good man, Leo Falkirk. I was wrong. Very wrong.'

'What did I do?' Leo shouts, as I pull Marc back to the car.

'Think it over,' says Marc, without turning. 'I'm sure you'll work it out.'

'He's fucking crazy,' I hear Leo tell the crowd.

Marc stops walking. 'You want to tell your story here, Leo? In front of everyone? Or have you humiliated your fiancée enough already?'

Leo's bronzed face goes pale. 'Oh shit. How did you—'

'You were hardly discreet.' Marc turns. 'Next time, lock the door.'

Leo puts a hand to his forehead. 'Jesus Christ. Does Jen know?'

'Not yet,' says Marc through gritted teeth.

Leo's eyes brim with hurt. 'But she will soon, right? Listen, you have to know. There are two sides—'

'Nothing excuses your behaviour,' says Marc. 'Absolutely nothing.'

75

Back in the Venturi, Marc grips the steering wheel, his knuckles white.

'Maybe we should have listened to him,' I say. 'Sometimes things aren't as they seem.'

'You saw him stark naked, screwing another woman,' Marc barks. 'It's despicable.'

'But still,' I say. 'He deserves to tell his side.'

'You're very forgiving of that man, Sophia.' Marc spins the car onto the road. 'Is there something I should know?'

'Don't go getting jealous again,' I say.

He accelerates. 'Let's just find Jen, shall we?'

I pull out my phone, checking my messages. 'She's in Francesca Donà right now. A jewellery store. It's—'

'I know where it is.'

Marc waits in the car, as I head into Francesca Donà. This is news I want to deliver alone.

Predictably, Jen is gazing at larger than life jewellery – huge gold collar necklaces, cuff-length bangles and diamonds the size of golf balls.

She's wearing the perfect Saint-Tropez outfit – a sixties-style sundress that shows off her cleavage and waist, cork platforms and giant Audrey Hepburn sunglasses.

Designer shopping bags hang from her arms.

'Soph!' She grins pink lipstick at me, but I can see behind the sunglasses she looks a little tired. 'How come you got the afternoon off then?'

'The filming got cancelled today,' I say, as a sales girl approaches me with a tray of tall, fizzing drinks.

'Kir Royal, ladies?' the girl asks, looking at Jen, then me.

'Thanks,' I say, grabbing a drink and thinking, *I'm going to need this*.

'Hair of the dog,' says Jen, taking a glass. 'Well if you're game, I am. God – I was so hung over this morning, but then Leo and I started arguing over *everything* and now I'm exhausted.'

'Arguing?' My hand tightens on the glass.

'You know how it's been.' Jen knocks back half her drink.

'Listen,' I say, taking a much-needed gulp of fizzing pink cocktail. 'You've been shopping all morning. Shall we go sit somewhere? Get a coffee or something?'

'Great idea!' Jen hands her half-drunk cocktail back to the sales girl. 'Oh my god, I know the *best* place. This funky little patisserie around the corner. It is *so* French. They have the most amazing pastries.'

'Let's go.'

76

The patisserie is called Crème Anglais. It specialises in custard pastries, decorated with thick caramelised sugar.

Over coffee and buttery tarts, Jen tells me how fed up she is with Leo.

'He bought me all these clothes,' Jen moans. 'And then turns around and says *I'm* controlling for buying my *own* handbag!'

'Leo bought you clothes?' I say.

'I know,' says Jen. 'Weird, right? He even *suggested* the shopping trip. I thought for a moment that maybe we were sharing an interest for a change. But he barely lasted an hour before he got bored.'

'How is Leo?' I ask, trying to sound innocent.

'He's fine.' Jen cuts a square of pastry. 'Why?'

'Just asking.' I tap nervous fingers on my coffee cup.

'Come on Soph.' Jen drops a square of pastry in her mouth.

I turn my espresso cup on its pretty pink saucer. 'There's something I need to tell you.'

'Spill it,' says Jen, wiping pastry crumbs from her lips.

Oh God.

'It's … about Leo,' I admit.

Jen's eyes fill with concern. 'What is it?'

My stomach turns over.

Can I really do this? Can I really tear her world apart?

It's not really a choice. This sort of news gets out, one way or another. This is the least humiliating way.

'Nadia threw Cassandra off the movie today,' I begin.

'That's big news.' Jen leans forward. 'What happened?'

'Well, you know how Nadia sees a film set as one big family?' I reply.

'I didn't know that.' Jen cuts more pastry. 'But carry on.'

'Cassandra did something that hurt the family,' I say, looking at my coffee cup.

'Oh wow.' Jen's eyes widen. 'What did she do?'

'Something bad. Jen … this is to do with Leo.'

77

'Soph? What do you mean?' Jen lowers her fork to the plate.

'Cassandra and Leo ... oh God.' I shake my head. 'I can't even say it.'

'Soph?'

'I saw them together this morning,' I gabble.

Jen shakes her head, confused. 'But Leo was with me this morning.'

'Before that,' I continue. 'He was in Cassandra's room. Her ... her bedroom.'

Jen's eyes widen. 'In her bedroom? *Why?*'

Oh god.

'They were ... ' I let out a long sigh. 'Together.'

'You mean ...' Jen shakes her head, eyes wide. 'Like having sex together?'

I nod.

'He was *fucking* her? That old cow with the fake tits?' Jen puts a hand to her stomach. 'He *wouldn't*. Not Leo. I mean, I know we're not getting along so well, but he'd never ... I mean, he's not *like* that.'

'I know,' I say. 'He's a good man. I still can't believe it. But I saw them.'

'Tell me exactly what you saw.' Jen leans across the table, eyes manic.

'Jen, don't do that to yourself. This is already bad enough.'

'I'm serious, Soph. Maybe they were rehearsing a scene. Or … he was just visiting her or something.'

I take a deep breath. 'They were both naked, Jen. And … well you can work out the rest.'

'That bastard!' Jen screams so loud that half the café turn to look at us.

'Jen—'

'Bastard, bastard, bastard!' She pounds the table with her fist.

If there was anyone left in the café not looking at us, they are now.

'I'm so sorry …' I begin.

'I'm going to burn all his stuff and cut his bollocks off.' Jen leaps to her feet, 'Oh *God* Soph. What the fuck am I going to do? We were supposed to be getting married. That cheating scumbag son-of-a-bitch. I can't believe he'd do this. *Leo*. I thought he was one of the nice ones.'

'He *is* a good guy.' I stand to. 'That's what makes this all so weird.'

'Where's my bag?' She looks around, knocking her chair back into someone else's. 'He's a scumbag. Oh Jesus Christ … I knew something was wrong. But I had no idea he'd do something like this. I'm going to find him and kill him.'

'Um … Marc already found him,' I admit.

'He did?' Jen grabs her bag from the floor, flinging it over her shoulder.

'And knocked him out,' I say.

'Well that's a start I suppose.' Jen bundles her shopping bags over her arm. 'But I still owe him a punch or two. Are you coming with me?'

'Jen, maybe this isn't a good idea,' I say, following her out of the café. 'You're in shock. We should go back to the villa, just the two of us, and let you calm down.'

'I will not calm down,' says Jen, marching along. 'Not until I've done some physical harm to that cheating piece of shit.'

'I know you, Jen,' I say, hurrying after her, out onto the street. 'You don't make good decisions when you're angry.'

Jen isn't listening. 'And Cassandra!' she rages, flicking sunglasses on her eyes. 'That fucking bitch. Has she left the villa?'

'She's gone,' I say, blinking in the strong sunshine. 'You know, maybe you and Leo—'

'Forget it Soph. No way.' She marches along the pavement.

'You don't even know what I was going to say,' I say, catching up with her.

'You were going to say that maybe Leo and I can work things out,' says Jen. 'And it's not going to happen. No chance. Not ever.'

78

I spend the next half hour following Jen around the town, as she darts into Leo's favourite shops and calls his phone over and over again.

But his mobile doesn't answer, and we can't find him anywhere.

'He's probably waiting for you back at the villa,' I say.

'Hiding, more like,' Jen shrieks. 'The cowardly piece of shit can't even answer his phone.'

'Calm down, Jen.'

'That's not going to happen.'

Back at the villa, Jen heads straight to the suite she shares with Leo.

'If he's not in our room,' she shouts, climbing stairs two at a time. 'I'm going to take all his messy, scruffy fucking surfer bum clothes and throw them in the pool.'

I run upstairs after her.

When Jen flings open the bedroom, Leo is perched on the bed, forehead lined with worry.

He stands when he sees her. 'I was waiting for you. Please. Babe, listen – I wish you'd never found out this way.'

'You fucking bastard.' Jen throws shopping bags at him. 'Get out. Right now.'

'You have to listen to me,' Leo insists.

'No I don't,' Jen shouts.

'It was such a big mistake.' Leo stands. 'Everything was getting so heavy. So grown up. I couldn't handle it. I ... I fucked up big time.'

'Fine. If you won't leave, I will.' Jen goes to the wardrobe and flings clothes into her huge Armani suitcase.

Leo follows her to the wardrobe. 'We need to talk—'

'My solicitor will be in touch over all the wedding stuff,' Jen snaps.

'Jen, just *stop*.' Leo puts a hand on the wardrobe door. 'I'm a huge, massive shit. I know that. I just ... you made me feel like a child, you know? I wanted to feel like a man again.'

'What a fantastic man you are,' says Jen, flinging more clothes into the case. 'Cheating on your fiancée.'

'I don't love her, babe.' Leo puts a tentative hand on her arm. 'I love you. Please. It was just some stupid thing.'

Jen whirls around. 'How many times did it happen?'

'Twice.' He looks at the floor. 'And that last time, I knew it had to end. It was just ... sex, you know? She thought I was worth something. Made me feel I wasn't such a useless waste of space.'

'You're not a useless waste of space, Leo,' says Jen, zipping up her suitcase. 'But fucking hell, you need to grow up.'

'Oh come on.' Leo's hand drops from her arm. 'You think I'm worth shit – that's the problem.'

'That's not true.' She pulls her suitcase towards the door.

'No?' He follows her. 'When was the last time you let me choose where to take you out? Or pick something for our apartment? Or even go down on you, for fuck's sake?'

I take that as my cue to leave.

'Soph?' Jen catches up with me. 'Wait right there.'

'Maybe you two should have some time,' I say.

'We don't need time,' Jen insists, straightening her bag on its wheels.

'We do,' says Leo. 'We need to talk. Work things out.'

Jen turns to him. 'There's nothing to talk about. The trust has gone. That's it. I'm going straight to the airport.'

'Please Jen. Don't do this,' Leo begs.

Jen pulls her suitcase over the threshold. 'Come on Soph. Let's go.'

'Jen, *please*.' Leo rushes to the door, trying to bar her way.

Jen drops her sunglasses on her nose and pushes straight past Leo, bumping her suitcase over his bare foot.

'Times that pain by a million,' Jen shouts, 'and you'll know how I feel. You've just torn my life apart.'

79

I don't bother trying to talk Jen out of going to the airport. And I don't argue when she says she wants to travel alone.

I know Jen in this mood – she's not going to listen to reason. Maybe tomorrow, but not today.

As I watch the limo speed out the villa gates, I can't help thinking that she's being too hasty.

I know she's heartbroken. I'd probably want to run away too if I were her. But she loves Leo. I'm sure of that too.

As I watch the gates clank closed, Benjamin strides over the lawn. He's showered and changed after his run, and smells of soap and aftershave. Loose, checked shorts hang from his tanned legs and a straw hat shades his face.

'Where's your friend going?' he asks, watching the car.

'The airport,' I say.

'She left him?' Benjamin asks, incredulous.

I shrug. 'Jen doesn't mess around. One strike and you're out.'

Benjamin puts a hand on my shoulder. 'Are you okay?'

'Not really,' I admit. 'Those two were made for each other. They just don't realise it.'

'Do you want me to go after her?' Benjamin asks.

'Honestly, there's no point.' I give him a tired smile. 'She doesn't want to see anyone right now. Not even me.'

There's a line of limousines on the gravel, waiting to take villa guests into town. Benjamin waves one over.

'All the same,' he says, 'sometimes, people don't always know what's in their best interests.' He opens the car door. 'Let me try, okay?'

I frown at him, confused. 'You don't even know her.'

'Yes but …' He drops his hand from my shoulder. 'I want to do this for you. I can be very persuasive.'

'Honestly Benjamin, she didn't even want *me* going with her. She wants to be alone. I don't understand why—'

'She's wrong to be alone,' says Benjamin, climbing into the car. 'Right?'

'Probably,' I admit.

'Then let me try.' Benjamin slams the car door closed, and the limo creeps towards the gates.

Marc's long shadow falls over me. 'Where's Van Rosen going?'

'After Jen,' I say, watching the villa gates swing open and closed.

'Just when I thought life couldn't get any more interesting,' says Marc. 'Why did he have his hand on you?'

'No reason. He was just making a point, that's all.'

'Mm.' Marc puts an arm around my shoulder. 'And why would Van Rosen go after Jen?'

'He was being thoughtful,' I say.

Marc gives a curt laugh. 'That's a new one.'

'No. Honestly.' I lean into Marc's body. 'He didn't want her to be alone.'

'Ah. Now it makes sense.' He squeezes me tight. 'Jen is

vulnerable. So Van Rosen spies another easy conquest.'

'No, it's not like that at all.'

He did it for me.

But I don't want to tell Marc that.

'Well.' Marc kisses the top of my head. 'Perhaps he'll persuade her to come back. You never know.'

'Have you met Jen?' I say.

'Once or twice.' Marc offers half-smile of his. 'But you never know. In her vulnerable state, she might give in to Van Rosen's suggestions. Women are known to do that. Give in.'

'Is that what happened with us?' I say. 'I gave in to you?'

'Exactly right,' Marc replies. 'And in your case, I had no choice but to persist.'

'Oh really?' I laugh. 'Because as I remember, you were ready to give up on me at one point.'

'Never.' He kisses my head again. 'I would never have given up on you. But I fully expected you to give up on me.'

'Well you *are* a lot of hard work,' I say.

Marc squeezes me extra tight. 'You, Mrs Blackwell, need to be careful. Don't forget, I have a length of rope in the suitcase and many pairs of handcuffs.'

'Many pairs?' I say. 'I didn't realise you were so well prepared.'

'I was assuming you'd be disobedient,' says Marc. 'And I was right.'

'Are you referring to my night out?' I ask.

'Among other things.' Marc strokes my hair. 'Nights out are forbidden from now on. Except with your husband.'

'I hope you're joking,' I say, my voice firm.

'I'm not,' says Marc, equally firmly.

'I'll go out whenever I like,' I tell him, looking up. 'As long as Ivy is safe and well looked after.'

'Very well.' He looks down at me, eyes stern. 'I'll enjoy putting you in line afterwards.'

80

We spend the afternoon playing with Ivy in the swimming pool, while Nadia stalks around, making notes and shouting into her phone.

After an especially long and swear-word ridden phone conversation, she slumps by the pool on a wooden lounger.

'This is *shit*,' she tells no one in particular. 'All fucking day on the phone, and not one decent lead on a new Cassandra. Oh Jesus. I just hope we don't lose too much money over this. Or the movie will suffer.'

Marc, who's swirling a delighted Ivy in the water, comes to the pool edge.

'I have a good lead,' he says. 'And she can be available immediately.'

'You do?' Nadia's eyes brighten. 'Who?'

'Denise Crompton,' says Marc.

'Denise *Crompton*?' Nadia shakes her head. 'Marc, have you read the script? This mother isn't the nice, cuddly sort. Denise is totally wrong.'

'She can act anything you put in front of her,' Marc insists, bobbing Ivy up and down in the water.

'But she *looks* wrong,' says Nadia, coming to crouch at the water's edge.

'So change the script.' Marc swishes Ivy in the water again. 'Have the mother be supportive.'

Nadia stares at him for a moment. 'I suppose it *could* work. Let me think it over.'

'I can have her flown in tonight,' says Marc.

'*Tonight*?' Nadia's eyes widen. 'You're sure?'

'Positive.' Marc passes Ivy to me, and hauls himself out of the pool. 'I'll have a private jet organised and she'll be here by sunset.'

'Oh to hell with it,' says Nadia. 'Yes sure – we'll change the script. Jesus Christ. I've been on the phone all day, and you sort out my problem in five seconds.'

'You should have asked me in the first place.' Marc grabs his phone from the sun lounger.

'Sophia!' Nadia kneels by the poolside. 'Can you believe this man of yours?'

'Was Cassandra very upset?' I ask. 'When she left?'

Nadia glances back at Marc. 'It doesn't matter now. It was her own fault. If she was angry, well she'll just have to get over it.'

'So she *was* angry?' I ask.

'She was fucking furious,' shouts a cameraman, who's screwing together a tripod a few feet away. 'Hell hath no fury. That's what they say, isn't it? And those venomous parting words … *See you at the Riviera Film Festival …*'

A shiver goes through me.

'Oh Cassandra will calm down,' says Nadia, with a dismissive wave of her zebra-striped nails. 'She'll be in another movie within a week.'

I notice Marc is frowning. 'All the same, I've doubled security on set. I've had my share of vengeful women in the past.'

'I'll bet you have!' Nadia laughs. 'Keep them mean, keep them keen. Before Sophia came along, of course.'

'Oh I can be pretty mean to Sophia too,' says Marc, with a half smile.

'I don't want to know.' Nadia stands on blue high heels. 'Listen. I have the perfect idea. Let's all have a champagne dinner tonight to celebrate Denise's arrival. I'll have some script writers come along too – we can work out the new character.'

'Good idea,' says Marc. 'How about Caveau Vin?'

'Caveau Vin?' says Nadia. 'We won't get in there. No way.'

'I can get us in.' Marc gives a dismissive wave of his hand.

'You can?' Nadia is incredulous. '*All* of us?'

Marc nods.

Nadia claps her hands together. 'Perfect! You've got an evening gown in all those suitcases of yours, right Sophia?'

'Um ... sort of. How fancy are we talking?' I ask.

'Well put it this way,' says Nadia. 'France has the best restaurants in the world. And this is the best restaurant in France. So ... it's fancy. It's owned by a Swedish prince. I wouldn't be surprised if we bump into some members of the royal family. And the food – oh my god! Like works of art. You hardly want to eat it, it looks so beautiful.'

Marc frowns at me. 'Stop worrying. You'll be fine.'

'It's not the restaurant I'm worried about,' I say. '*See you at the Riviera Film Festival*. What does that mean?'

'Cassandra goes to Riviera every year,' says Nadia. 'That's all. You don't need to be worried. Security at the Riviera festival – wow. She'd never try anything stupid there.'

81

Later in the afternoon, I take Ivy for a walk around the grounds.

The gardens are beautiful, with bright purple lavender bushes, swirling privet hedge labyrinths and perfectly clipped, conical-shaped fir trees.

As I'm pushing the stroller back towards the main house, I see a limo crawling through the gates.

It pulls to a stop, and Benjamin climbs out holding his straw hat on his head.

'No Jen?' I ask, pushing the stroller over gravel.

'I was too late,' he says, walking to meet me. 'She was already on the plane.'

'Thank you.' I touch his wrist. 'For going.'

He shrugs, taking my hand and kissing the back of it. 'Just something you wanted. So ...'

'Benjamin.' I take my hand from his. 'About what you said earlier. On the beach.'

'Oh, that.' He tilts his hat back, and I see hurt in his blue eyes. 'It's all right. I'm not going to do anything stupid. Make any other wild confessions. But just so you know, I'd do anything for you.'

'Thank you. I ... I don't know what to say.'

His eyes find mine. 'Karma, huh? It's a bitch. You don't have any sisters or anything, do you?'

I laugh. 'No. Sadly not.'

'Shame.' He puts a hand on my shoulder. 'Listen. It's been good for me. This feeling. It's taught me a few things. I'll learn from it.'

I nod. 'Okay.'

'This movie will be great.' He plants a swift kiss on my cheek. 'Stay perfect. And if Marc ever gives you a hard time, you know where to come.' He gives me one last smile, then turns and walks towards the house.

'We're all out for dinner tonight,' I call after him. 'To meet Cassandra's replacement. Can you make it?'

He turns. 'Marc too?'

'Everyone.'

'Thanks,' he calls back. 'I think I'll skip it.'

'*This* is a restaurant?' I ask, as the limo drives Marc and I down a long gravel path, lined with tall, thin trees.

Up ahead is a stately home kind-of-place, with perfect lawns and lavender bushes.

'It was a royal holiday home, once upon a time,' says Marc.

The car pulls to a stop by an extremely grand winged building, and a suited man rushes to open our door.

'Welcome, Mr and Mrs Blackwell,' says the man, offering us a little bow. 'Please come this way.'

'Have you ever met the royal family before?' I whisper to Marc, as I climb out of the car.

'Once or twice.' Marc helps me out.

'Well which one is it? Once or twice?' I step onto gravel.

Marc climbs out after me. 'On several occasions. Ascot. Wimbledon. They're charming. Good people. Extremely polite.'

'I've never been anywhere like this.' I look over the building. 'What if I say the wrong thing? Or use the wrong fork or something?'

'There is nothing you could do wrong,' says Marc, taking my hand.

'But *royalty* come here,' I insist, still feeling nervous.

He squeezes my fingers. 'You'll be fine.'

82

Marc and I are shown into a marble-floored ballroom, the walls hung with gold-framed oil paintings.

We're served canapés on swirling dry ice, and champagne from magnum bottles.

'Where are the tables?' I ask, accepting a fizzing glass of champagne.

Marc points to golden doors up ahead. 'Through there. Relax.'

I nod, trying for a smile as a passing waiter offers me bright red triangles of caviar.

'Um ... thank you.' I take a canapé, but my shaking hand drops it on the marble floor.

'Oh my god. I'm so sorry.' I take a nervous sip of champagne.

'Not a problem, madam.' The waiter rests his tray. 'I'll have it dealt with.'

'Sophia, it's okay.' Marc squeezes my arm.

'No it's not.' I gulp more champagne. 'I'm dying of embarrassment.'

'It's fine. The waiters have seen worse.' Marc takes my champagne glass. 'Don't drink so quick. Or you'll be drunk.'

'That's the plan.' I'm joking. Sort of.

Marc frowns.

'Where's Nadia?' I ask.

'Late,' says Marc, handing my half-empty glass to a passing waiter. 'She's always late.'

'And what about Denise?' I ask, looking around. 'Shouldn't she be here by now?'

'She'll be here soon,' says Marc.

Behind us, an orchestra begins a slow classical piece.

'Mrs Blackwell?' Marc takes my hand. 'May I have this dance?'

'Here?' I say.

'Of course, here. Where else were you thinking?' Marc arranges my hands, positioning me in the right way.

'How did you learn to dance?' I ask, as he leads me around the room.

'For a movie.' He turns me quickly, catching me before I lose my footing. 'The Divine Act. There was a ballroom scene.'

'That scene was all of thirty seconds,' I say, following his feet.

'I'm dedicated to my craft.'

'I like dancing with you,' I whisper.

Marc presses his cheek to mine. 'I'll let you into a secret. I like dancing with you too.'

'It's a secret, is it?' I whisper back.

'Yes. You know, this is a good tutoring opportunity. Don't you think?'

'Here?' I ask.

'Why not?' Marc turns me again, and this time I follow his lead more gracefully.

'Well, we're in public for one,' I say, enjoying the strength of his locked arms.

'You may not have realised this, Sophia,' says Marc. 'But when the movie airs, it will be seen by millions of people.'

'Marc, I really don't think now is the time,' I insist.

'It's the perfect time. Look at where we are.' He leads me around the floor. 'Do you remember your lines for the ballroom dancing scene?'

'Of course.' I try to keep my balance as I'm whirled around. 'I've read them a hundred times.'

'Good.' Suddenly, Marc snaps into character. 'I knew you'd be lousy. I had no idea you'd be this lousy.'

I can't help smiling. He's so amazing – the way he transforms like this.

The actress in me can't help but play along. 'I'm *trying*, okay?' I pretend to lose my footing. 'It's my first time.'

'Your first time?' Marc shakes his head. 'Try harder, princess.'

'Just give me a chance.'

Our feet move together, picking out the music.

'Better,' says Marc, leading me into another turn.

We're in perfect rhythm now, and Marc swirls me around the room.

'Hey. Not too bad.' Marc lifts me and drops me down. 'What happened? You finally remembered there's music playing?'

'You'd know all about music, wouldn't you?' I say, hair swinging as he pulls me upright.

'Meaning?' His face is inches from mine.

'Oh come on.' I glare back at him. 'Everyone on this ship has heard the rumours. About your family.'

I steal myself, knowing that the script tells him to shake me and shout at me. But he doesn't.

'Marc?' I say, as he whirls me around the dance floor.

'I'm not going to shake you,' he replies.

'Because we're in public?' I ask.

'No.' He turns me again. 'Because I'm not doing it.'

'But it's in the script,' I insist, a little disorientated.

'I don't care.' His arms lock tight, and he leads me around.

'It's part of the character.'

'Call this my actor's prerogative,' says Marc. 'A man should never shake a woman.'

I laugh. 'That's a little hypocritical, don't you think? Considering you had me handcuffed to the bed a few days ago.'

'Different. Entirely different.' He pulls my body to his, then pushes me away again. 'That was consensual.'

'Oh look – there's Denise!' I turn. 'And Nadia.'

Denise stands by the entrance, a huge fur coat around her shoulders, smiling softly at the beautiful room. Her fluffy, blonde-grey hair is short and lightly curled, and laughter lines crinkle her eyes.

Nadia has an arm around Denise's shoulder and is chattering away. She's dressed in a black-sequinned fishtail gown, her bright-red nails gesturing around the room.

'Sophia! Marc!' Nadia waves at us, accepting a glass of champagne from a passing waiter. 'Hey – you ready for dinner?'

83

Over poached fish, champagne and buttered vegetables, Nadia, Marc and I rewrite Denise's script, covering her scenes with thick black pen.

'You know,' Nadia announces, as a mountain of spun-sugar profiteroles is set down, 'I think we're there. Now all we have to do is shoot the movie.'

'You make it sound so easy,' Denise laughs.

'It will be easy.' Nadia takes a long sip of chilled white wine. 'You'll see. The hard thing will be the Riviera Film Festival. I am *so* nervous about that night, I can't even tell you.'

'You? Nervous?' Marc raises an eyebrow.

'Oh yes. My god, I am *so* nervous. Best director? I've spent my life wanting that award. The Riviera Film Festival is what I live for.'

'You have a good chance,' says Marc. 'You know you do.'

'A good chance isn't the same as winning,' Nadia points out.

'You never know how those judges make their choices,' says Marc. 'It's a lottery. Don't invest yourself too heavily in it.'

'Okay for you to say,' Nadia snorts. 'You've already won best actor at the Riviera.'

'And it means nothing to me,' says Marc. 'The only thing that matters is what the audience thinks.'

'Don't remind me,' Nadia moans. 'We have them to please as well.'

With Cassandra gone, filming goes smoothly. The villa scenes are shot within a few weeks, and then we move back onto the cruise ship to finish filming there.

Often, the ship takes us out to sea. I love those days when we can see nothing but ocean and sky.

Benjamin is courteous and professional – much to Nadia's surprise.

'I don't know what's happened to him,' she confides in me. 'This isn't the Benjamin I know. Here he is, a little pussycat. Have you been spiking his drinks or something?'

'Maybe he's just grown up a bit,' I decide.

In the end, I really enjoy the scenes I shoot with Benjamin. We're friends. Good friends. And I respect that he keeps his word and doesn't try for more.

Leo is a shadow of himself, barely socialising and refusing all offers of company.

I know he's tried to call Jen a hundred times. And I also know she won't answer him.

One day after lunch, I find Leo at the third-deck cocktail bar looking out to sea.

There are four empty beer bottles on the table, and he's halfway through a fifth.

'You didn't fancy joining us for lunch?' I ask.

Leo gives a humourless laugh. 'Not much in the mood for socialising.'

'You're not okay, are you?' I offer.

'Probably never will be again,' he says, picking at a beer bottle label. 'Why did I have to be such an idiot, huh?'

'I don't know.' I take a seat opposite him. 'You tell me.'

'Where's Rocky?' Leo asks.

'In our suite. Working.'

'Quite a right hook Marc has.' Leo stares out to sea. 'I'm not trying to make excuses. Jen's amazing, but … she can be a real force. I just wanted to feel … like a man, I guess.'

'She certainly knows what she wants,' I admit.

Leo takes a long gulp of beer. 'I mean, Cassandra was into some kinky shit. It got pretty weird. But … I liked being in charge for a change. Look, don't tell Jen this, but I sort of needed it. With Jen, everything I did was wrong.'

'Why didn't you just *talk* to Jen?' I say.

'Have you ever tried talking to Jen?'

I lean forward. 'Oh she's not so scary. Once you get to know her.'

'Will she ever take me back?' Leo asks, sad eyes finding mine.

I let out a long breath. 'Um …'

No.

Leo takes another gulp of beer. 'Let's change the subject. So. You all ready for the Riviera Film Festival?'

'Not at all,' I say. 'I don't even have a dress. Marc is taking me shopping before we leave.'

'I never had you as a dressed up sort of girl,' says Leo, waving at a waiter and pointing to his beer bottle.

'I'm not really,' I say. 'But … it's the Riviera Film Festival, you know? It's special.'

'Well I hope Marc picks you out a good dress. I'm sure you'll look beautiful.'

'I'll choose my own dress, Leo. You know that.'

'Really?' Leo accepts a full, cold beer from the waiter. 'I thought Marc liked things his way.'

'He does,' I say. 'But I still have a mind of my own.'

'You know, Cassandra will be at the Riviera Film Festival.' Leo takes a swig of beer. 'Talk about awkward. I gotta make sure I'm sat a million miles away from her. Because if the cameras get us in the same shot, there is no *way* Jen will ever take me back.'

84

'You needn't look so nervous,' says Marc, squeezing my hand.

We're on Rue François Sibilli – a major shopping street in Saint-Tropez.

The buildings are peach and sandy pink coloured, with white shutters and sparkling glass windows. Words like, 'Valentino', 'Miu Miu' and 'Gucci' are painted on the soft stone shop fronts.

'I can't help it.' I stare at myself in a gleaming glass window. 'I never know what to do with myself in designer shops.'

Behind me, an immaculate French woman strolls past in a white linen suit. She has perfectly coiffed blonde hair and a snakeskin envelope handbag under her arm. At her feet, trots a pure white poodle.

'You'll be fine,' says Marc, kissing my head. 'You look like a model. Any designer would be delighted to dress you.'

Sun warms the wide, spotless pavements.

'I don't feel that way.' In my loose, white summer dress, I am way too scruffy for the well-put-together crowd milling around the shopping district. Everyone is so coiffed. So made-up.

'You should,' Marc insists.

'I'm just not used to expensive clothes,' I say, as we walk past Valentino. 'Oh my god. Marc. Did you see who was in that shop?'

'Who?' He turns.

'*Mick* Jagger.'

'Ah … Mick's here.' Marc raises an eyebrow. 'Surprise, surprise. He loves Saint-Tropez. Would you like to say hello? He's a friend of mine.'

'I'd be *way* too shy.'

'Of Mick?' Marc looks surprised. 'There's no need. He'll love you.'

'You're telling me not to be nervous?' I whisper. 'These shops are for celebrities.'

'What do you think you are?' says Marc.

'I'm … just ordinary.' I see myself in another shiny window – just a normal twenty-something girl, with brown hair and eyes. Nothing special.

'No you're not,' says Marc, leading me along the pavement. 'Trust me. Ah – this is the place.'

Marc takes me into a shop of elegant trouser suits and astonishing gowns.

'*Enchanté!*' A tiny, pale lady rushes to greet us. She has a perfect, geometric white bob and darts of black eyeliner. '*Marc* Blackwell. It's been too long.'

'Claudette.' Marc allows himself to be kissed on both cheeks. 'I've brought someone for you to dress.' He takes my hand and offers me forward. 'My perfect wife. Sophia.'

'Oh, I'm not perfect,' I mumble.

'*Certainment!*' Claudette grabs my hand and twirls me round. 'My goodness! What a body! I love her, Marc. For

French fashion, there is no better shape. Come sit down here, Sophia.'

Claudette pats a pink velvet chaise longue and drops me down. 'Now, my gorgeous girl. Wait there while I find beautiful gowns. You're dressing for the Riviera Film Festival, right? Why else could you be here?'

'Yes.' I catch a glimpse of myself in a full-length mirror – long, wavy brown hair falling around my shoulders and eyes staring in surprise.

I have to admit, the French sun has given me a certain glow. But I'm just so ordinary. Nothing like the women in this town.

'Ah. *Perfect*.' Claudette pulls a full-skirted pink dress from a show rail, draping it across my body. '*So* Riviera. Don't you think? Bold and beautiful.'

I look down at the elaborate fabric, wondering how anyone could walk with all the whirls and twirls bunched around their body.

'Umm …' I don't know how to tell her I hate it.

'No?' Claudette steps back. 'You don't think so?'

'It's … um … I like simple things,' I say tentatively.

'Simple? You *cannot* have simple,' Claudette insists. 'Marc will tell you. Not for the *Riviera Film Festival*. What is that English phrase? Go big or go home.'

At the window, a line of pretty, giggling girls have gathered, their noses pressed to the glass.

Marc frowns. 'Do you have a private dressing area?'

'*Certainment*.'

85

Claudette leads us to a pretty, walled garden full of flowering honeysuckle and lavender.

There's a wrought-iron table and chairs, and a woven, wicker garden sofa.

'You can change out here.' Claudette bumps a wheeled clothing rail onto the patio. Then she props a full-length mirror against the wall. 'It is totally secluded.'

The rail is hung with gowns she's selected for me, and a few I've chosen myself.

'I've never been in an open-air changing room before,' I say, smiling at the feel of sunshine.

'Perfect weather today, huh?' says Claudette.

'Perfect,' I agree.

'You know, I never thought Marc would marry.' Claudette fluffs out gowns. 'Sophia, you have to tell me. How did you win him around?'

'It was me who won her around,' says Marc, gruffly.

'So now we have some of the story,' says Claudette. 'But how did you meet?'

'I was Sophia's teacher at Ivy College,' Marc tells her. 'And I fell in love with her the first moment we met. Very inconvenient, I must say.'

'Her teacher? Scandalous!' Claudette laughs. 'I love it. Wait there – you both need a glass of wine in this heat.'

'So Claudette never thought you'd get married,' I tease Marc, when Claudette disappears inside. 'How does this woman know you so well?'

'I would never have married anyone but you,' says Marc. 'How do you know Claudette?'

Marc's lips tilt into a smile. 'I shot a movie here. Years ago.'

'I think I know which one. *Drug Money*.'

He raises an eyebrow. 'You're quite the Marc Blackwell fan.'

'I've seen all your movies.' I falter. 'Even the one with Cassandra …'

My insides burn as I remember the scene between Marc and Cassandra. It's passionate and animalistic. The characters are supposed to have sex in the school locker room, but you don't see that – only frenzied kissing.

It's not the only movie Marc kisses a woman in. But it's the only one, to my knowledge, where he had a relationship with her off screen too.

I look away from Marc.

'Sophia,' Marc says softly. 'It was a million years ago. I was a different person.'

I nod, blinking at a rim of tears. 'I know. I just … wish it had never happened.'

'So do I.' Marc puts his arms around me.

'Here we are.' Claudette returns with two glasses of chilled white wine, and an elaborate gown over her arm. 'I found another dress too – something you just *have* to try, Sophia.'

The gown is covered in giant, silk roses and flows along the floor behind Claudette.

'I know, I know.' Claudette places wine glasses on the table. 'You said simple. But just try this one, okay?' She hangs the gown on the rail, fingers lingering over the fabric roses. 'It's the perfect colour for you.'

'I think plain will suit me better,' I insist.

'At the Riviera Film Festival you *cannot* be plain,' says Claudette. 'Just *try* it. Marc – you're her husband. Can't you convince her? The man always has the last word. Right?' She laughs. 'They're the ones with the wallets.'

'Sophia can choose whatever she likes,' says Marc. 'I don't tell her what to wear.'

'You don't?' Claudette looks surprised.

'Sophia isn't my possession,' says Marc. 'She's my wife.'

'Not how most men around here think,' Claudette muses. 'You should see them – dressing their wives in gold Rolexes and diamonds, wanting everyone to see how much money they have. Okay – so I'll leave you to try on, okay? Call me if you need anything.'

Claudette vanishes back into the shop, swishing a big, black curtain across the glass doors.

'Sophia –' Marc begins.

'It's okay Marc.' I attempt a bright smile. 'You're right. The past is the past. It hurts, but … that's how it is. You're my husband. We have a baby together. There's nothing for me to be jealous of.'

'And yet you are jealous. Aren't you?' His eyes bore down on me.

'I can't stand to think of you with that woman,' I admit.

'Does it help if I tell you I can't stand the thought either?'

'A little,' I say.

'You're the girl who changed me,' says Marc. 'Who gave me a beautiful daughter. Who made me fall in love. No one else will ever come close to you.'

He finds the small of my back, stroking back and forth, eyes holding mine. 'So choose your dress, Mrs Blackwell.'

'It's difficult. I need to look elegant. But … I hate being all trussed up.'

'Mm … interesting choice of words.' Marc raises an eyebrow. 'You always look elegant. Even when tied to the bed. You should trust Claudette. She's been in this business a long time.'

'This sort of thing just isn't me,' I insist, taking the cloth-rose gown and holding it against my body. 'I mean, can you imagine me in this?'

'I think you'd look incredible in it,' says Marc. 'Maybe it's time to push your boundaries.'

'You don't think you've pushed them enough already?'

'Not nearly enough. Let me help you undress.'

'Do you think that's a good idea?' I ask.

'One of my better ones.' His eyes have taken on that dangerous look.

'Like marrying me, you mean?' I say, hanging the gown back on the rail.

'Exactly right.' Marc comes to stand behind me, lifting my dress up over my head. He throws the dress over the rail, then runs a knuckle from my neck all the way down my spine.

I stand in plain, cream-pink underwear, shivering with pleasure.

326

'Hold onto the dress rail,' he says, lifting my hands to the cool, metal bar between swinging gowns.

As my fingers adjust to the cold, Marc slides my panties down my legs. As I feel them drop to my feet, his fingers come between my thighs, moving back and forth, sending delicious shivers all over my body, building up friction where I'm most sensitive.

'Oh god Marc,' I whisper, leaning into the rail. 'We shouldn't do this here.'

His hand falls away, and hear the zip of his trousers.

'*Marc.*'

Firm hands clasp my backside.

I swallow and close my eyes, waiting.

Marc squeezes and releases, squeezes and releases my buttocks, until I have to stifle a little moan. Then he parts my backside.

I gasp, gripping the rail, as he enters me in one long stroke.

'OH!'

I yelp with the tightness, and Marc stops.

'Okay?' he whispers.

I nod, not trusting myself to speak.

When I don't make any other sound, Marc slides further in, little by little, until he's all the way in.

Then he starts to move.

'Oh *Marc.*'

I feel his hand clamp my mouth, and the other come between my legs, rubbing where I'm hot and sensitive.

He moves slow and steady, getting deeper with every stroke.

My eyes are tight shut now, and I'm moaning against his hand as he builds up pace.

The slow, gentle movements become faster and harder, his hips smacking into my backside, my hair jerking tight in his hand.

I'm so caught up with him, so outside of myself with pleasure, that my orgasm takes me by surprise. It burns and sparkles, building to a hot flame between my legs that melts into gentle heat.

Marc grasps my hips again and pulls himself into me, his body throbbing and rigid as he comes inside me.

His fingers clench me tightly, digging into my skin, and I feel him jolt.

'*Sophia,*' he whispers, and I hear his hard breathing.

I hold tight to the rail, panting and a little sore. I feel like my backside is glowing bright red.

After a moment, Marc's gentle fingers glide down my buttocks and he slides out of me.

'Well Mrs Blackwell,' he growls 'Have you decided which outfit you like best?'

86

I feel Marc pull up my panties, as I cling to the dress rail for support.

'God, Marc. You certainly choose your moments.'

His lips quirk into a smile. 'From time to time, I like to remind you who's in charge.'

'Oh, so you're in charge of me, are you?' I turn to him, smiling.

'Just then I was,' he says. 'Could you have stopped?'

'No,' I admit.

Marc pulls me into his arms. 'Good.'

I catch a sideways glance of myself in the mirror, tangled up in Marc's body.

'How do I look?' I ask.

'You want my opinion now?' says Marc.

'I always want your opinion.'

'I think you look beautiful in everything.' Marc watches us in the mirror. 'But you're going to the Riviera Film Festival – why not wear the biggest, showiest gown there is? You won't look out of place.'

'Maybe I *will* try that dress with the roses,' I say, reaching for the rail. 'Even though I'm not a rose anymore.'

'A rose by any other name ...' Marc gives me his half smile.

The dress is covered in roses of different sizes and colours, even on the shoulder straps. A palette of soft grey, ballerina pink and ice white falls from collar to ankle.

I stroke the giant silk roses with my fingers. 'Romeo, Romeo. Will you help me with this?'

'Gladly.' Marc takes the dress and helps me step into it.

'You're good at this,' I say. 'Have you helped many women to dress?'

As soon as I ask the question, I regret it. It's not funny. Not with Cassandra's ghost still floating around.

'I don't remember other women,' says Marc, pulling the zip up my back. 'Not now I have you.'

'Good answer.'

'It's true.' Marc is still watching me in the mirror. He sweeps my hair around my shoulder, exposing my neck.

I see myself, hardly believing the girl who looks back at me. The dress. It's stunning.

I thought the fabric would be loose, but it clings tight to every curve of my body. Like a work of art. I'm cocooned in a nest of crushed silk, held from shoulders to feet in softness and beauty.

'What do you think?' I ask Marc.

'You know what I think. You look astonishing.' He plants a kiss on my neck. 'Absolutely astonishing. But I prefer you with no clothes at all.'

I don't want to take the dress off. But I let Claudette wrap it carefully in tissue paper, smoothing and folding so it fits perfectly in a matt-pink dress box.

Claudette drops rose petals in to fragrance the dress,

then slides the lid into place and wraps a jet-black ribbon around, finishing with a bow.

'*Voilà!*' she announces. 'Now. I have the perfect pair of shoes, also.'

She takes a pink and black striped shoebox from a shelf, and folds back the tissue paper.

Inside the box, I see silk stilettos with a fabric rose on each toe strap.

'They're beautiful,' I admit.

'They're yours,' says Claudette. 'No charge – I insist.'

I glance at Marc.

'Claudette,' says Marc. 'I've never been a fan of complimentary. Charge them to my account.'

'No, no, I absolutely insist.' Claudette waves a dismissive hand. 'By the end of the week, Sophia's photograph will be in every fashion magazine in Europe. That's payment enough.'

87

That afternoon, Marc and I shoot our last scene on the cruise ship, as we sail from Saint-Tropez to the Riviera Film Festival.

I know the moving ship will look great against the sunset, but it means we have a time pressure.

Once we arrive at the Riviera, the noise and light of the film festival will ruin the shot.

'Just relax,' Marc tells me, as I mess up yet another take. 'You're over thinking it.'

The sunset is beautiful. Perfect. And I know my lines. Marc and I have rehearsed this scene a dozen times. But he's right – I am over thinking it. And putting too much pressure on myself to be perfect.

Marc takes my arms, shaking them loose like that first time I was on stage with him. He turns to Nadia. 'Let's go.'

We shoot the scene, and as Marc and I share a passionate kiss for the cameras, I know we've got it right. We're in character. And there's chemistry. Lots of chemistry. How could there not be with he and I?

'Great,' Nadia shouts. 'Just great, you guys. Wow! We did it. Everything in the bag. Next stop, the Riviera Film Festival.'

The shouts and cheers become deafening as our tender boat reaches the Village International Riviera.

'Oh *wow*.' I grab Marc's hand, grinning at the Palais des Festivals lit by neon pink and green strobe lights.

A red carpet runs the length of the building.

'This is crazy.' I watch fans screaming outside, as the tender comes in to dock.

Marc frowns. 'Lucky Ivy stayed on the cruise ship.'

'I'm just sorry Tanya had to miss this,' I say, fingers drumming the boat's fibreglass superstructure.

'It was invitation only honey,' Nadia interrupts, leaning into our conversation. 'I'm sorry to leave the *Cruise* gang behind too. But it's all about *Rapunzel* now. Hey – *this* is the way to travel, don't you think?' She takes a sip from a tumbler of ice and whisky, then hands it to a wobbly waiter, struggling to keep his footing on the waving boat. 'Last year, I was stuck in traffic for hours.'

As the tender docks, Nadia smooths her beautiful, feathered black gown and looks me up and down. 'My God, Sophia. Do you need someone to help you carry that dress? It looks like it weighs a tonne.'

'Actually it's not that bad,' I say, gathering up the layers.

'It's stunning.' Nadia bends to stroke one of the silk roses. 'Utterly stunning. Cover your eyes honey. Because those cameras are going to snap, snap, snap at you the moment you step ashore.'

Marc puts a protective arm around my shoulder. 'Stay close to me.'

'*Bonsoir*, Mr and Mrs Blackwell.' A girl with a clipboard and slicked down blonde hair meets us at the Palais des Festival.

We've already been escorted along the red carpet, beside a screaming crowd.

I'm overwhelmed, wanting to laugh when the crowd call my name and shout back to them, *I'm just ordinary.*

'You're with the Malbeck party,' the girl tells us. 'Your table is ready.'

Nadia comes tottering up behind us, throwing her arms over our shoulders. 'Okay guys! Let's go party.'

The clipboard woman blinks politely at Nadia. 'And you are?'

'Nadia Malbeck.'

'Oh! Ms Malbeck. Of course. Right this way.'

88

'Don't let go of my hand,' I whisper to Marc, as we're led into the giant ceremony room.

There are film cameras everywhere, their cables covered with red carpet.

A suited waiter leads us through a sea of tables.

'Oh my god.' I cling to Marc. 'There are so many famous people here.'

Marc squeezes my fingers. He looks like Hollywood royalty in his black and white tuxedo, and fits this place like a glove.

I, on the other hand, feel extremely self-conscious. How did someone like me end up here?

For a moment, I am star struck.

Meryl Streep. Leonardo DiCaprio. Scarlett Johansson …

There are so many famous actors. People I adore and admire.

We're seated right near the stage, and when I see who's sitting at our table, I break into a smile.

'Baz!' I wave. 'Sigourney!'

Baz is stuffed into a tuxedo, looking decidedly awkward, his scuffed and scarred face at odds with the starchy white collar.

Beside him sits Sigourney, who looks skinny and miserable in a tight gold gown.

It seems like a lifetime since we all shot *Rapunzel* together. But unbelievably they're still together. Baz has finally found someone as crazy as him to settle down with.

'All right people.' Baz stands to shake our hands. 'Fucking good to see you. I hate these stuffed shirt parties. Can't wait to get out of here and down the pub.'

'Hi everyone,' says Sigourney, not standing, but offering a surprisingly genuine smile. 'You look really pretty, Sophia. Um … I never got to thank you before. You know, when we were filming. For being kind to me. So … thanks.'

'That's fine,' I say, not really sure what to make of her comment.

'See?' says Baz, putting an arm around Sigourney. 'Told you it would be easy. You can be nice. When you're off the booze.'

Sigourncy smiles again, and it's a sweet smile. Vulnerable.

'Where's Leo?' I ask. 'He came by car — why isn't he sitting at our table?'

Nadia points across the room. 'He's over there. Working the crowd.'

I see Leo, laughing and slapping backs.

'He's cheered up,' I remark, taking a seat.

'Hasn't he?' Marc sits beside me.

Nadia arranges herself in the seat on my other side, and we all watch Leo grin at a beautiful blonde, then drape his arm over her shoulder.

'I thought he was sitting with us,' I say.

'He should be.' Nadia stands, black feathers flying. 'HEY! Falkirk. Get your butt over here.'

'Just a minute,' Leo shouts back. 'I've got some important business to attend to.' He slides into the seat beside the blonde.

Nadia shakes her head, arranging feathers again as she takes a seat. 'That boy. He'll never get his fiancée back if he plays that game.' She surveys the table. 'Hey – something isn't right here. There's an extra chair.'

'What's Leo doing?' I ask Nadia. 'He's desperate to win Jen back. I know he is. Why is he flirting with that woman?'

'Maybe he's trying to show her what she's missing,' says Baz. 'Won't work though. Women aren't that stupid.'

'You got that right.' Nadia grabs a passing waiter. 'Hey listen – there are seven chairs here. You need to tell the organisers.'

The waiter looks confused. 'But all the seats are accounted for, madam.'

'No,' Nadia insists. 'There's only six of us. And we're all here.'

'You have someone else arriving,' says the waiter. 'Cassandra Kilburn.'

I stiffen, turning to Marc, who has gone equally rigid.

Nadia's eyes widen. 'Cassandra Kilburn? Oh no, no. That is a *big* mistake. She wasn't even *in* Rapunzel.'

The waiter turns. 'Ah. Here comes Ms Kilburn now.'

89

Through tables of suited celebrities, Cassandra glides towards us.

She is immaculate in a tight red-silk dress, shiny black hair lying straight down her back.

When she reaches us, Cassandra puts a diamante-encrusted silk glove on Nadia's shoulder. 'Good to see you again, chica. I hope we can all be grown-ups and put any bad feeling behind us.'

'There's been a mistake.' Nadia shakes her head. 'You can't be at this table, honey. I'm sorry. But Leo will be sitting here soon, and … look I have to think of the family.'

'A mistake?' Hurt flashes in Cassandra's eyes. 'Surely you're not going to say I can't sit with you?'

'But you're not even *in* Rapunzel,' Nadia insists. 'Look – I'm sure we can find you another seat. How did you even end up here anyway?'

A waiter leans in. 'It was understood Ms Kilburn is currently shooting a movie with you. So this was her table request.'

'Was it indeed?' Nadia mutters. 'Well listen.' She claps her hands together. 'This can all be smoothed out, right? Let's arrange another seat for Ms Kilburn.'

'I'm afraid all the other seats are taken,' the waiter explains.

'You wouldn't send me home, would you?' Cassandra flutters her long, black eyelashes.

Nadia looks between Cassandra and the waiter, clearly weighing up her options. 'Can't we move people around?' she asks the waiter. 'Make a space?'

'It is impossible madam.' The waiter gives a curt shake of his head. 'Changes are not allowed.'

Nadia sinks defeated into her chair. 'Oh for Christ's sake. Well listen – Cassandra, don't sit next to Leo. That's all I ask.'

Marc glares up at the waiter. 'This isn't appropriate. Cassandra needs to be re-seated.'

'What can he do?' Nadia spreads her hands. 'He can't magic a chair from thin air. He already said. All the other seats are taken.'

Cassandra lowers herself into the seat opposite me and pours wine.

'Here's to The Riviera Film Festival,' she says, raising her glass.

Awkward glances are exchanged.

'ATTENTION EVERYONE!' a voice booms from the speaker system. 'The ceremony is about to begin. Please do not leave your seats.'

90

'Where's Leo?' Nadia cranes her neck. 'He needs to hurry up and sit the fuck down. Leo. Hey. LEO!'

Leo bounds towards the table, but slows when he sees Cassandra.

'You know,' says Cassandra, elbows staking out the table. 'We should make a toast to Leo. To celebrate his new status. I hear he's recently single.' She smiles at Marc and raises her glass to him.

'What the fuck?' Leo appears by Nadia's shoulder. 'How come she's at our table?'

'Hey, why is everyone coming down on me?' Nadia snaps. 'I didn't make the table arrangements. She just turned up.'

'Look, no offence Cassandra.' Leo takes a chair. 'But I want my fiancée back. I don't want anything to do with you. So don't get in my shot. Okay?'

If you want Jen back, I wonder, *why were you flirting with that woman over there?*

'But we had such *fun*,' Cassandra smiles.

'SILENCE PLEASE,' booms the sound system. 'The ceremony will now begin.'

On the stage, a huge projection screen lights up, and a slender, blonde lady strolls towards a silver lotus-flower podium. Actually, she's not just any blonde. She's the woman Leo was flirting with earlier. And something clicks.

She's … *Aurelie Reynard*. The French actress. Now I'm even more confused, because Aurelie Reynard is happily married to director, Pierre Reynard.

'Greetings everyone and welcome to the Riviera Film Festival,' says Aurelie, her small frame disappearing behind the podium.

The auditorium is dark, but I feel Cassandra's eyes on me.

'You know, before we get started I have a special announcement to make,' says Aurelie. 'A good friend of mine – Leo Falkirk – has a message he wants me to deliver.'

The film cameras turn to our table.

'Leo wants to send love to his fiancée Jen. And tell her he's thinking of her. And he's sorry.'

A collective *awww* flows around the auditorium.

So that's what all that flirting was about, I realise. *Leo was charming Aurelie into making his announcement.*

Cassandra's lips pinch together, and she takes a long drink of wine.

'Sweet, huh?' Aurelie claps her hands. 'Okay. So let's begin the ceremony.'

91

I hold Marc's hand tight and focus on the stage.

As film clips roll and awards are handed out, I notice Leo's eyes glued to his phone.

Cassandra fixes me with glittering, angry eyes. 'This isn't over,' she whispers. 'All I have to do is make sure the cameraman gets a shot of us together. And that message will mean nothing.'

'Why are you doing this, Cassandra?' I whisper back. 'Why are you messing with Jen and Leo's relationship? They're nothing to do with you.'

Cassandra smiles, drinking wine through red lips. 'To punish you. For taking my man.'

'How is this punishing me?' I hiss.

'I'm hurting you through your friends,' she replies coolly. 'You don't live in Hollywood as long as I have without learning to play the game.'

My hand clenches a wineglass.

'I wouldn't throw that if I were you,' says Cassandra casually. 'If you do, the tabloids will have you down as a crazed, bi-polar jealous wife. I'll make sure of it. You see how it works?'

'Jen isn't stupid,' I say. 'She'll see through you. She'll know what you're doing.'

'Jealous women rarely see sense,' says Cassandra. 'Most likely she'll decide her boyfriend can't stay away from me. And you know the best part? Leo can't say a word in his defence. Because if he does, his career will be over.'

I sense Leo is listening. His jaw is hard, his fingers white as they grip his phone.

92

The ceremony rolls on, but I find it hard to focus on the film clips. All I can think about is the game Cassandra is playing. The worst part is, she's winning.

Leo's phone stays black; no messages flash or sound.

Finally, it's time for the Best Director award.

'This is it,' says Nadia. 'Hey listen – if I don't win this year, I don't care. Okay?' She gives me a wink.

'Let's all have a drink,' Cassandra announces, pouring more wine. She fills Leo's glass, then goes to fill mine.

'No thanks,' I say. 'I can fill my own glass.'

I see a camera turn to our table.

God.

Cassandra shrugs, filling everyone else's glasses. 'Suit yourself. If you don't want to toast your director.'

Something inside me sinks, as I realise they'll now be a shot of me snatching my glass away from Cassandra. She really does know how to play the game.

There are murmurs from nearby tables, and someone whispers, '*Shush!*'

'And now,' Aurelie announces, tapping a silver envelope on the podium, 'the award for best director.'

Suddenly, my naked body is projected onto a 20-foot high screen, as Leo and I make love in *Rapunzel*.

My back moves back and forth above Leo, and the camera films my face, pretending to be lost in ecstasy.

'Oh great.' I half cover my eyes.

Beside me, I feel Marc tense.

It seems to take forever, but finally my scene disappears, and Leo and I fade into another movie clip.

The audience falls silent, as Aurelie opens the silver envelope.

'And the winner for best director goes to …' Aurelie pauses. 'Nadia Malbeck.'

Applause explodes around the auditorium.

'OH MY GOD!' Nadia screeches. 'OH MY GOD!' She leaps to her feet, nearly knocking over her wine glass. 'Jesus Christ.'

Leo, who has just caught her glass, stands and takes her arm. 'Come on, best director. I'll walk you up there.'

93

Up on stage, a microphone is thrust into Nadia's face. But she just opens and closes her mouth, spluttering, 'Um … err …'

Leo puts a friendly arm around her shoulder and takes the mike. 'I think our best director is a little lost for words. For once.'

He pauses for a laugh, and gets one.

'I gotta tell you all, I love this girl,' Leo continues. 'She's just the best. Well done Nadia.' He kisses her cheek.

'Oh my God,' Nadia stutters. 'I can't believe this. Honestly, I can't. Jesus Christ. There are so many people I should thank. My husband. Of course …' She reels off a long list of people, including Marc and I, Baz, Sigourney and pretty much every cast and crew member she's ever worked with.

Everyone claps good-naturedly as the thanks go on and on.

When Nadia finally runs out of names, Leo takes the mike. 'Are you done telling everyone how fantastic they are Nadia?'

Nadia laughs. 'All done, Leo.'

'Good.' Leo turns to camera one. 'Because I've got something to say.'

The crowd falls silent.

Leo's good-natured smile fades. 'I have a fiancée,' he says. 'The most amazing woman I've ever met. But I totally fucked up. I … I slept with someone else.'

A deathly hush falls over the audience.

Through the gloom, I see Nadia approaching our table, Silver Lotus award under her arm. She slides into the seat beside me. '*What the fuck is he doing?*' she whispers.

'No idea,' I whisper back.

Leo looks earnestly into the camera. 'Jen. I never cared about Cassandra Kilburn.'

'Oh Jesus Christ.' Nadia puts her head in her hands. 'And now he's given them a name.'

'I was weak and stupid,' Leo continues. 'Cassandra took advantage when I was lost, but I'm found again. And Jen … I just love you so much.'

Big tears slide down Leo's cheeks. 'I can't imagine life without you. So Jen. Please. Please take me back. We'll get counselling. We'll get help. And I'll spend my life proving how much I love you. That's all.'

He hands the mike to Aurelie and bounds off stage.

'Um … well, thank you Leo,' says Aurelie, throwing a confused glance at camera one, then shuffling with podium papers, clearly a little thrown.

Cameras swivel to our table – I guess to get a close-up of Cassandra's reaction. And seeing Cassandra's surprised face and wide eyes, I know they're going to get exactly the shot they want.

We're not seeing the usual cool, calm Cassandra, but a caged animal, red lips parted in panic.

As a cameraman sprints across the room to get his shot, Leo saunters back to our table.

'Cassandra,' Leo says, picking up a champagne bottle and swigging directly from it. 'Never underestimate what a man will do for true love.'

94

For a moment, I think Cassandra might slap Leo – her eyes are so hate-filled. But instead she bolts up, leaving our table and weaving her way across the room. She's followed by a stampede of cameramen and photographers.

'Oh my god,' I breathe, watching her head to the exit.

'Well done Leo,' says Marc, leaning to pat him on the back. 'Admirably done.'

'It was for Jen.' Leo toasts the nearest cameraman. 'Oh Jesus fucking Christ, God in heaven. I hope she forgives me.'

'I hope you know what you're doing, Leo,' Nadia remarks, stroking her Silver Lotus award. 'The public have long memories when it comes to cheating fiancés. You, golden boy – well let's just say you won't be offered any roles for a while. Movie goers don't like men who cheat.'

Dimly, I'm aware of more film cameras turning our way. I guess they still want a shot of Leo, after his big announcement.

'It's a chance I was willing to take,' says Leo, downing his glass of champagne.

Sigourney puts a hand on my shoulder. 'Um … Sophia?'

I turn to her. 'Yes?'

'You might want to look at the stage.' Sigourney points.

'Why?' I ask, looking around in confusion.

Sigourney smiles. 'Because Aurelie just said your name.'

On stage, Aurelie holds a torn silver envelope. 'Sophia Blackwell?'

I blink at her, more confused than ever as more cameras turn to our table.

Aurelie smiles down at me. 'Shall I do this again? Dum, dum, dum.' She pretends to do a drum roll on the podium. 'So. The award for best actress goes to … Sophia Blackwell. For *Rapunzel*.'

I turn to Marc. 'I … is this a joke?' My stomach flips over and over.

Marc stands. 'Come along, Mrs Blackwell. You're wanted on stage.'

'*Me*? Best actress?' Shakily, I get to my feet.

'Go on girl.' Baz beats his hands together.

'But I wasn't nominated. Was I?' I blink at the smiling faces around our table.

'Evidently you were.' Marc takes my arm. 'Let's go collect your award.'

I nearly fall over my feet as Marc leads me through the crowd.

Thank god I have his arm to hang on to.

Everyone is clapping and cheering.

I don't really know how I reach the stage, but somehow I'm there, staring out at bright lights and famous faces.

'So how does it feel, Sophia?' Aurelie asks, holding out a mike.

I look down at the mesh of silver.

'Oh wow.' My voice booms all around the auditorium. 'Um … I wasn't expecting this.'

On the big screen, live images of the other nominees flash up.

'Seriously.' I take the mike. 'This is … it's incredible. Nadia is incredible. The whole cast and crew … Leo … you were amazing. And Marc.' I turn to him. 'You are the most amazing husband, father and teacher. And you're right. I still have so much to learn.'

After I've been presented with my award, I navigate a sea of back pats and handshakes on the way back to our table.

I sit heavily in my chair, staring at my award and trying to work out how on earth this happened.

'It's real,' says Marc, putting a hand over mine. 'I promise you.'

'I'm not so sure about that,' I whisper back, smiling at my cheering, clapping table mates. 'I think I could be dreaming. Hey. Where's Leo.'

'Gone, honey,' says Nadia, filling my champagne glass. 'Leo has balls. I'll give him that. But Jesus, surely there was a better way. I mean, throwing his fucking career away …'

'The man's in love,' says Baz, putting an arm around Sigourney. 'You do stupid things for love.'

'Like messing up your whole life?' says Nadia, filling everyone else's glasses. 'It took him years to build up his career. What woman will want to see him playing the nice guy now? When they know in real life he can be not so nice.'

'I dunno,' says Baz. 'The great movie-going public have short memories. I thought my career was over when I got done for that drug charge. But they had me back again. God love 'em.'

'But *where* did Leo go?' I ask, scanning the crowd.

'He left the building,' says Sigourney. 'The paps followed him out.'

I hunt around for my phone. 'I should try and call Jen.'

95

Jen doesn't answer her phone all night. Or reply to my text messages. By the time the ceremony finishes, I'm getting worried.

'She always answers her phone to me,' I tell Marc, as festival staff escort us out.

'Maybe she needs time alone,' says Marc, steering me past cameramen and glaring at any one stupid enough to try and get us in shot.

'That's not how it works with us,' I insist, nodding thanks as we're presented with woven-silver goodie bags. 'Wow.' I stop walking, glimpsing inside the bag. 'I think there's a Rolex watch in here.'

Sigourney leans in and whispers, 'That's not the half of it. The women get Cartier love bracelets too. And a luxury Caribbean holiday. Award-ceremony goodie bags are half the reason I date actors.'

Behind us, Baz slaps Sigourney's behind and says, 'Oi!'

Sigourney winks. 'Just joking, love of my life. You know it's the sex I'm dating you for.'

'Too right,' says Baz, pulling her into a rough hug.

Outside, the night air is warm and fresh, and smells of expensive catering and lavender. Marc and I bid everyone goodnight, and head towards our limousine.

Marc opens the car door for me. 'I'm glad the Riviera Festival saw what I see in you,' he says.

'And what would that be?' I ask.

'Extraordinary talent. Truth. Purity. And light.'

'And what about when you won your award?' I ask. 'What did they see in you?'

Marc's lips tilt into a dangerous smile. 'I believe they saw my dark side. And enjoyed it. Just like you do.'

The limo takes us to the airport, where we're reunited with Ivy. Then Tanya boards the private jet with us, and we all fly back to London at gone midnight.

I can barely keep my eyes open on the short flight, and find myself falling asleep on Marc's shoulder. I'm extremely grateful Tanya is on hand to help with Ivy.

'It's fine Soph,' Tanya insists, as we begin our descent to London. 'I have good energy reserves. Plus I've just drunk a can of Red Bull. I'm totally good to go.'

The moment the plane touches down, I take out my phone and check for messages from Jen. But there are none.

'I'm really worried about her,' I tell Marc.

'Jen can take care of herself,' says Marc. 'She's a tough cookie.'

'Not as tough as people think,' I say. 'And she *always* answers the phone to me. It's one of our rules. I need to go see her. What if something's happened?'

Marc strokes my hair. 'I'll have one of my people go over and check she's safe in her apartment. Will that make you happy?'

'A bit,' I say. 'But I still need to see her.'

'You'll see her tomorrow,' says Marc. 'You're exhausted right now. And Jen, if she has any sense, will be asleep. Patience, Miss Blackwell. Keith will drive you into London in the morning.'

Outside Jen's new office in Piccadilly, black cabs and red buses trundle past.

After so many days at sea, my legs hardly know what to make of London's still pavements and slow sky.

I call into Jen's office intercom: 'Hey. Can I speak to Jen please?'

'Soph?' Jen's voice crackles through the speaker.

'Hello stranger,' I call back, relief flooding through my body. I already knew she was safe and sound, because Marc's security man reported back to us in the early hours of the morning. But to hear her voice … I'm just so glad.

'Can I come in?' I ask.

The glass door buzzes open, and I walk into Jen's flashy reception area, lost amid huge bamboo stalks and orchids. There's a glass bar on one wall with silver stools underneath, and a seating area with *Vogue* magazines laid out tastefully on a metal coffee table.

'Jen?' I call out.

I hear tip tapping, and see Jen striding towards me, looking fabulous in a light-pink pencil-skirt suit and Chanel scarf.

'Soph!' She kisses me on both cheeks. 'Oh my God, best actress? I am *so* proud of you. You must be over the moon!'

'I'm more interested in how you're doing,' I say. 'Why didn't you answer my calls?'

Jen hesitates. 'Do you want an espresso or anything? We've got this amazing new machine.'

'*Jen.*'

Jen click-clacks to the glass bar, fiddling with an espresso machine. 'I was … I had a lot on yesterday. A *lot* on.'

'I was worried about you,' I say, feeling like the parent of a wayward teenager.

'Sorry,' says Jen. 'Yesterday was … sort of a blur.' She let's out a yawn, quickly covering her mouth.

'We *always* answer our phones to each other,' I insist.

'I know, I know.' Jen rubs her eyes, and I notice there are grey bags under them. 'Look – it was a one off. I won't do it again. Listen, that's all in the past now. Let's move forward.'

'You look tired,' I say. 'Is Leo back in London? Have you spoken to him?'

Jen slots a capsule into the espresso machine. 'I don't give second chances …'

'I know you don't.'

But Jen has a funny little smile on her face.

'Jen?' I ask.

'Of course,' she says, 'there's always a first time.'

My eyes widen. 'Jen?'

She clicks the espresso machine, and it begins to whir. 'Oh Soph, what's happened to me? I used to be so sensible.'

'Are you giving Leo a second chance?' I ask, a smile growing.

Jen's face explodes into a grin. 'Yes! And … we're getting married!' She holds her finger out, and I see a glittering blue diamond. 'He bought me a new ring and everything. You know, to symbolise a fresh start.'

'Oh my GOD!' I shriek. 'Oh Jen. That's amazing. But … when did all this happen?'

'Leo flew back last night. He'd already bought the ring. And we spent all night … reconciling.'

I laugh.

'And do you know what?' Jen continues. 'We're going to fly out to Vegas, just the two of us. No press. No fuss. Like Leo said, cut out all the nonsense. Make it all about the love. Of course, we know we have work to do. Leo knows this great counsellor and … wait. You're not hurt that you weren't a bridesmaid, are you? Because we're going to have another ceremony—'

'Not at all,' I laugh. 'Oh Jen, that's fantastic.'

'I really do love him, you know?' Jen says, her eyes going soft and dreamy. 'Do you think that maybe, just maybe, we could live happily ever after?'

I nod emphatically. 'I do.'

96

The Silver Lotus Flower sparkles on the mantelpiece, held tight in its glass cube.

I love seeing my name inscribed on the glass.

Sophia Rose – Best Actress

Marc slides an arm around my shoulder. 'You're rather captivated by that piece of modern art, aren't you?'

'Piece of modern art?' I turn in mock outrage. 'That award, Mr Blackwell, is the highlight of my acting career.'

He smiles. 'So far.'

'So far.'

I hear a thump, thump upstairs and look up. 'Uh oh. What's Michael doing with Ivy now? Jumping around the bedroom with her?'

'He's teaching her to be a terror,' says Marc, glancing fondly at the ceiling. 'I should never have agreed to these visits.'

I put my arms around his neck. 'I'm glad you changed your mind.'

'You were very persuasive.' His stern, blue eyes bear down on me. 'This seems to be the year for second chances, doesn't it?'

'It certainly is.' I smile up at him. 'And learning from mistakes.'

'On the subject of learning, isn't it time for our next lesson?' says Marc, his hands coming to my waist. 'Or are you above tuition, now you've won yourself a Silver Lotus?'

'Never.'

Marc fixes me with dangerous eyes. 'How do you like your new classroom?'

I look across the garden at the small theatre Marc built by my favourite oak tree.

The classroom is totally private, looking out onto fields and farmland. No one can see what we get up to in there. Which is just how we like it.

'I love it,' I tell Marc. 'But you already know that.'

'Of course, you can always return to Ivy College,' says Marc, his eyes darkening. 'Should you ever wish to become more adventurous …'

'I think we've been quite adventurous already,' I reply, thinking of the wide away of equipment in our small theatre.

Ropes. Handcuffs. Canes.

Marc certainly takes his role as teacher seriously.

'Come along, Mrs Blackwell,' says Marc. 'Time for class. There's so much you still have to learn.'

What next?
I've written a short novella about
Marc and his dark past.
'Mr Blackwell', is out now on Amazon:

UK   US

http://amzn.to/1Q19NQG   http://amzn.to/1WrTa5M

JOIN OUR
DEVOTED READERS

You are an AMAZING reader –
which makes you part of our Devoted family.
Devoted readers find out about special-offers
and secret release days before anyone else.
Join our favoured reader list below ...

Sign Me Up ⌄

Join Devoted Readers List HERE

And a quick word about AMAZON REVIEWS …

I read ALL my Amazon reviews (and yes, the bad ones do make me cry) and pay special attention to my favourite reviews and sometimes send special gifts as a thank you.

Reviews don't have to be fancy. In fact, just one word is great (hope that word isn't 'shit', but you're free to pick whichever word you want …).

So GO AHEAD and review – I would LOVE to see what you have to say, and some of you will receive a thank you presents.

Huge hugs and kisses

Suzy K Quinn xx

The BESTSELLING IVY SERIES
TEACHER + STUDENT
= PASSION FORBIDDEN

  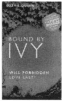  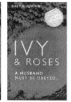

What next? Search for the novella,
Mr Blackwell by SK Quinn, on Amazon …

Exclusive Sample: The Bad Mother's Diary

I know many of you are mothers doing an amazing job. So I've written a romantic comedy called the Bad Mother's Diary that I hope will make you laugh, cry and fall in love ☺.

I don't know if it will be your sort of thing, or whether you prefer just straight romance. Turn the page for your sample chapters – I've given you 50% more than you'll get on Amazon.

Juliette Duffy's Guide to Baby Brit-Speak

Baby gro – A 'onesie' in the US. Basically it's a sleepy suit.

Cot – Crib. (In England, crib is a game of cards or another word for cheating.)

Dummy – Pacifier. I like the word pacifier so much better! Awww … so peaceful!

Pram – Baby carriage. Pram is a bit of a crap word really. I think I'll call Daisy's pram a baby carriage from now on. Or what about perambulator? I LOVE that one!

Pushchair/buggy/pram – Stroller. And yes, confusingly we call a stroller a pram too.

Knackered – Tired. We use this word a lot when we have babies …

Nappies – Diapers. I think 'nappy' is short for napkin or something.

Rusks – Baby biscuits with lots of added vitamins. They taste like cardboard.

Sleepy suit – Onesie.

Stag and hen party – Bachelor and bachelorette party.

Tea – This can be a cup of tea. If you're a commoner like me, it can also be an evening meal.

Whinge/grizzle – Complain.

Yorkshire pudding – Sort of like a big puffy pancake. You eat it with meat and potatoes. Then instantly put on five pounds …

Thursday January 1st

New Year's Day

Nick wouldn't cheat on me. He *wouldn't*. Right? I mean, he was a player in the past, but we have a baby now.

I'm just being paranoid and sleep deprived.

Just because he bought himself a new set of Star Wars underpants and has started using dental floss … that's no reason to be suspicious.

We're getting married, for goodness sake. He just proposed.

New Year's resolutions:

MOVE HOUSE!!! This is urgent. The glass balcony alone is a health and safety issue. Even the pigeons slip over.

Set up regular donations to Save the Children, NSPCC, Child Action and Stop Child Poverty.

Phone Nana Joan every Saturday, like I did before I had Daisy. Feel terrible I keep forgetting, but something has happened to my brain.

Stop watching the news. It's just depressing – especially now I'm a mum. Horrible to think about the things that happen to children.

Lose baby weight. Post-pregnancy, I look like a Renaissance nude.

And on a lesser note:

Use bags for life.

Stop playing Candy Crush Saga / online bingo.

Learn how to fold up the stroller without slicing my fingers open and find out what those black cushiony things are for.

Try REALLY hard not to swear at Nick's mum. Even when she lets herself into our flat unannounced.

By the time I had a baby, I thought we'd live in a proper house with tasteful wooden board games and a vegetable patch.

I also thought I would own a rolling pin.

Nick says we should count our blessings. Plenty of Londoners would kill to live so near the Tate Modern.

But they don't have a three-month old who wakes at car horn noise and businessmen yelling on their mobile phones.

Will give Nick a good kick up the arse this year, because good houses in our price range sell fast.

The only ones that hang around for more than a few days are 'in an up-and-coming area' (shit area), 'delightfully cosy' (shit size), 'priced to sell' (massive shit hole) or 'remarkably energy efficient' (shit-smelling basement).

Nick tried to stay in bed this morning claiming he 'wasn't feeling well' (10 bottles of Corona last night), so I threatened to spray him with window cleaner until he got up and helped me clean the panoramic glass.

Am taking Daisy to see Nana Joan this afternoon. Haven't seen her in ages, and Nick and I could do with some space.

Afternoon

No trains today, so drove the 50 miles to Nana Joan's care home in Great Oakley.

It should have been an hour's journey, but we got stuck in M25 holiday traffic.

Kept glimpsing my tired face in the rear-view mirror and wishing I'd worn makeup.

I have an English-rose complexion (pale skin, instant sunburn) that usually looks okay natural, but right now a bit of colour wouldn't hurt.

My hair (which my hairdresser politely calls 'not quite blonde, not quite brown') could do with some attention too. It's been ages since I had highlights, and my curls are past my shoulders and need a trim.

Oh well. I suppose I'll sort myself out when Daisy sleeps through the night.

Had to turn up Radio Two progressively louder and louder to stop Daisy crying. By the time we reached Nana's care home, the car windows were shaking.

Such a relief to finally give Daisy a cuddle and get inside.

There was a big sign on the visitor's notice board:

BEWARE! JOAN JENKINS SOMETIMES TAPES KNIVES TO HER WALKING FRAME AND CHASES ANY VISITOR WEARING RED.

Nana was so pleased to see us. She hugged me for ages and talked to Daisy in her funny pigeon voice. 'Ooooeee! Coo coo coo!'

She was especially happy because her toenails hadn't been cut in ages. I'm the only one who can do it without breaking the clippers.

After I'd done Nana's bath, I washed her hair and helped dye it 'Vibrant Cherry'. Then I showed her how to play Angry Birds on her phone.

Nana asked about the wedding, and I told her we were marrying at St Mary's church in Great Oakley.

Nana said, 'What does Nick's mum think about that?'

I told her that Helen wants us to marry in London. And that she comes around three times a week with glossy bridal magazines.

Nana said, 'That big-nosed cow. Hasn't she had enough of her own weddings?'

Helen has been married twice. Her first wedding was featured in Vogue, the second in Harper's Bazaar.

When Nana asked about house hunting, I had to admit that we're STILL living in Helen's apartment.

Nana said, 'Oh Jules, love. You haven't got your own place yet? That Nick's a useless little bugger isn't he?'

She's right – Nick does need to change his priorities. But a house is my responsibility too. We're not living in the 1950s.

It was nice seeing Nana. She called Daisy and I her 'blue-eyed girls' and took photos of us with her new selfie stick.

Nana also warned me I was getting too skinny and told me not to 'catch an eating disorder.'

I never trust her views on weight, though. She's lost most of her teeth because of all the Walnut Whips she eats.

Friday January 2nd

I love being a mum, but sometimes I miss going to work.

As a charity executive manager, I was respected. Valued.

My team tackled third-world poverty and childhood diseases. Also, I wore nice suits from Karen Millen and drank vanilla lattes.

Got a picture message from Helen today.

It showed a rail-thin, pouty model bride wearing a huge lion's mane on her head.

Helen had written, '*So* stylish, don't you think? Viv West at her best.'

I texted back a picture of Pamela Anderson in her wedding bikini and wrote, 'I prefer minimalism.'

Saturday January 3rd

Nick and I spent the morning house hunting on Rightmove.

I'm happy Nick is finally getting involved, but he can't seem to grasp the 'family home' concept.

A garden is more important than a marble wet-room with waterfall shower.

We have a budget and there are priorities. Sacrifices have to be made.

Nick was grumpy anyway, because his new casting photograph had arrived. It's black and white, so doesn't show the 'dazzling contrast' of his blue eyes and dark-brown hair. Plus, according to Nick, the angle doesn't highlight his 'manly' jaw.

In my opinion, the photographer got it right. Nick is good-looking. But when he poses looking all serious and brooding, jutting his jaw, it just looks stupid. Far better that he comes across natural.

Already broken a New Year's resolution, but Candy Crush is SO addictive.

Spent the afternoon making Christmas thank you letters, supposedly from Daisy. I got a bit ambitious and decided to photograph Daisy with each and every present. Then she fell asleep, and it all looked a bit weird.

Nick's mum turned up and asked me what the hell I was doing arranging a set of Neal's Yard toiletries around a sleeping baby.

I said, 'Helen, for once could you knock?'

But I don't think she heard me properly, because she said, 'Yes alright then, I'll have a decaf.'

Sunday January 4th

Train back to Great Oakley to see Mum and Dad.

Nick had scripts to read, so he couldn't make it. Probably for the best – he hates the countryside.

Oakley-on-Thames station is only an hour from London, but that's a long time with a baby.

Daisy cried from the minute the train door closed. She only calmed down when a nice old lady rattled a box of denture cream at her.

I love Oakley village. It really is the perfect place to get married.

Helen just doesn't get it – this is where I grew up. I spent my childhood running around these woods and paddling in the river. That's a million times more special than some fancy London hotel.

Laura and Brandi met me at the train station, and we had lovely warm sister hugs. Then we walked up the little woodland trail, along the waterfront and across the maypole green to Mum and Dad's pub.

Dad had scrubbed the Tudor beams and whitewashed the walls for the Christmas, so everything looked like a pretty winter postcard – all frosty, lattice windows and cosy, uneven walls.

Shame Mum's neon-pink nativity scene was still flashing away on the roof.

Choice of beef, chicken or pork for Sunday lunch, plus half a pint of Guinness. It's great being a landlord's daughter.

As usual, Mum wanted to give Daisy a teaspoon of beer for her runny nose, and I had to wrestle the spoon away.

How does she not get that alcohol isn't good for a baby?

Mum said, 'Don't be so paranoid. You *lived* off Guinness when you were her age. And you turned out just fine.'

The 'just fine' argument.

According to Mum, Laura, Brandi and I crawled around on broken glass eating lumps of raw chicken. And turned out 'just fine'.

Ate our family lunch upstairs, away from the regulars, and had a good old catch-up over beef, Yorkshire puddings, roast potatoes, peas and gravy.

Laura is thinking of becoming a vegan.

Brandi has (another) new boyfriend.

Dad saw a meteor in the sky last night.

Mum's been teaching next-door's dog to sing 'Let it Go'.

Everyone asked me about Big Nose. Meaning Nick's mum.

I admitted that Helen had let herself into the apartment this morning and checked the stainless steel windowsills for dust.

She found plenty. I have a baby. I hardly ever dust. I barely have time to use the toilet.

Everyone told me off (again) for letting Helen come round unannounced. But they don't get it – Helen isn't like a normal person. I've told her hundreds of times to let us know she's coming, but she doesn't listen.

Brandi pointed out that Nick and I pay rent, and that we could take Helen to court under the Landlord and Tenant Act for unauthorised visits.

True. But Helen gives us a pretty hefty discount. When I think of all my London friends, I'm the only one whose elevator doesn't smell of piss.

I said, 'Helen probably won't be around so much after the wedding. She only visits to nag us about place settings and colour schemes.'

'So the wedding's still on then?' Mum asked.

I said of course.

We had the usual family 'discussion' (row) about me

marrying Nick.

I mean, yes – he does wear his sunglasses indoors. And yes – he needs to realise he's not a child star anymore and roles aren't handed to him on a silver platter. But he's Daisy's dad, and we're in this together, for better or worse. I want Daisy to have a real, proper family life.

I told everyone I was dieting for the wedding, and Mum said, 'Righty-o. Just four potatoes for you then. Don't you worry. I've cooked this whole roast in olive oil.'

I showed her the calories on the Aunt Bessie's roast potato packet.

She said, 'Two hundred. Is that a lot?'

Yes – if you add olive oil when you're cooking them. And eat four.

Considering Mum is overweight and has type II diabetes, it's pretty shocking she knows nothing about calories.

She had eight roast potatoes on her plate, a mountain of buttery mash, oven chips and three huge slices of beef. And last week she asked me if coffee beans counted as one of her five a day.

I worry about her (we all do) but I've given up nagging. Mum just calls me 'obsessive' and warns me about getting an eating disorder.

She said, 'Men like a bit of something to hold onto. Isn't that right Bob?'

Dad replied, 'It certainly is!'

Mum still dresses in skimpy tops and skin-tight leggings. And Dad still wolf-whistles at her. If anyone criticises Mum's weight, she says, 'I'm a complete original. Which makes me absolutely fucking priceless.'

Dad asked me if Nick and I had 'any joy' looking for houses.

I told him no – everything in London is way over our budget. But we have to live in the city because Nick has almost all his auditions in London.

Nick wouldn't move back to Oakley village anyway, even if we could.

It's too near his parents (I didn't admit he'd said it was too near Mum and Dad's pub too).Plus, muddy fields and shiny leather shoes don't go well together.

Dad said, 'You can't rent his mum's place forever you know.'

I know.

Monday January 5th

All the trains are buggered, so Daisy and I are still in Great Oakley.

Nick was distraught when I said we'd be staying away overnight. He asked me to send video footage of Daisy's bedtime, plus email instructions for the coffee machine, microwave and television.

I relented about the bedtime video. Didn't get much footage though, because Daisy kept trying to eat my phone.

Ended up having a nice country walk with Laura, Brandi and little Callum (Daisy bobbing along in the sling), and afternoon tea at Mary and John's Family Farm Café.

Mary and John hate children, so we had to sit outdoors by the pig pens.

Alex Dalton was in the farm shop, frowning at jars of honey.

He was immaculate as always – black suit and tie, cleanly shaven, jet black eyes.

I have never, ever seen Alex in jeans. He was born to be a businessman.

When Alex saw me, he said, 'Hello Juliette', in his usual formal way.

I said, 'Are you doing your own shopping? I thought you had staff for that sort of thing.'

Alex said, 'I'm sourcing British produce for the Dalton Hotel Group. New business strategy.'

'That's wonderful,' I said.

Alex said, 'Customers pay more for British. Plus it cuts transportation costs.'

Typical Alex.

When I went back outside, Zach Dalton was sitting at our table.

Zach and Alex are *so* different. Night and day, the two of them. Weird that they're brothers.

Zachary is like sunshine – round face, blond hair, always smiling. Comes to all the village parties and pub crawls. Has a beard, goes travelling.

Alex lives in business clothes and could freeze water with his stare.

I couldn't help noticing that Zach was right sitting next to Laura, even though there was loads of room around the big wooden picnic table.

Laura had gone a little bit pink.

'Juliette!' Zach bellowed. 'Laura says they threw you out

of the café. Still, they do stock fairtrade, so all is forgiven. I'm gate-crashing your table – hope you don't mind.'

Then he asked me if 'that scoundrel Nicholas Spencer' had made an honest woman of me yet.

I said yes, Nick had finally proposed and we'd be marrying in Great Oakley this year.

Then Alex came out, swinging honey jars in a brown-paper bag.

Zach said, 'What ho, brother Alex. Let's stay for a cup of tea, shall we?'

Alex said, 'Tea by the pig pens?'

Brandi snorted with laughter and said, 'Shame Nick isn't here, Jules – he would have felt right at home.'

Honestly!

I told Brandi that Nick was the father of my child, and she should be more respectful. And that anyway, she was too young to understand adult relationships.

Brandi said she'd had 'way more boyfriends' than me, and that I was only still with Nick because he got me pregnant.

That was a low blow and TOTALLY not true.

Brandi and I ended up having a massive row, with me defending Nick and her picking him apart.

I think we must have got pretty loud, because the café curtains started twitching and even the pigs were staring.

Little Callum said, 'What does fuck up mean?'

Alex announced he had a meeting in London, and marched off to his vintage MG.

Zach lingered for a bit, asking Laura how she was finding studying in London.

When he finally left, Brandi teased Laura about how girly she got around Zach.

'Oooo Zachary Dalton. You are just *tooo* dishy. Will you take me round the world on your yacht?'

I laughed along. It was SO true.

Then Brandi teased me about fancying Alex when I was at school.

I told her to shut up.

Tuesday January 6th

The trouble with motherhood is you're expected to:

Be slim, attractive, and fashionably dressed, with a brightly coloured designer baby bag covered in little forest animals.

Have a perfect IKEA home with quirky little child-friendly details, like a colourful chalkboard stuck on the fridge and designer robot toys.

Be an all-natural, organic earth mother and not use any nasty plastic Tupperware with chemicals in it, only buy organic vegetables, breastfeed, have a drug-free birth, etc. BUT at the same time …

Be a super-clean chemical spray freak with hygienic clean surfaces and floors at all times, plus wash your hands ten times a day.

All this AND get out of the house without mysterious white stains all over you.

How do women do it?

Don't get me wrong, I wouldn't swap being with Daisy. But sometimes a *tiny* break would be nice.

To be fair, Nick did suggest taking it in turns at night. The trouble is, I'm the only one who can get Daisy to sleep. I think it's because Nick's an actor – he's just too exciting. I've told him a million times that song and dance routines won't help Daisy relax, but he never listens.

Wednesday January 7th

Poor little Daisy had a cold last night. ☹

She woke up every two hours, all snuffly.

I was so worried I couldn't sleep – I just lay next to her, checking she was still breathing.

I know I should nap today, but I just can't seem to nod off. Plus I've nearly cracked level 50 on Candy Crush Saga.

5pm
Sooooooo tired. But can't sleep.

8pm
Daisy has woken up.
She's making all these cute little noises.

11pm
Daisy still awake! Desperately looking for sleep apps on my phone.

11.30pm

Found an app that makes hairdryer noises. Seems to have done the trick. Daisy asleep. My turn now, thank goodness.

Thursday January 8th

3am

Daisy just woke up!

Nick was sound asleep, so I phoned Mum in sleep-deprived tears.

Mum said, 'The Duffy family have never been good sleepers. Remember Brandi? She used to suicide dive out of the cot.'

I broke down, sobbing, 'Why doesn't she have an off switch? Why are there no answers?'

Mum said, 'Feeling confused is what motherhood is all about.'

Then I remembered the iPhone app that makes hairdryer noises.

I shouted, 'I need my phone, Mum. I can't find it! I've lost my phone!'

Mum pointed out that I was holding my phone.

I am so sleep-deprived!

Then Dad came on the line and suggested I put cinnamon in Daisy's milk.

I sobbed that I didn't have any sodding cinnamon.

Mum said she'd drive over with some. Then she remembered she'd lost the car keys.

While she was looking for them (and arguing with dad),

Daisy fell asleep.

SO tired.

4am

Can't sleep! Keep thinking that Daisy will wake up any minute.

5am

Still can't sleep.

6am

Daisy just woke up.

Thank God for Nick – he's giving her milk and singing 'Food Glorious Food' from *Oliver!*

Friday January 9th

Needed to research good-value (cheap) buffet food for the wedding, so Mum stopped by to help with Daisy this morning.

Helen would have gone mad if she'd seen me checking the Aldi, Lidl and Iceland websites. She wants Nick and I to have a three-course wedding breakfast in some fancy hotel. But a wedding is about love, not frills.

Anyway, once the reception gets going, I'm sure Helen will be as glad of a sausage roll as anyone.

This is a new beginning for Nick and I. A commitment to family life. We should celebrate with fun and laughter, not some formal silk-tablecloth nonsense.

When Mum arrived, she'd bought me some bits from the wholesale supermarket: 2000 teabags, five litres of washing up liquid and a lemon torte that said '*serves 50*'.

The torte wouldn't fit in the fridge, so Mum cut us a big slice each for 'elevenses', then sawed up the rest and filled every fridge shelf and half the freezer.

After that, she showed me how to clean the toilet with her 'Wonder Woman technique' (squirting half a bottle of bleach over everything and blasting it off with the shower), threw Daisy around and sang 'YMCA' with all the hand movements.

Quite a few passersby stared through the big glass window at her dancing, but Mum never cares what people think. If she did, she wouldn't wear leopard and zebra prints at the same time.

Before she left, Mum asked if I had a spare feather boa. She and her old school friends are dressing up in '70s clothes to watch the *Mamma Mia* musical.

Mum absolutely can't wait. She's already ordered silver platform boots from eBay.

Saturday January 10th

January sales shopping with Laura and Brandi today.

We stopped for coffee at Barnes and Noble – skinny decaf for me, espresso for Laura and a big frothy whipped strawberry thing for Brandi (bloody twenty-one-year-olds – Brandi is skinny as anything and eats exactly what she likes).

Then we looked at books (well, Laura and I did. Brandi browsed magazines, then moaned that book shops were BORING).

I browsed the diet section. I used to think diets were bullshit, but that's before I had a baby. Really would like to lose a bit of weight before the wedding.

There were so many diet books to choose from:

Fat Around the Middle (But I'm fat *everywhere*!)

The 5:2 Diet (Can't starve myself two days a week, I might pass out when I'm carrying Daisy upstairs or something.)

The Atkins Diet (There's that bad breath rumour …)

Weight Watchers (Sarah Ferguson did it and, without sounding horrible, she's still fat.)

The Slow Carb Diet (Ugh, who likes beans?)

Bought the *Food Guru* book in the end.

Healthy, sensible eating. No fads or false promises. But you *could* lose ten pounds in a week …

Sunday January 11th

Went to Regent's Park with Althea and baby Wolfgang today.

Wolfgang is twelve months old, but he looks much older. He has one menacing front tooth and can snap a bundle of twenty coffee stirrers in half.

I love Althea. She's the most laid-back parent I know. Not many first-time mums would drive their baby around on a moped.

Althea lives in a big, rambling Victorian house in Bethnal Green. It's worth a fortune, but you'd never guess because Althea has decorated it in what she calls, 'kindergarten fusion style'.

Her artistic vision is lost on me, though – all I see is a lot of sprayed silver egg boxes and Wolfgang's handprints.

Today, Althea wore her big Afghan coat, Jackie O shades and bright red cowboy boots. Her curly gypsy hair was tied with a fluorescent yellow ribbon.

Althea's laugh is just brilliant. It could break plates. She sort of goes, '*Nah, nah, nah!*' and shows all her teeth.

From some angles, Althea looks a *tiny* bit like a frog. But a pretty one. With a temper.

Wolfgang was dressed in a little blue mod suit. God knows where Althea found that. It gave him a slightly sinister 'Brighton Rock' air – especially when he was pulling kids off the roundabout.

When Wolfgang bit one of the other children, Althea laughed and said, 'Aw, bless him. He's having such fun.'

Then she tried to put him in his sling, but Wolfgang clung onto the roundabout and neither of us could budge him. Eventually, Althea lured him away with beef jerky.

I told her about my diet, but Althea shouted about diets being sexist crap.

She said, 'You were a measly size twelve. Now you're a measly size sixteen. I weigh far more than you and *I* don't care. The universe made us all perfect. So get over it.'

I said Nick had finally set a date for the wedding.

Althea barked, 'So fucking what? He's no bloody prize pigeon is he? Has he got himself a decent job yet? He should be crawling over broken glass to marry a girl like you.'

I told Althea about me and Nick's meal on New Year's Eve and asked if she thought it was anything to worry about.

She said, 'That he drank six bottles of beer in two hours?'

I said, 'No. That we couldn't agree on anything about the wedding.'

She said, 'You're different. So you're bound to want different things.'

I said, 'They say opposites attract.'

Althea said, 'Hmm.'

Monday January 12th

Bought all the stuff for the *Food Guru* diet.

The Food Guru guy says you can't put a price on health. But you can. It's about two hundred quid.

Bought stuff like steak, salmon, asparagus, and a load of things I've never heard of like chia seeds and psyllium husk.

Dad took me to the supermarket because he's the only one who can work Daisy's car seat.

He was such a proud granddad, telling any shopper who'd listen Daisy's age, birth weight and toilet habits.

Tuesday January 13th

10am

So far today I have eaten:

Two boiled eggs (no toast or anything – wheat is the work of the devil).

A handful of nuts.

Celery with pumpkin seed butter.

11am

Must be lunchtime by now?! I'm going to eat my own leg if I don't have lunch soon.

Awww lovely Daisy. So adorable.

People say I post too many pictures of her on Facebook, but Nick posts way more. Over 500 at last count. His wall is just a long stream of him holding Daisy in different poses.

11.30am

Cooked stir-fry without any soy sauce or flavour of any kind.

Ate it.

Nick's mum came in just as I was washing up and sniffed the air with distaste.

She said, 'Smells like some horrible Chinese restaurant in here.'

I told her I was on a healthy diet.

She blinked at me with her manic blue eyes and said, 'Good for *you*, darling. In time for the wedding?'

I said no – I was losing weight because lap-dancing has child-friendly hours and good rates of pay.

Helen didn't laugh.

Often, she makes me think of a raven bobbing its nasty head around the insides of an animal.

When she smiles she looks like Mr Punch.

I asked Helen if she'd put on any weight after Nick was born.

She stroked her bony hips in skinny black jeans, pulled her cashmere cardigan around her bony ribs and said, 'No, I *lost* weight actually. The whole experience was so traumatic.'

Then she frowned at a tiny fingerprint on the kitchen cupboard and polished it with a tea towel.

The trouble with living in a posh executive apartment is everything is so *shiny*. Shiny stuff shows up everything. I fried an egg once. Never again.

Helen asked me what Mum would wear to the wedding.

I said probably something ten years too young for her.

Helen blinked frantically and said, 'Please persuade her to wear something *tasteful*. Maybe with a shawl? For the pictures …'

I had a good laugh about that. *My* mother! In a shawl! I suppose Helen can dream.

The idea of *anyone* persuading Mum to wear something that isn't skintight is hilarious.

Mum face-timed me earlier to show off her '70s *Mamma Mia* outfit. It would have made Christina Aguilera blush.

Quite sweet really – Mum is SO excited about seeing her old friends. They only get together once a year. I just hope the theatre knows what it's letting itself in for.

Wednesday January 14th

Nick's got a job up north again. He's playing a road sweeper in Coronation Street.

He has one line: 'That always happens if you eat too much chicken pie.'

So I'm staying at Mum and Dad's for a few days.

Nick got all stressed, worrying about what to wear. I reassured him that he's still good-looking and that no – he doesn't look his age (35).

Liked this sample? Find the full book here:

UK

US

http://amzn.to/1TG6SyY   http://amzn.to/1KrY79H

www.devoted-ebooks.com

21723929R00234

Printed in Great Britain
by Amazon